The Lamp in the Valley

Arthur Stringer

The Lamp in the Valley

Arthur Stringer

WILDSIDE PRESS

Originally published in 1338.

Published by Wildside Press.

Visit us online at wildsidepress.com.

Introduction
Karl Wurf

Arthur Stringer (1874–1950) was a Canadian poet, novelist, and screenwriter whose work often explored the intersection of wilderness life, modern industry, and human relationships. Born in Chatham, Ontario, Stringer became known for his versatility: he wrote detective stories, romances, early science fiction, and some of the first Canadian pulp fiction. He published more than forty novels and many volumes of poetry, while also contributing to magazines on both sides of the border. Several of his works were adapted into silent films, marking him as one of the Canadian writers whose career bridged print and early cinema.

Stringer's literary influences were wide-ranging. He admired the craftsmanship of Robert Louis Stevenson and the naturalism of Jack London, whose portrayals of frontier survival helped shape his own depictions of Canada's and Alaska's northern landscapes. He also absorbed the popular traditions of adventure and romance that circulated in pulp magazines, blending them with a modern awareness of social change. In this respect, he was part of a broader movement of early twentieth-century North American writers who sought to connect frontier mythology with contemporary themes of industrial progress, labor unrest, and women's independence.

The Lamp in the Valley reflects these concerns. Set against the backdrop of Alaska's frontier, it combines elements of romance, social observation, and adventure. Stringer portrays not only the wilderness environment but also the tensions between old sourdough prospectors and new corporate mining interests, echoing broader struggles between individualism and modern industry. At the same time, he gives attention to women's roles in the frontier—often placing them at the center of the story in ways that challenge stereotypes of the period.

Though his reputation faded after mid-century, Stringer holds an important place in Canadian and popular literature as a writer who linked the romance of northern landscapes with the pulse of modern life. His books capture both the excitement and the contradictions of the last great frontiers.

CHAPTER I

I OPENED THE CABIN window and felt the night air blow in on my face. It blew clean and cool, cutting through the softness of the Kuroshio and making me think of a knife blade wrapped in black velvet.

As I stood there sniffing that sharper air, like a fox flairing the breeze, I realized some ghostly presence just over the peaks, sparkling blue-white in the starlight. Above those receding peaks I could see the pointers of the Great Dipper as it swung regally about its lodestar. And between that steadfast star and the line of the black-toothed hilltops I could make out a faint showing of the northern lights, a few wavering bands of green and opal to remind me that I was heading north again.

There was no mistaking the smell of that air. It carried with it the scent of wide sprucelands and the sparkle of highland ice fields and the razor-edged aroma of valleys where the sun falls thin on balsam and alder and buckcrop. It was more than an aroma; it was an essence, mysterious but unmistakable. It was the breath of Alaska, calling me back to the home of my youth.

And I wanted to meet it face to face. That little ship's cabin became suddenly hateful to me. I was tired of the noise and the accordion music of the drunken groups swarming north to their cannery work. I was tired of tobacco smoke and alcoholic song and crying babies and squawking radios that cheapened the midnight quietness of the Inland Passage twisting between the headlands where the stars came close. I wanted to be alone with that whispered greeting from my old world.

So I reached for a wrap and made my way up on deck, where all was quiet and not a ship's lamp showed between the shadowy bow and the equally shadowy bridge. But in the gloom there, I remembered, anxious eyes were deciphering our passage through the narrows, our tortuous passage that swung the Dipper first to one side and then to the other.

I crept as far forward as I could, groping about the deck freight waiting to be left ashore at the next port of call. I finally found a seat on what proved to be a slatted crate of chickens. The feathered bodies under me moved and clucked sleepily at that midnight intrusion. Then everything was quiet again.

It was so quiet that I could feel the tremor of the *Yukon's* screw as she plowed northward through the night. I could feel the fir-scented wind on my face and sniff a new keenness in the air that awakened something ancestral in my bones. I could see the gloomy slopes of mountains stippled with spruce, the remoter peaks of white that sparkled in the starlight, the silver and green of the channel water as we skirted black-wooded islands and twisted about obstructing headlands, lonely headlands from which little lighthouses blinked like cat's eyes in the dark. At times it seemed as though we were steaming straight into a mountain side. But the hills, as always, moved apart and let us pass through and as casually came together again in our wake. And as the channel widened out I could see a spangle of lights where some nameless little salmon town sprawled hemlock-stilted along its narrow shelf between tidewater and hilltop. And down from the gloomy slopes of spruce and pine that swept endlessly up to the black-notched sky, striking through the balmier breath of the Japanese Current, I could feel stronger than ever the tang of the North, the true North in whose hills lay the beginnings of my life.

I felt less alone in the world, for all the quietness about me, as I sat watching the faint and far-off waver of the northern lights. They seemed like quiet hands, friendly but ghostly hands, beckoning me to the hills of my childhood. And as I sat there, with the night wind fanning my face, I felt that my mission was not a trivial one. I owed something to Alaska. And I had to justify myself through my work there, in what men called the last frontier.

It would be different, of course. That new world would have all the roughness of wilderness life. And, jackaroo that I was, I'd have to begin all over again. I'd be a cheechako once more in the colony of old-timers. But my country was never ashamed of its pioneer women. And there was something moving and mysterious, I felt, in man's eternal quest for new frontiers. For hope always lies just over the horizon. And the outland trail always carries a hint of glamour and high adventure. Even the *Yukon* itself, as it plowed on through the starlit water, took on a momentary air of mystery. It seemed to turn into something epic and stirring, a world in itself, weaving its dark way through shadowy uncertainties.

Then the light of mystery faded from the picture. For I woke up to the fact that I was no longer alone on that silent and starlit foredeck.

A man, none too steady on his feet, wavered past me in the darkness. He stopped, on his way aft again, and leaned a little closer over my crate seat. He wanted, apparently, to make sure it was a woman there.

He laughed as he passed an exploring hand over the softness of my polo coat. Then he sat down on the crate beside me. His repeated laugh impressed me as both reckless and slightly defiant.

I sat silent, without moving, as he turned and tried to throw a bottle overboard. The bottle fell short, crashing noisily against an iron windlass.

"Good-by, sweetheart," he said with thick-voiced indifference. He was, I concluded, one of the West Coast wanderers who had been turning the lower decks of the *Yukon* into a cross between a faro joint and a water-front saloon. But he was sober enough to resent my sustained silence.

"Can't you talk, pretty one?" he asked, with his face insolently close to mine. I wasn't afraid of him. I'd seen camp drunkards enough in my day. But I hated him for corrupting the quiet beauty of that midnight vigil. And in him I recognized a type that was the curse of the North Country. So I continued to confront him with the thunders of silence.

As I did so he rose unsteadily to his feet and reached into his pocket. From it he took out a flashlight which he even more insolently held up in front of my face. The sudden glare made me blink.

"Not a bad looker," he had the grace to acknowledge. But it in no way added to my happiness. "Why in hell are *you* heading for the land of the sourdoughs?"

That question I also declined to answer. I even moved a little to one side, to avoid the wavering flashlight. But he made the beam follow me, laughing a little as he did so.

"Put out that light," a deep voice commanded from the darkness of the bridge. It was no easy matter, I remembered, to navigate the waters of the Inland Passage.

My tormentor did as he was told. But he took his time about it. And after staring a minute or two at the distant bridge he reseated himself on the crate beside me.

"We like it dark, don't we?" he said as he reached for my hand. The vigor with which I removed it from his clasp caused him to lose his balance for a moment or two. But he steadied himself and sat beside me in morose silence.

"What's taking a peach like you to that tin-can territory?" he finally inquired.

"That," I was foolish enough to answer, "is entirely my own affair."

But it was plain that I puzzled him.

"You're a cheechako," he maunderingly proclaimed. "That fact, my pink and white friend, is written all over you."

It didn't seem worth while telling him I was Alaska born.

"And you're still an unpicked peach," he insolently went on, "for no woman who's married is going to be up here stargazing in the dark. But you don't fit in with our fish-pack females. And you're sure not the dance-hall type. On the other hand, you're no low-brow. You've got class. You've been places and seen things. But you're sure no panhandle chalk-wrangler." He nodded his head in confirmation of his own alcoholic discernment. "No, sir; you're no camptown schoolteacher."

"Why couldn't I be?" I quietly inquired, resenting his effort to paw about my personality. It was bad enough having him paw about my polo coat.

"Because you've still got too much to learn, my little glacier worm," he announced. "But why in God's name are you coming to Alaska to learn it?"

"It so happens," I informed him, "that I'm going to teach in the Indian school at Toklutna."

That seemed to hold him for a moment. But his laugh, this time, was more caustic than ever.

"Then your first lesson to those little frostbitten Siwashes ought to be that a bunch of rubber-stamp bureaucrats can't run a country the size of Alaska. Look what they've done with the power rights. Look at their fool laws about salmon fishing. And look how they've let the big interests come in and choke the life out of the territory. No wonder it turns an honest worker into a Red."

I resisted the temptation to ask if he regarded himself as an honest worker. But he was satisfied to be carried along on a wave of his own alcoholic indignation.

"I know this country and I know what they're doing to it. And I'm not going to take it lying down. I may be down-and-outer enough to gut cohos for a couple of months. But I'm a freeborn citizen and I know my rights. And, if they won't give the laboring man a chance, he's going to stand up and go after it. They've got an idea they can turn us workers into an army of tongue-tied sheep. They think——"

"They don't seem to have left you tongue-tied," I ventured.

"You bet they haven't," he announced. "And that's why I'm known as Eric the Red. I can talk to 'em one at a time or five hundred strong. And before I get through, sweetie, they'll be sitting up and taking notice."

He seemed to resent both my silence and my small movement away from his unsteady body.

"Am I right?" he challenged.

I glanced up at the wavering gold and green and opal of the lights that were growing dimmer along the far-off northern sky line.

"I have no wish to discuss it," I said with my best pedagogic iciness.

"Haven't you now!" mocked my quite unimpressed tormentor. "Since you know all the answers, I s'pose you'd rather be laying down the law to a roomful of half-grown Nitchies."

But I'd had enough of his soapbox oratory. And I was tired of being played on by both his alcoholic breath and his equally sour theories of reorganized labor.

"I wish you'd go away," I told him.

His movement, as he leaned closer over me, was an exasperatingly intimate one.

"On a night like this," he murmured, "with the stars up there singing together over the mountain tops? Not on your life, lady!"

I knew my first tingle of fear as I felt his arm creep like a snake's head about the loose folds of my polo coat. The *Yukon*, at that moment, seemed a terribly empty ship.

"Kindly go away," I said. I said it slowly and distinctly and with all the severity I could command.

He only laughed at me.

"Not on your life," he said for the second time. And he laughed still again as I tried to writhe free of his encircling arm.

The sound of that carelessly defiant laugh was still in the air when I saw a shadow detach itself from the shadowy iron bulwark toward the bow of the boat.

It was a man there.

It was a man, I realized, who'd been leaning against the rail and watching the starlit water. He moved toward me, in the uncertain light, with rather unhurried steps. But there was no hesitation in them.

"Is this mucker annoying you?" he asked.

I couldn't make out his face. But from the moment I first heard it I liked his voice. It was a casually deep and full-timbred voice, with a reassuring note of quietness that made my foolishly quickened heart slow down a little. I could see, as he stood over me, that he was tall and lean. And I knew, in some way, that I could depend on him.

"I wanted to be alone here," I found the courage to protest.

But the man on the crate beside me declined to move. It was the tall and shadowy figure above me that came a step or two closer.

"Did you hear what the lady said?" he prompted. The quiet-before-the-storm tone of his voice sent a little chill needling up and down my spine. But still my tormentor held his ground.

"Who asked you to barge in on this?" he was reckless enough to challenge.

The tall stranger stood silent a moment, in a sort of patiently impatient tolerance.

"Isn't your name Ericson?" he finally demanded.

"You're tootin' right it is," came the prompt reply.

"Well, Ericson, you're not quite sober," said the other. "You haven't been sober a day since we pulled out of Seattle. And at the present moment you're not wanted here."

"Who says I'm not wanted?"

"I do."

"What's that to me?" said the man at my side.

"It's this," was the unexpectedly prompt reply. And before I knew it I was alone on the crate.

I couldn't quite make out what was taking place in the darkness that wasn't altogether darkness. But what startled me, after a quick moment of struggle, was that the young man who answered to the name of Eric the Red had not only been lifted bodily from where he sat, but had been shaken as a rag is shaken by a terrier and had been swung out over the ship's rail. He was held there by the scruff of the neck, writhing and kicking. He began, in fact, to emit muffled little rat squeals as he hung over open space, with nothing but the star-riffled, black water under his heels.

"Don't," I gasped, with a hand on the unrelenting long arm. And that arm, I discovered as I tugged at it, was as firm as iron.

"A few gallons of sea water," said the untroubled deep voice beside me, "would wash a little of the fireworks out of his system."

"Please don't," I implored, remembering that a moment's unexpected rending of cloth might send the man tumbling down into the channel.

My rescuer turned to me and apparently tried to study my face in that misty midnight duskiness. Then he swung out his second long arm and lifted the still struggling figure back over the rail.

"Now you get down where you belong," said the tall man as he gave his captive a final shake. "And if you talk to this girl again, Ericson, I'll break every bone in your body."

It took time for Ericson to get his breath back.

"You don't own her," he shrilly announced. "And you don't own me. And if you——"

But the other cut him short.

"Are you going?" he demanded.

Ericson fell back a step or two as the other advanced.

"I'll do more than talk before I'm through with her," he proclaimed. It was a final effort, I felt, to save his face. But it fell short of its mark. For as the menacing long arm once more reached out he dodged away between a row of gas drums. From there, after a silent moment or two that impressed me as heavy with hate, he retreated into the darkness.

The tall man stooped to pick up the fallen flashlight. And I sat there wondering at the foolish sense of security his sustained silence was bringing back to me.

"They've been hitting it up pretty hard for three days now," he finally observed. I was glad to find him without the impulse to kick a man already down.

"I suppose," I ventured, "it's because they're so hopeless and homeless."

"That's the curse," he said, "of our West Coast. It's too full of bums and bindle stiffs. They never stay long enough in one place to take root. And then these soapbox agitators come along and spout communism at them." He looked away, for a moment, and then turned back to me. "But that fire-eater had no right getting rough with a woman. With a woman like you, I mean."

"Why with a woman like me?" I questioned, for, like a horse, I was already feeling quieter with the knowledge that the reins were in a quieter hand.

"I spotted you the first day out," he said, "as a girl who rather wanted to be let alone."

"I do," I said. But that, I felt, might frighten him away. And I didn't want him to go away. "I mean I *did*," I amended.

"You naturally don't belong among those roughnecks."

"I'm afraid I do," I told him. "I'm north born."

That seemed to surprise him.

"You've been out for quite a time?" he suggested, as we stood there side by side looking at the wavering opal and gold of the aurora borealis beyond the white-capped mountains.

"For seven long years," I told him, feeling a little alone in the world. But I kept my chin up. I even laughed a little as I inhaled some newer sweetness in the air, some sharper fragrance from the spruce-clad hills all around me, the immeasurable hills with their immeasurable tang of wildness.

"She's a great country," he said out of the silence. And, being north born, I agreed with him. "But it's no place for a woman," he added.

"Why not?" I demanded. He laughed a little at that quick challenge.

"Because women want anchorage. They're not satisfied with wildness and roughness. And there's been a sort of conspiracy to keep Seward's Icebox uncivilized."

"Why," I promptly questioned, "can't Alaska be civilized?"

"Oh, it will in time," he quietly conceded. "But it has some bad habits to get over. It's too proud of its shirt-sleeve past. It's too fond of calling itself the last frontier and doing things on the dime-novel basis. It's banked too long on the bush-rat with a skillet and a slab of sowbelly."

"What's wrong with the bush-rat?" I demanded, remembering that I was the daughter of one.

"Nothing," was the deliberated reply, "except that he's outlived his usefulness. That's what's the matter with your country. It's too full of grubstaked sourdoughs who go out on the creeks with a tomrocker and imagine they're mining. They scratch at the rubble and hill-cracks for a month or two, and wash out a poke of dust and stay drunk for two-thirds of the year. They're hobos at heart. They do nothing for the country. They don't even know the meaning of real mine work."

I had seen those lone-fire wanderers in their lonely valley bottoms, hawking float-gold from the sand of icy creeks, lugging timber down snowy slopes for their cribwork, thawing out the frozen silt of their test pits with hot stones and a hand winch, facing hunger and hardship and pushing deeper and deeper into the unmapped wilderness for their precarious ounce or two of yellow metal.

"To me," I maintained, "they're all terribly brave."

"And terribly inadequate," amended my companion.

"How would *you* have done it?" I asked. I could hear his quiet chuckle at the challenge in my voice.

"The only way it *can* be done," he answered. "By big business, by the geologist and the engineer who does more than tickle the surface of things. Then you get something better than claim-jumpers and gun-toters and fly-by-night camps. You get roads and honest workers and towns and settlements and something permanent, while your old sourdough squats beside a saloon drum stove and dreams about the strike he's going to make when he gets back to the hill claim he hasn't even done assessment work on."

"You seem to know all about Alaska," I ventured. But he disregarded the barb in my voice.

"Not as much as I'm going to," he said. "I fell for the North, my first year out of Lehigh. The bug bit me when I prospected the Michikamau country in Labrador and had to dig in for the winter. Then I went to Flin Flon for a year. Then I headed for Fairbanks and had a couple of seasons on the gold dredges along the Tanana, where the work's plotted out three and four years in advance. That's what you'd call real mining."

"Where you're really a part of a machine," I amended.

"Sure," he agreed. "But she's a grand old machine. Why, the barge I worked had a million dollars sunk in her before she turned a wheel."

"And you're still on the Tanana?" I questioned, absurdly chilled by the aroma of big business.

"No; the next summer I did field work for a big company along the upper Yukon. Then I swung in with the Trumbull outfit."

"And now?" I prompted.

"Now I'm headed for the valley of the Chakitana, where the Trumbull company is going to consolidate its claims and tackle that territory in earnest. It's got something to work with there."

"The Chakitana," I echoed, ignoring the quiet exultation in his voice. The once-familiar sound of the Chakitana came back to me, across the years, with an oddly disturbing ring.

"Do you know that country well?" I asked.

"Not yet, of course," he said. "But I know something big is going to break before we get through with it. We'll dig a little deeper than the old pan-tilters who've been fussing around the fringes there. And I want to be in on the show when the color comes."

"Where you'll be safe and well fed and getting the news of the world by radio," I said, thinking of the lone-fire old-timers.

"But merely a hired man," my companion added with an unexpected note of regret. Then he laughed, a little defensively, and leaned closer to me in the starlight. "What I'd rather know is more about *you*. And why you're heading north again. And what you're going to do with yourself up there on the last frontier."

"I promised my father I'd come back and work for Alaska," I told him.

"Dig in and civilize the sourdough?" he said with a flippancy I resented.

"No," I answered, "just do my bit toward getting a great country on its feet."

"He gave you quite a job. How are you going to do it?"

I told him that I was going to teach in the Indian school at Toklutna.

"But twenty thousand teachers couldn't tame that country. She was born wild and she seems to want to stay wild."

"I have a promise to keep," I told him. "And I've my father's claim to look into."

"Why'd he ever send you down to the States?"

"He and I were alone, back in the Waceeta hills. And when he struck through to prospect in the Ghost Lake country he felt it wasn't fair to me. He felt I ought to better myself, as he put it. So he sent me out to get civilized."

My companion's laugh was curt but not unkindly.

"It seems to have succeeded," he said. "Where'd you go for your slice of civilization?"

"All the way to Michigan," I told him. "I had an aunt there who was supposed to look after me. But she died the year I entered Ann Arbor."

"Then you weren't as happy as you had expected to be?"

It was my turn to laugh.

"I was only a bush-rat's daughter. They made fun of my clothes and my hillbilly ways. I had to learn life all over again. And I was so late in getting started. It was that, I think, made me work harder than the others."

"Then you had to shift for yourself? Or was your father in Alaska still helping you?"

"He'd promised to come down to the States, but he kept putting it off. I think he was afraid of that outside world he knew nothing about. Then he went back in the hills, and I had trouble keeping in touch with him. Nearly a year went by, once, before I got a letter."

"That's not so nice," observed my new-found friend. "How did you keep going?"

"By working in a girls' camp for a summer. Then by teaching for a year in a north-side Saginaw school. Then by tutoring a lumberman's feather-headed daughter. And after my final year at Ann Arbor I got a chance to go to England for the summer. I was taken along as a sort of companion for a Detroit automobile-maker's daughter. She wasn't very strong. But she got to like me. And when the family went to Amalfi for the winter they kept me on. Then in the spring they went north to Florence, where they leased a villa just above Fiesole."

"I'd call that quite a break," said the man beside me.

"It was," I agreed. "It was all rather wonderful. But it made me feel like a deserter. And it was too good to last. Just when I was telling myself I had about everything one could ask for, I got a letter from Alaska, nearly seven months old."

"Telling you what?" prompted the voice at my side.

"Telling me my father had been found dead on the open trail," I answered, doing my best to be casual about it. "He'd been found there, frozen to death, between his Chakitana claim and Trail-End Camp. His grub bag was empty. Two of his dogs had died and the others must have left him in the night. I can't help thinking of that lonely grave between the hills when you talk about the uselessness of the sourdough."

"I'm sorry," said my companion, with a quick note of contrition. He stood beside me, for a full minute of silence. "Where was your father's claim on the Chakitana?"

"That's what I've got to find out," I told him. "But it seems to be somewhere along the Three-Finger Range between the Cranberry and Blackwater Pass. Father, you see, was just an old-fashioned sourdough. He was always brooding about some final strike that was going to make him a millionaire. And he always felt there was a fortune in that mine of his, once it was opened up. It was his secret. And he hugged it tight, even from me."

"But the important point is, did he establish his claim?"

"I'm afraid not," I had to admit. "That's one of the things I've got to find out."

He leaned closer, as though trying to decipher my face in the starlight.

"That shouldn't be hard for an old-timer," he observed.

"I sometimes wonder," I found myself saying, "if I've gone soft. That's the worst thing, it seems to me, that could happen to a north-born girl. I don't want to be soft, like a husky that's lived too close to a stove."

He laughed a little.

"You won't be," he assured me. "But there are other battles in life, remember, besides bucking a snowbank."

"But I haven't much use," I told him, "for people who turn back."

"You wouldn't," he said out of the darkness. And that darkness, I felt, had been making us both a little less afraid of ourselves. We were two travel-worn wanderers, alone in the world, with all our yesterdays and tomorrows dissolved in the sea and the starlight and the wavering aurora above the snow-clad mountains. Yet when he leaned closer, so that my shoulder brushed against the hardness of his arm, I found myself moving away a little. Lonely ladies, after midnight on starlit nights at sea, needed the feel of something solid under their feet.

"It was kind of you," I said as I drew my polo coat closer about me, "to help me as you did."

But he disregarded that valedictory note.

"I don't even know your name," he reminded me.

Names, on a night like that, didn't seem to mean much. We were up between the stars, I wanted to tell him, where time and titles didn't count. For the *Yukon*, as she floated on between towering cliffs that shut out half the planet-spangled sky, seemed merely a ghost ship wandering on through ghostly aisles of gloom.

"Who *are* you?" I heard him ask. And I laughed a little, for it still didn't seem important. *He* impressed me as the one important thing there. For mysterious men with Herbert Marshall voices had no right bending over a heart-free girl when the Kuroshio was already playing ducks and drakes with her peace of mind.

"Who are *you*?" I found myself asking, foolishly glad because of his nearness.

He didn't answer me at once. And in that moment of silence I summoned up courage to reach for the forgotten flashlight. Then I pressed the button and framed his stooping head in a sudden shaft of light.

I gulped as the light fell on his face. That face was strong and bronzed and touched with a quiet audacity that went well with his big frame. But I had seen it before, in an altogether different setting. For this was the mackintoshed man who had stood in the rain with a blonde and blue-eyed girl in his arms before the *Yukon* pulled out from the Seattle wharf. He had been so absorbed in that last clasp that he almost missed getting aboard. A little cheer, I recalled, had gone up from the passengers lining the dripping deck rail as he broke away and leaped up a gangplank already in motion.

The memory of that scene promptly chilled and steadied me. An ice wall as wide as the Columbia Glacier seemed to drift in between us.

I turned away and lifted my face up to the hills, from which the night wind was blowing down so clean and strong. And my companion, plainly enough, was conscious of that prolonged silence.

"I don't suppose it makes much difference," he said out of that silence, "but my name is Lander, Sidney Lander."

"No, it doesn't make much difference," I heard myself saying in an oddly thinned voice.

"Why?" he demanded, conscious of that remoter note.

"We'll probably never see each other again," I said with a limping enough effort at indifference.

"But I think we will," he corrected with unexpected solemnity. My hand, resting on the rail, could feel his bigger hand close over it.

"Hasn't Eric the Red done enough of that?" I asked in an adequately frosted voice.

The man who called himself Sidney Lander promptly lifted his hand away.

"But I still want to know your name," he quietly reminded me. "I think you owe me that much."

I laughed and stood silent a moment.

"My name's Carol Coburn," I finally admitted, "free, white, and twenty-one, and heading back to the icebound hills of her birth."

I tried to be flippant about it, since I found something chilling in a too abrupt relapse to actuality. But my levity was lost on the man beside me.

"Coburn?" he repeated. And his voice impressed me as almost a startled one.

"Carol Koyukuk Coburn," I announced, "with the Koyukuk usually suppressed."

"What was your father's name?" he asked.

"His real name," I said, "was Kenneth Coburn. But back on the creeks he was known as Klondike Coburn."

That brought silence between us again. And when the man beside me spoke, it was in an oddly altered voice.

"It's a small world, isn't it?"

I didn't, at the moment, see much point to that observation.

"I was beginning to feel it was an oppressively big one," I said as I stared out over the lonely hills. And it was about time, I remembered, to go back to my cabin.

"How long," he asked, "will you be at Toklutna?"

"For at least a year," I told him. "But why do you ask?"

"Because I think I'll be seeing you," he said, without the slightest trace of levity.

"Why?" I inquired, doing my best to make that query a matter-of-fact one.

"Trails have the habit of crossing in this North Country of yours," he said with a curt little laugh.

"I hope yours leads to success," I said with an answering small laugh that wasn't as light in note as I'd intended.

But to that, as he piloted me down between the chicken crate and the bales of deck freight, he ventured no immediate reply. And I had a feeling, as I undressed and stretched out in my berth no wider than a tombstone, that low-voiced strangers who belong to someone else had no right to talk to lonely-hearted girls in the starlight and then have to say good-by with nothing more than the most solemn of handclasps. It was apt to do things, I discovered, to the lady's dreams.

CHAPTER II

IT WASN'T UNTIL THE crowding and confusion of our shore stop at Cordova that I saw Sidney Lander again. Then I caught sight of him on the dock, stooping over a wire-covered crate that had just been swung down from the ship's deck. He plainly didn't like the roughness with which that piece of baggage was being handled. But his face cleared as he opened the crate end and let out a long-haired sheep dog which disdained the chop bone held out in front of it. The quivering animal merely flung itself on its master, whimpering and crazy with joy as it rested a paw on either wide shoulder.

Lander rubbed the shaggy ears and patted the russet flank and was staring so intently into those adoring canine eyes that he failed, at first, to see me. He looked very tall and brown in the open sunlight. He looked, in fact, very much as I expected him to look. And I felt a little catch in the throat at his quick smile of recognition.

"This is Sandy," he said as he stroked the dog's nose. "There's just Sandy and me."

It was the duffel bags and the equipment piled about him, I suppose, that depressed me a little by their suggestion of flight.

"I'm flying in to the Chakitana," he said. "But Sandy doesn't like air travel." I could feel his eyes on my face. "You go on to Seward, of course?"

"Then in to Toklutna," I said, wondering at the sense of incompletion that hung like a plumb bob from my heart.

"You won't have much to work on at Toklutna," he observed. "They're a spineless lot, those north-coast redskins."

"I've another mission in Alaska," I reminded him. And that brought his eyes back to my face again.

"I know it," he acknowledged.

I wondered, as I looked up at him, why his abruptly hardening eyes made me think of a window with its curtains quickly drawn. Even his smile seemed edged with ice. "It would be funny, wouldn't it, if we found ourselves on the same trail there?"

"What does that mean?" I asked, when the *Yukon's* warning whistle gave me a chance to speak again.

Instead of answering me he led me toward the gangplank over which the last of the passengers were crowding aboard. The smile faded from his face as he stood there, with my hand in his. He neither spoke nor said good-by. But his eyes, as he looked down at me, did things to my heart action. For my woman's instinct told me that something was stirring deep in that bear cave of silence. Those eyes, I felt, were saying something that his lips seemed afraid to put into words.

He was stooping over his Sandy as the ship swung out into the harbor. And the *Yukon,* as we headed for open water, impressed me with an altogether unlooked-for sense of emptiness.

All the way to Resurrection Bay, in fact, I felt oddly alone in the world. It seemed less and less like going home.

Yet I knew, once we reached Seward, that I was back on the frontier. I knew it by the smell of the sub-Arctic air, by the glint of sunlight on glacial ice, by the lightly timbered hills, by the wooden-fronted shops and saloons and the loungers in shoepacks, by the smoke-crowded day coaches that went creaking and twisting up a shack-strewn valley of jack pine. I'd feel better, I told myself, when I got to Toklutna.

But when I found myself face to face with that solemn big schoolhouse surrounded by a straggle of cabins that made it look like a mother hen surrounded by her chicks, no sense of high adventure reposed in my arrival.

It was Miss Teetzel, I think, who spoiled everything. For Miss Teetzel, the school head who met me there with two scrofulous-looking Indian boys at her heels, proved to be a somewhat dehydrated spinster with an eye like a bald-headed eagle's and a jaw like a lemon squeezer. I could see her disapproving glance go over my person, from my gray tweed cap with its rather cocky Tyrolean feather to my frivolous suede pumps. I plainly didn't fit in with her idea of what a teacher should be. I'd been outside so long that I failed to remember the law of the rugged North which inclines even the daughter of those great open spaces to a certain sturdy roughness of attire.

What they expect of you there, I soon learned, was something with the bark on. And it didn't take me long to find out I wasn't as welcome at Toklutna as I'd fondly imagined. I didn't much mind being consigned to the smallest and meanest room in the big old building. I could have forgiven that building itself, which was one-half reservation school and one-half hospital and always smelled of soap and disinfectants, for being as ugly and barren-looking as a middle-aged pesthouse. But I couldn't overlook the spirit of hostility with which I was ushered into my far-north mission. For that spirit expressed itself, once I'd unpacked, in the first task with which Miss Teetzel confronted me. It was to take charge of the washing from the children's ward. And it was rather a septic mess to get clean, even with the power machine which Miss O'Connell showed me how to operate. But I knew the lemon-squeezer lady was playing an operatic air or two on the keyboard of my endurance. So I put on my rubber gloves, and shut my teeth, and went through with my job.

It wasn't until my third day at Toklutna that I had a chance to humanize the cell-like baldness of my room. But it looked less like the box stall of a stable after I'd put out my pet books and thumbtacked my Amalfi snapshots and my prints from Florence on the walls. I found something friendly and consoling in the old college groups clustered about the larger photograph of a basketball team wherein a stern-eyed and rather leggy Carol Coburn looked like a bobbed Artemis in shorts.

Miss O'Connell helped me do the decorating. And this same Katie O'Connell proved herself the one girl I liked in that new valley of loneliness. She had Irish gray eyes, a sense of humor, and a frame like a man's. She was, I discovered, really a graduate nurse and should have worn a uniform. But she bowed to the law of the frontier and dressed that muscular body of hers in mannish-looking flannel shirts and khaki breeches and high-laced hunting boots. She swung an ax and managed a boat and handled a rifle as casually as any old-timer. In winter, I learned, she drove a tractor and opened up roads with a "snow-go" or tooled a dog-team along the back-hill trails of her bailiwick. Twice, since she came to Toklutna, she had slipped away to Kodiak to shoot brown bear. She was in a San Bernardino sanitarium for three years, making a specialty of tubercular cases. Then she worked for a year with the Indian children at the Sherman Institute in Riverside.

At Toklutna she plainly found plenty to do. For of the thirty-seven children in our school three had tubercular neck glands, two had congenital hip disease, and another dozen either ear trouble or ominous chest coughs. They were the offspring of the once stalwart Eskimo and the noble red man of the North, proving how merciless the hand of mercy could sometimes be. Our civilization, plainly, hadn't done much for those misfits. We thought we'd been helping them, but all we did was take away their stamina and pauperize them. We left them so improvident they came to regard it as foolish to go out and fish and hunt and trap.

So they let the white man bask in the glory of the white man's burden. They gave up and wallowed in shiftlessness and loafed about in rags and mated and reproduced and passed their ill-begotten offspring over to Toklutna to feed and clothe and make into good little Americans.

Miss Teetzel, I soon discovered, did her best to keep the native girls in the school from talking with the old women of the outside settlement. For these verminous old squaws had a lot of tribal superstitions they tried to pass on to the youngsters. According to Miss O'Connell, for example, they made a practice of not letting their first-born children live, especially the Copper River Indians who believed that if their first little papoose lasted only until he was eight or nine months old his father went straight to the Happy Hunting Grounds. So they quietly forgot to feed the child, or casually exposed it to the cold. And when it was frozen stiff they felt a parent's life had been saved.

Katie O'Connell, in fact, was on the warpath because of an Indian couple who sneaked over into the Matanuska Valley with their seven-months-old baby, ostensibly on a hunting trip. But if they came back without that papoose, our grim-eyed nurse proclaimed, she was going to have them locked up for life. It wasn't that they didn't love their children. It was merely one of those absurd old superstitions that brought unnecessary tragedy into their lives. They even thought it unlucky to have twins. An Indian mother would refuse to nurse the weaker of the two until it just quietly curled up and died. And that was the sort of thing, I remembered, my poor old dad wanted me to fight against.

But Miss Teetzel took the savor out of my mission. She also quietly contrived to make me as uncomfortable as possible. She seemed to feel that the scrub brush was a major factor in pedagogics. When she delegated me to clean out Katie's medicine closet I was rather at sea about what to salvage and what to discard. It was Katie who came to my rescue. She made a clean sweep of things. She threw out, in fact, enough medical supplies to stock a drugstore, quarts of old icthyol and mercury ointment and countless boxes of pills and bottles of yellow iodide tablets and an antique gallon or two of cascara sagrada which she said wasn't fit to flush a tractor crankcase.

But Sidney Lander was right. I hadn't much to work on at Toklutna. And I wasn't very proud of my teaching, if it could be called teaching. The little slant-eyed Eskimos, I found, were both brighter and merrier-minded than the Siwash children. They all seemed fond of music, though, especially the march music Katie and I pounded out on the old school organ. So the two of us concluded that a little dancing might brighten up the emptiness of their evenings. We tried putting them through an old-fashioned square dance or two. And just when the fun was at its highest Miss Teetzel appeared and looked me over with that sardonic eye of hers.

"I'm afraid," she observed, "that you're a trifle too modern for us old-timers."

"I don't see," I was foolish enough to retort, "that teaching calls for the 'Dead March' from *Saul*."

The lemon-squeezer jaw promptly hardened.

"You may have mixed with the crowned heads of Europe," announced my enemy, "but it would be unsafe, I think, to regard that as an excuse for insolence."

I had to swallow it, of course. But after that we were restricted to group-singing and saluting the flag and a handful of dolorous old hymns which my Siwash charges translated into a pagan chant of woe.

And I was guilty of a second lapse when, after washing the blue ointment off five of my little Indian girls, I bowed to their hunger to be up-to-date and have what they called "buffalo heads." I thoughtlessly agreed to bob their hair, the thickest and coarsest hair I ever saw on human skulls. They looked rather like plucked robins when I got through with them. And I looked like something worse when Miss Teetzel got through with *me*. I had to go out and tramp over the spruce hills for an hour, to compose my soul. For the mountains were always there, in a friendly huddle on every side of one. And I loved to watch the wine glow deepen on their snow-clad peaks as the sun went down. That high-arching sky, when the air was clear, was the bluest blue I've ever seen.

As I quartered back across the schoolyard, after stopping a fight between two of my little redskin warriors (based on a can of tinned cow stolen from the kitchen), I bumped into Doctor Ruddock, who looked us over once a week. He stopped, with his black bag in his hand, and rather solemnly looked *me* over.

"You're not very happy here," he said. "How'd you like a whack at a school over at Wasilla?"

My first impulse was to tell him that I didn't believe in running away from things. But I said, instead, that I was waiting for rather an important report from the Record Office at Juneau.

"Got a mine claim?" he said with his quick and kindly smile.

"That's what I have to find out," I told him.

He glanced at the shabby old barracks that overshadowed us.

"Well, if they crowd you too hard here, let me know. I can pull a string or two, when you're ready. And that Matanuska Valley, if I don't miss my guess, is going to be very much on the map."

The memory of that message didn't stay with me as long as it might have. For on my way to my room Katie O'Connell handed me a letter from Sidney Lander. It had come out from Chakitana by airplane and had been mailed at Fairbanks. The writer of that letter said that I had been very much in his thoughts. But the comforting little glow a message like that could bring just under one's floating ribs was cut short by the further message that the sooner I could marshal all data and documents in connection with my father's Chakitana claim the more definite it would make Lander's course of action in the immediate future. "The Trumbull outfit and I are parting company," it concluded, "and what I prophesied about our trails coming closer may happen a little sooner than either of us imagined."

CHAPTER III

I COULDN'T, OF COURSE, send documents which I didn't possess on to Sidney Lander. And I couldn't get any response to my repeated letters to the high-and-mighty Record Office officials at Juneau. I had to wait, as women so often have to do in this world, and marvel at the manner in which busy days could slip away and the ever earlier hour at which our northern sun went to bed.

For summer, up here under the shadow of the pole, seemed a very short season. And also a very beautiful one, though I'd scant time to luxuriate in its loveliness. For I'd classes to conduct, and my supplies to pass out, and my mending to do, and mercury iodide to apply to five pairs of little Indian eyes. And at night, when our tinny old radio brought us echoes of a faraway world, I'd my papers to mark and my reports to make out. I was no longer afraid of the power washer. I'd learned how to process salmon and look at my snapshots from Fiesole and Amalfi without any pucker of pain just under my fifth rib. I could get along quite nicely without grapefruit. I'd even helped to make berry jam to add to our winter stores. I'd been three times to the Russian church in the village. And I'd been twice to Anchorage, to explore the wooden-fronted shops and buy things to cover my nakedness and bring home an armful of month-old magazines. And through it all, as the voice over our tinny radio announced, "Time marches on."

For the sun was swinging lower and lower and the birch leaves were turning and the wild fowl heading south. The fireweed was red on the hillsides and I once more faced the familiar old task of stoking a drum stove with spruce logs. There was a sheeting of ice on the trail pools in the morning and we breakfasted by lamplight. Doctor Ruddock brought Katie O'Connell seven wild ducks which he'd shot on the Inlet, explaining that the six mallards were for the staff, and the spoonbill for the principal. With the coming of the first untimely snowfall, in fact, I'd taken to whipcord riding breeches and invested in a pair of pacs, high boots made of rubber, with generous enough foot room to allow for at least two pairs of woolen socks. Katie, when she saw me thus attired, proclaimed that I once more looked like an old-timer. Then she went over her combination rifle and shotgun, which she called a "game-getter," and asked if I'd swing in with her on a moose hunt across the Inlet.

But instead of a moose hunt we went on a baby hunt. For Katie had been right about her vanished papoose. Word came that our poor little redskinned Oedipus had been found abandoned in a poplar grove east of Wasilla. Doctor Ruddock, who brought the news to Toklutna, said there was a passable trail through the hills and delegated Katie and me to motor over to Matanuska Valley and bring the outcast back.

Katie, who would have started out for Timbuctoo at a word from that doctor of hers, lost no time in getting ready. She togged me up in an old caribou parka and a pair of bearskin gauntlets that came to my elbows. And we started out, with plenty of food and blankets and a medicine bag that held two pints of brandy. It wasn't an entirely dignified departure, for it took place in the school's old wood-toting motor truck. And our traveling wasn't exactly a triumphal procession. For the doctor hadn't been entirely right about the trail. That road was passable only in parts. An autumn thaw had softened the surface soil, making some of our way more like muskeg than wagon road. There were times when we were hub deep in mire. There were other times when we had to cut brush and make a bridging mattress across mud swales. And there were still other times when we had to snub onto a wayside tree stump and ratchet our truck out of the engulfing ooze.

But no complaint came from either Katie or me. It took me back to the days when I was truly a bush-rat's daughter. And I preferred trail mud to Miss Teetzel. When I glanced up and saw a black bear, not two hundred yards from where we were standing, my road mate merely laughed. She waded back to the truck, to get her rifle. By the time she had crawled up over the hill shoulder, however, the bear was no longer in sight. So we made a fire and cooked a surprisingly good supper and slept in the truck that night.

By noon the next day we won through to the Matanuska River, where we were told to push on eastward along the valley toward what was called the Butte. High up in the hills, as we went, I could see mountain sheep, looking like little snow clouds anchored to the rock ledges. I spotted one long-horned ram, perched out on a purple-tinted parapet. He stood snow-white in the clear mountain air, as motionless as a statue. Katie accused him of posing. But I knew he was there on the lookout for wolves.

Then Katie snorted aloud. For at a turn in the road we came face to face with a bewhiskered old-timer with a holstered hunting knife and a six-gun swinging at his hip, to say nothing of a long-barreled rifle in the crook of his arm. He looked, for some reason, like a picture out of the past. The light in his saturnine old eye was none too kindly as he studied us and then inspected our mud-covered truck.

"Them contraptions," he mordantly announced, "weren't built for North Country mushin', no more'n women were."

Katie, after agreeing with him, made an effort to explain our mission there. The rugged and defiant old figure assailed the trail ruts with a barrage of tobacco-juice shrapnel.

"Injins like that ought t' be shot. And in the good old days," he said as he slapped his six-gun, "I'd a done it on sight." He spat again. "That's what's the matter with this whole gol-darned country. She's gone soft on us. And 'stead o' spoon feedin' them copper-bellied sons o' she-dogs she should be puttin' a bounty on their scalps." And still again he spat. "That's what's spilin' this ol' territory. Too much gover'ment. I've trapped her and prospected her from Keewalki down t' Wrangell. And in the ol' days———"

"We're from the Toklutna Mission," interrupted Katie, "on an emergency case."

"So I savvied," was the unhurried response. "But in the ol' days, as I was sayin', we could run our own camp. But now it's your Uncle Sam who steps in and runs us same as he runs the Injins. He makes a raft o' fool minin' laws, slaps a closed season on beaver, and gits a game warden after us if we shoot a lady-caribou t' keep body and soul together. He tells us t' settle down and grow turnips. But once we clear an acre or two he claims we ain't provin' her up right and puts her back in the public domain."

The old-timer, when he spat again, was able to convert the movement into a sweeping gesture of repudiation.

"And right now a thievin' lot o' politicians is set on turnin' this valley into a truck garden for a bunch o' broken-down corn-rustlers on relief. They've got their survey men over there, markin' out road lines and drivin' stakes and claimin' they're pavin' the way for the resurrection of Alaska. And next spring they're countin' on plantin' an army o' pie-eaters on the valley tundra and watchin' 'em git rich growin' spinach for themselves."

He shifted his cud and brushed aside the mittened hand with which Katie was semaphoring for silence.

"This ain't no place for college doods," he doggedly pursued. "I got one o' them know-it-all engineers over t' my shack right now. He kin talk big about g'ology and machine-minin', but he could no more take a tomrocker back in the hills and wash out a poke o' dust than I could pilot one o' them airplanes that's stampedin' our good ol' brand o' husky-dogs off the trails of Alaska."

Katie, very plainly, could stand for no more.

"That's all very interesting," she bellowed. "But we're here to find an Indian baby. And if you can help us in our search I'd rather like to know it."

The challenge in Katie's voice brought a keener look of animosity from the bewhiskered old face.

"I was a-comin' to that, lady, if you'll only keep your shirt on." And still again he spat with deliberation. "Your Injin baby's over there in my wickyup."

"It's *where*?" cried Katie, reminding me of a coiled cobra.

The old stranger seemed to relish her bewilderment.

"It's over yonder in my wickyup, with that dood engineer tryin' to wet-nurse a little life into it. And I'll be doggoned if he ain't got it squallin' again like a two-year-old."

"Take me to it," commanded Katie. Her lips were grim as she motioned for the old-timer to climb up on the truck. She was, apparently, too exasperated to talk to him. So I did the conversing.

"Where," I asked as we rocked along the rough trail, "was the baby found?"

"Why, this long-legged quartz-cracker came mushin' down through the hills with a sheep dog at his heels, a right smart dog with a nose like a weasel's. Fact is, that hound smelt out something in a poplar grove jus' over the knoll beyont my clearin'. Kept whimperin' and whinin' and circlin' back there until his owner jus' had t' investigate. And there he finds an Injin baby wrapped up in a ragged blanket. And then comes stampedin' t' my shack door sayin' we've sure got t' save that little Injin's life. It looked plumb dead t' me. But I'll be gol-darned if that dood didn't get some signs o' life out o' the little varmint, after workin' over her half the night and warmin' her up with hot milk and my last bottle o' hootch. And he may git his own privit satisfaction out o' sweatin' over a whimperin' bunch o' skin and bones that-away, but, pussonally, I'll sleep easier when that little she-Injin is took from under my roof."

"What's your name?" I asked, primarily to cover Katie's open groan of indignation.

"You can call me Sock-Eye," he answered, "Sock-Eye Schlupp. What's yourn?"

"It's Coburn," I told him. And the deep-set old eyes studied me with a livelier interest.

"You ain't Alaska born?" he ventured.

"I was born," I proudly explained, "on the Koyukuk."

The man who called himself Sock-Eye stared at me.

"A Coburn from the Koyukuk? You ain't meanin' to tell me you're ol' Klondike Coburn's girl?"

I announced that I was.

"Why, I mushed many a trail with that leather-necked ol' pan-swizzler," was his slightly retarded rejoinder. "And I seen you when you was a squallin' little brat no bigger 'n a minute, over back o' Pickle Crick Camp. Why, it was me helped tote you down t' the sky-pilot at Elk Crossin', when you was christened. And consoomed my share o' the moose-milk after that sky-pilot'd mushed on t' his next mission post. They called you Carol in them days."

"Carol Koyukuk Coburn," I said, feeling a little closer to him.

"Sure it was, girlie," said my new-found friend. "Your pappy'd been pannin' pay dirt along the Koyukuk and held he was handin' luck on t' you with that name." Sock-Eye spat luxuriously, indicated the right trail fork for Katie to take, and turned back to me. "But his own luck didn't hold out. It sure didn't." Still again Sock-Eye spat. "That was a dirty deal they gave him over on the Chakitana."

"He died there," I said, with reproving quietness in my tone.

"And died fightin' for his rights, tryin' to push through t' the Record Office to git his patent from bein' canceled on him. But he was buckin' something too big for him. Seems like you got t' be a college g'ologist and a law sharp before you can stake a claim in this country nowadays."

"Then somebody else should be keeping up the fight," I said with a sort of she-wolf fierceness that brought the deep-set old eyes back to a study of my face.

" 'Tain't a fight where a pinfeather cluck like you'd have a look-in," observed Sock-Eye Schlupp. He spat wide into the fringing spruce. "And nothin' much is gained by bellyachin' over water that's gone down the flume, girlie. You should be satisfied Klondike sent you outside t' git eddicated proper."

"Perhaps I'm not," I said, embittered by a sense of relapse in the face of some old loyalty.

"Then what're you set on doin' with yourself?" my companion coolly inquired.

I told him, briefly, about my work at Toklutna. But it didn't impress him much.

"You're sure wastin' your time on them no-account Nitchies," he averred. His morose eye ranged along the far-off mountain peaks. "Same as I'm wastin' my time in this valley, batchin' it in a ten-by-twelve wickyup and bakin' my own sourdough, when I was known in the ol' days as the best shot on the Yukon. The best shot on the Yukon, fallen t' hoein' taters all summer and mushin' a run-down trap line all winter! But, by jiminy, I ain't give up. I've got me a minin' claim up between the Little Squaw and the Goldstream where the mother lode runs as thick as your leg and once I get back there and open her up she's sure goin' t' be a second El Dorado."

I could feel Katie's elbow prod my ribs.

"They all say that," she muttered.

I remembered that she was right. I'd seen them broken and wasted from bad diet, and arthritic from bad teeth and burnt out with bad whisky, but still nursing their dream of some lucky strike that was going to make them millionaires overnight. And in it, I felt, lay both the curse and the glory of all Alaska.

"Here we be," cried Sock-Eye as we rounded a trail bend and rolled up in front of a log shack with a pair of weather-bleached moose horns over the door. A blue column of smoke, going up from the slanting chimney pipe, seemed to endow it with both a sense of valor and a sense of hominess.

I was the last to pass in through the narrow door that squeaked on its leather hinges as it was swung back. The light wasn't strong in the shadowy warm room, where a tea kettle sang on the cookstove and a few telltale squares of flannelette hung from a drying line. So I didn't see any too well. But I could make out a dog, lying beside the stove, and a man in his shirt-sleeves, stooping over a blanket-lined basket without a handle.

I stared at that man, rather stupidly. Then I looked back at the dog, in an effort to verify the incredible. For I had seen that dog before, on the wharf at Cordova. And the man stooping over the blanket-lined basket was Sidney Lander.

I could feel my heart beating a little faster as I stood staring at him. He wasn't, I could see, giving us much attention. But he looked a little leaner and older, I thought, than when I'd last seen him. And a little too big for that narrow and low-ceilinged room. I could see Katie O'Connell's eyes widen as she inspected the nursing flask he'd made out of what looked suspiciously like a beer bottle with a glove finger tied over its end. It wasn't working right, apparently, from the thin wails of protest that came from the basket.

"Leave this to me," said the nurse as she tossed her parka over a chair back and reached for her handbag.

Sidney Lander, thus elbowed aside, stood watching the expeditious hands that betrayed none of the hesitations marking his own clumsy movements. His laugh, I felt, was one of discomfort at being discovered in a task for which he was plainly ill fitted. His gaze passed over the others and slewed about to his dog Sandy, who had crossed to my side and was sniffing at my ankles. When the dog lifted his pointed nose and rubbed it in a friendly way against my knee his owner raised his eyes and stared straight into my face.

He saw, for the first time, just who it was under that worn old parka. But he didn't speak and he didn't smile. He merely stood there, with wonder in his eyes. Then, after reaching for his coat and putting it on, he stepped over to where I stood.

"I didn't expect this," he said as Sock-Eye Schlupp busied himself stoking the stove. "I was on my way down to Toklutna."

"Why to Toklutna?" I asked. I could see, over my shoulder, where Katie O'Connell was opening her hypodermic case.

"To find out why you hadn't much faith in me," he said with his clipped smile.

"In what did I fail you?" I questioned, a little resentful of his power to dampen or quicken my spirits.

"I asked for the data and documents to back up your Chakitana claim," he reminded me.

"I don't happen to have any documents, as yet," I told him. "But even if I had, why should they go to you?"

I was thinking, at the moment, of the girl in the raincoat on a fog-draped wharf in Seattle.

"I wanted to lay them before John Trumbull," replied Lander, puzzling me by the grimness of his jaw-line. "He's the big smoke in the Chakitana Development Company."

"But also your boss," I said. I was glad to have Sandy's sleek neck to stroke. It seemed to make everything more casual.

"I'm afraid he won't be for long," was Lander's unexpectedly embittered reply.

"Why not?" I naturally enough inquired.

"Because you happen to be Klondike Coburn's daughter. And I don't relish the thought of working against you."

"Why should you work against me?" I asked, wondering at the foolish little spasm that was tightening my throat.

"Because I've been finding out a thing or two," he quietly affirmed. "I know, now, it's *you* they're trying to double-cross. It's your father's claim they're trying to swallow up on a clouded title."

"But I'm not sure that claim was ever established."

And it was equally obvious that his right either to champion my cause or control my destiny had never been established. But, for all that, an absurd little robin of happiness stood up on the tip of my heart and started to sing.

"We can't go into that now," Lander said as old Schlupp came in with an armful of stovewood. And Katie, a moment later, was announcing that you couldn't kill some children with a club. All this little papoose needed, she called out to us, was food.

"Then she ain't a-goin' to kick the bucket?" questioned Sock-Eye.

"Of course she isn't," said Katie. "But if I could lay hands on her fool redskin father I'd have him drawn and quartered."

The old fire-eater's face brightened up with a new eagerness.

"I'll do it for you, lady," he said with a large and rounded oath. "Sam Bryson was a-tellin' me that no-account Injin's hidin' out in a hill camp up above the Happy Day Mine. And I'd sure relish roundin' him up and ventilatin' his good-for-nothin' carcass."

"No," Katie said, "that's a luxury we can't afford. But he's going to be made an example of by due process of law. And if either of you men will take Miss Coburn and the baby back to Toklutna in the truck I'll get help and push on to the Happy Day and see that this baby-killer is put where he belongs."

Sidney Lander, who had been looking down at the blanket-wrapped papoose, lifted his head and caught my eye.

"I'll take Miss Coburn through to Toklutna," he quietly announced. And I could feel my pulse skip a beat, casual as I tried to appear about it all.

Even Katie's voice, as she outlined her instructions to me, seemed very far away. "And the sooner we get this little mite under Doctor Ruddock's wing the better," she concluded.

It was Sock-Eye who crossed to the door and looked out.

"There's sure a smell o' snow in the air," he warned. "We'd best fix up that truck more comfortable and stick a shovel in between the blankets and grub bags."

Through the window, when they left us, I could see the two men bedding down the body of the truck with fresh hay. Then over it I could see them bending and fitting a series of bows, and over these, in turn, adjust and fasten a canvas tarpaulin. As I watched I could see the truck being transformed into something startlingly like one of those covered wagons in which an earlier generation, down in the states, had crawled westward across the plains.

"She's all set," asserted Sock-Eye as he returned to the shack. He studied me for a moment of silence. Then his somber old eyes rested on Lander, who was busy filling the primus stove.

"I figger you out as a square-shootin' *hombre*," he announced. "But if you try any dirty work with this daughter o' Klondike Coburn's I'll fill your good-for-nothin' carcass so full o' lead you'll look like a range butt after a day o' target practice."

Sidney Lander, as he screwed the top on the primus stove, refused even to smile.

"She'll be safe with me," he said without even lifting his head.

CHAPTER IV

I FELT SAFE ENOUGH with Sidney Lander on that ride back to Toklutna. I had my papoose to look after and my trail mate had his truck to manage. He even refused to smile when I said it rather reminded me of *The Flight into Egypt*.

Something always happens, of course, to keep life from being too happy. For before we were an hour out on the road snow began to fall from the darkening sky. It fell heavier, before we were out of the valley, with a rising wind that blew the whipping flakes in streaks, and made it hard to see. It seemed to shut us up in a gray world all our own. And it gave us something more than our puny little emotions to think about.

By the time we were up in the hills we had drifts to buck. When it was necessary for Lander to stop and get busy with his shovel, I'd give my Indian baby its needed attention and nest it down in its cocoon of blanket-wool again, with only its pinched little yellow face showing like a seal's at the bottom of a blowhole. Then we'd fight our way on for another hundred yards or two. And I was almost ready to agree with Sock-Eye Schlupp that such contraptions as motor trucks weren't made for Alaska travel.

It wasn't until my companion got down from his seat and waded forward through a battalion of heavier drifts, to make sure of the trail that twisted so crazily about its narrow mountain shelf, that I had my first qualm of doubt.

"D'you think we can get through?" I asked, wondering why I was so contentedly facing hardship and peril.

Lander's laugh, as he turned and studied my face, was quiet and assuring.

"Aren't we of the breed," he demanded, "who never turn back?"

So we ploughed on again, feeling out our way in the uncertain light. Twice, when we slewed perilously close to the ravine that yawned at our car wheels, I thought the end had come. And twice, where the trail wound so vaguely about the upper slopes, we had to cut our way through drifts, with the help of the shovel. We did very little talking. But I could breathe more easily when we were over the hump and dropping down into the next valley.

Yet even there the drifts and darkness were too much for us. We got off the road and bumped head-on into a spruce stump. The old truck, with indignation boiling from its radiator cap, refused to go farther. I could see Lander's grim smile as I sat there staring out at the flailing snow. There wasn't a shack or settler, I felt sure, within ten miles of us.

"What'll we do?" I asked with a gulp.

It was Lander's turn to blink about at the snow-clad wastes surrounding us.

"I suppose we'll have to sleep out here," he casually announced.

"I suppose so," I agreed. But I wasn't as placid-minded about it as I pretended. Lander, in fact, stared into my face for a moment or two before swinging down from his driver's seat. Then he lighted the primus stove and hung a lantern from one of the bows of our little covered-wagon truck-tent. And then, after shutting out the snow and wind by closing the end flaps of the tarpaulin, he announced that he was going to have a look ahead along the trail.

He stayed away longer than I expected. By the time he got back, in fact, I'd melted snow and had our coffee boiling on the primus stove. The smell of that coffee made our little canvas-covered cave seem rather homelike. And my cave mate watched me with a ruminative eye as I warmed milk and fed the quietly complaining Indian baby. When our papoose was back in its blanket-muffled basket, and we sat eating, with the primus stove between us, it seemed oddly paleolithic to be squatting there on a bundle of hay, dining on bacon and beans and sourdough bread.

Lander helped me pack things away when the meal was over.

"You're facing this like an old-timer," he said as he closed a tarp-vent through which the wind was whistling. My answering smile was altogether a forced one.

"I used to go out on the trail with my father," I reminded him.

"That's what I want to talk to you about," he said. "Can you remember his camp on the Chakitana?"

"I was never there," I had to admit.

"Then it won't be easy to explain what I want to," he went on. "Your father had a real mine there. And he must have known it."

"Of course he did," I said, recalling ghostly scraps of talk from my childhood.

"Well, so does the Trumbull outfit," proclaimed my companion. The grimness of his voice made me prick up my ears. "The Chakitana Development Company always wanted a clean sweep of that valley bottom. They even sent me up there as field engineer to find out how the land lay and corral any territory needed to round out their development work. It was your father's claim which cut their field in two and kept them from having full control."

"He always said he'd never sell out," I explained.

"Of course he did," cried Lander. "He may have been a lone-fire prospector, but he knew he held a key position there. And when they couldn't buy him out they did what they could to cancel on him."

"Then he had his patent?" I asked.

"Yes; but they tried to cloud his title by claiming his location lines were wrong. The official survey, when his first twenty acres were patented, showed the eastern limits of the claim to border on the Big Squaw where that creek ran into the Chakitana. The Big Squaw, in the open season, has a fine flow of water. And you can't mine in Alaska without water. I saw the Fairbanks Exploration Company spend a year and a half bringing water to their placer fields. And Trumbull wants that water for his upper shelf just about as much as he wants the claim."

"How do you know all this?" I asked.

"Because I've seen the Trumbull papers. And I made it my business to investigate some of the Trumbull moves. I know, for example, that while his engineers pretended to be doing development work their powdermen planted enough dynamite in the right place to change the course of Big Squaw Creek. Then they brought in a Record Office surveyor who naturally found the Coburn location stakes all wrong."

"But the mining laws were framed to protect the finder of new claims," I argued. "And the records are still the records."

"But now and then a big corporation seems able to steamroller the rights out of them. A man like Trumbull, remember, can always pull strings at either Juneau or Washington. He can always find a palm to grease."

"The thing that puzzles me," I interposed, "is why you're not loyal to the man you're working for."

Lander's laugh was curt.

"If you can't sense that," he said, "I can't explain it to you." He laughed again, less harshly. "Let's put it down to the fact that a man can't work for a boss he doesn't believe in."

I still found a blaze or two missing along that trail.

"But why should he call my father's claim a fraudulent one?"

"Klondike Coburn, he contends, was born on the Canadian side of the line."

"That's true enough," I conceded. "But what about it?"

"A great deal. It means he wasn't a citizen. And the law says a patent can be allotted only to citizens."

"But my father was naturalized," I told him, "a year or two before I was born. He even used to talk about when he moved up out of the Indian class and got a right to vote."

Lander's spine suddenly stiffened.

"Are you sure of that?" he demanded. "Trumbull claims there's no record of it."

"But I have his papers," I explained. "He sent them out to me so I could get my passports when I was sailing for Europe."

I wondered at the grimness with which my companion said, "Good work!" And I remembered the faded and dog-eared certificate, with the photo attached, also slightly faded, showing my father looking young and strong, in the pride of his early manhood. I'd always treasured that picture of him, the only one I possessed.

"That means our battle's half won," proclaimed Lander.

"Why do you say *our* battle?" I asked. Lander's face, as our glances locked, hardened a little. Then he laughed his curt laugh.

"Since I muddled into this thing," he said, "I'm going to be bullheaded enough to see it through."

"Why should you?" I asked, recalling earlier days when my ears had caught so many echoes of quarrels over location posts, water rights, metes and bounds.

"Let's write it down," he finally said, "to the fact that I like a straight shooter."

What was above suspicion as an ideal of conduct proved slightly disappointing as a personal response.

"But it's all so long ago," I objected. "And you can't wreck your career championing lost causes."

Still again Lander laughed.

"My career isn't wrecked. I'm thinking of swinging in with the Happy Day outfit, in fact, just beyond the Matanuska."

"Why?" I asked.

"Because then we won't be so far apart," he said.

I sat silent a minute or two, listening to the howling of the wind. I was thinking, as I studied the man sitting beside me on the truck hay, how close people could seem and yet be an ocean apart.

"You've been very kind to me," I said with a sort of let's-turn-the-page listlessness.

"You're easy to be kind to," Lander retorted with a quiet intensity that should have shifted my heart action into high. But I had certain things to remember.

"What does that mean?" I exacted, challengingly calm-eyed.

He leaned a little closer under the swaying lantern.

"It means I'm happier being with you than with anyone who walks this good green earth."

I was able to laugh a little. "It isn't green," I reminded him. "And you might also remember why you so nearly missed the boat at Seattle?"

That took the wind out of his sails. I could see his jaw muscles harden as he sat staring at me in the dim light from the lantern. Then he reached for his blanket roll.

"I guess I'm running a little ahead of schedule," he said as he rose to his feet. I watched him, with a small tingle of disappointment, as he backed out of the tent opening and began tying the flap cords together again.

"You're not going away?" I cried out above the whining of the wind. His quiet laugh, I suppose, was at the womanish quaver in my voice.

"I'll bed down up in the driver's seat," he casually remarked. And in a few minutes I could feel the tremor of the truck as he climbed aboard, up in front. I could hear him, a moment later, as he nested himself under his double blankets.

He wouldn't, I knew, be very comfortable there. But I consoled myself with the thought that it was something of his own choosing. I even wondered, as I stretched out on the hay next to my blanket-swathed little papoose, if wind and cold wouldn't drive him back under cover, where he had a perfect right to be.

But when I wakened, in the middle of the night, I was still alone. And our Alaska blizzard was still slapping the tarp sides against the truck stays. And the snow, I knew, was piling deeper and deeper about that open-throated little cave of a driver's seat.

CHAPTER V

I WAS AWAKENED, EARLY the next morning, by Lander reaching in for the lantern. The drifter was over, he explained, but he'd have an hour of shovel work before we could hope to climb back to the trail bed.

He hadn't slept any too well, I'm afraid, up on his wind-swept driver's seat. I detected a sort of glum fury in his movements as he shoveled at the snowdrift that embedded us. Even after I'd boiled coffee and cooked breakfast for him he impressed me as unnecessarily constrained and silent. And he must have found little to lighten his spirits, once we had got under way again, as we fell to battling that deep-drifted trail.

Yet the world, to me, looked very lovely under its undulating blanket of snow. It looked clean and virginal and mysterious in the opal-gray of early morning. And as the light grew clearer my spirits grew blither.

"What's on your mind?" I challenged as he stopped to look into his fuel tank.

He was worried, he explained without looking up at me, about his gasoline giving out.

"And in a week or two," I babbled, "we'd be found by a searching-party, eating spruce bark and stewed mukluks and ready to murder each other."

He saw no humor in that, apparently. For all he did was climb back in his driver's seat and busy himself bucking the windrowed trail that wound down through the hills.

And the gasoline, after all, didn't give out. But it was late in the afternoon when we got through to Toklutna and drew up at the old wooden barracks that was our destination.

There we were received by Miss Teetzel, who promptly ordered the Indian baby to the infirmary and sent for Doctor Ruddock. Lander, ignoring the lady's glacial eye, quietly asked me if I'd be good enough to give him my father's naturalization papers.

I could feel something pregnant in the silence I left behind me as I went to my room and dug out the dog-eared old document.

I had no way of knowing, of course, what Miss Teetzel said to Lander during my absence. But I didn't like the heat-lightning fire that glowed in those deep-set eyes of his as he took the proffered document from me. He studied it, for a moment, the lines of his mouth still grim.

"I'll take this, if you don't mind," he said as he tucked it away. "It'll help to clear things up."

I wasn't unconscious, all the while, of Miss Teetzel's narrowed eye fixed on my face.

"There's one point I should like to see cleared up," she announced, her lips pressed into a foreboding straight line.

"What?" said Lander, almost in a bark. But Miss Teetzel's attentions, obviously, were being directed toward me.

"How long," she asked, "did it take you to get here?"

"Since yesterday afternoon," I said, rather light-hearted with the knowledge of obstacles overcome and dangers past.

"Where," demanded Miss Teetzel, with a disapproving glance at my silent companion, "did you spend the night?"

"Why, in the truck, of course," I answered. "There was no place to go."

"And this man?" she questioned, with a second stony glance at the altogether unimpressed Lander.

"Naturally, he slept in the truck too," I quietly acknowledged.

The lemon-squeezer jaw took on a new line of grimness.

"I've an idea, Miss Coburn," said the lady of unpolluted purity so icily confronting me, "that your days in this school are quite definitely numbered."

It was Lander who spoke first. I could see the color deepen a little on his weathered brown face.

"What does that mean?" he challenged.

"It means, sir," was the icily enunciated reply, "that there are certain things this institution will not stand for. And you and your perilously modern traveling companion have just been guilty of one of them."

Lander merely turned his back on the poker-spined Miss Teetzel.

"Are you going to stand for stuff like this?" he demanded, towering over me with a quick flame of indignation lighting up his eyes. Those eyes, I noticed, were a mahogany-brown stippled with hazel. "And from a mean-spirited old bureaucrat like that?"

Behind me I could sense the last boat of hope burning up on the coast of desperation. Instead of looking at Lander I looked at the audibly wheezing Miss Teetzel, who had an Adam's apple that moved engagingly up and down as she swallowed. I knew, when I spoke, that I was issuing an ultimatum.

"I don't intend to," I quietly announced.

"That," proclaimed the thin-lipped Miss Teetzel, "simplifies my problem." And with a gesture as though she were removing herself from something unclean she flounced out of the room.

Lander, when we were alone, stood a little closer over me.

"I got you into this," he said, "and it's up to me to get you out of it."

I was conscious of his bigness as I let my gaze lock with his. My laughter, I'm afraid, was a little reckless.

"There's nothing to be done about it," I told him. But deep in the ashes of disaster I could feel a small glow of happiness at the thought that he was there to lean on.

"Why not come back with me?" he finally inquired.

"What good would that do?" I said, doing what I could to keep my voice steady. For, womanlike, I felt the shadow of a disturbingly wide issue fall across that empty room.

Lander, after looking down at me for what must have been a full half-minute of silence, walked to the window and then returned to my side.

"It wouldn't do *any* good," he said, with just a trace of the color ebbing from his face. "It's all happening a little too late."

"What's happening too late?" I asked him, wondering why I should wring a forlorn sort of comfort out of the trouble I could see in his eyes.

"Our coming together," he said. I thought he was going to reach for my hand, but he didn't. "There are things," he went on, "not easily talked about."

"But we can at least be honest with each other," I announced, for instinct had already told me what he was groping toward.

"Yes, we must be honest," he agreed. And the unhappiness in his eyes made my heart beat a little faster.

"I'm pretty practical-minded," I told him, doing my best to speak calmly. "And I think I know what you're trying to tell me."

"I'm not trying to tell you," he retorted. "But as I said before, there are things a man doesn't talk about."

"Just as there are things he doesn't *do*," I amended. "I mean, of course, a man of honor."

"I'm not altogether a cad," he cried, "just as you're not what that Teetzel woman thinks you are."

"So it's time," I said, "that we both came down to earth."

"What do you mean by that?" exacted my grim-jawed companion.

"I saw the girl back on the Seattle wharf, the girl you said good-by to. And I can understand why you must play fair with her."

Lander's glance came slowly back to my face.

"I've been engaged to her," he said, quite simply, "for over two years now."

If I reached for a chair back, to steady myself, I at least managed to laugh a little.

"That's fine," I said, with my chin up.

"Fine?" he echoed, plainly puzzled by that lilting lightness of mine.

"Of course," I maintained. "For now we can go on being good friends, without any worry or threat of—of complications."

"Can we?" he asked as his eyes once more rested on my face.

"Good pals," I cried, "to the end of the trail. So let's shake hands on it, like two old-timers."

He failed to observe, as we shook hands, that I had to swallow a lump in my throat.

"Would you mind telling me," I said when that was over, "just who she is?"

It wasn't easy for him, of course. But he faced it with a forlorn sort of casualness.

"She's Barbara Trumbull," he explained. "John Trumbull's daughter. We practically grew up together."

"Then you must have a great deal in common."

He studied my face, as though in search of second meanings.

"We had," he finally acknowledged.

"But you talk of fighting her father," I reminded him.

"And I intend to fight him," said the wide-shouldered man beside me. "But she'd feel things like that shouldn't count between us."

When I spoke, after thinking this over, I was able to keep my voice steady.

"How do *you* feel about it?" I asked.

"I can't answer that," was Lander's slightly retarded reply. "You see, she's coming to Alaska to get things straightened out. She doesn't agree with her father that I've been disloyal to the Trumbulls."

That also gave me a moment of thought.

"Then she must be very fond of you," I heard myself saying.

To that, however, Lander offered no answer. His smile, as he looked down at me, was wry and rather mirthless.

"But we've still got a battle on our hands," he reminded me.

I preferred accepting that in its more practical implications.

"But I can't ask you to fight for me," I said, trying not to feel as though I were standing alone in a world that was only a burnt-out planet lost in space.

"You can't stop me," he said, catching me almost roughly by the shoulders. And he was still staring down at me with a sort of Nunc-Dimittus solemnity when the outraged Miss Teetzel stepped into the room.

CHAPTER VI

TOKLUTNA DIDN'T GET RID of me so soon as it expected. Two days after my scene with the acidulous Miss Teetzel I was interrupted in my packing by Katie O'Connell, who seated herself with an air of triumph on my battered old trunk.

That triumphal smile of hers, I thought, stemmed from the fact she'd just that morning returned from Matanuska with her Indian prisoner and promptly obtained his commitment for trial. But I was wrong there.

"You can back away from all that," she said with a hand wave at my half-packed bags. "You're anchored here, old dear."

I asked her what gave her that idea.

"Because we're in quarantine," she announced, "with two cases of scarlet fever in the infirmary. And Ruddy says you can't walk out on him."

"Miss Teetzel," I reminded her, "said otherwise."

"But old Teetzel's out of the picture. She's in bed with bronchitis—and that's about the only thing she ever *will* go to bed with. And Ruddy says we've got to carry on."

Ruddy, of course, was Doctor Ruddock. And even though his word hadn't been law, at such a time, the Ruddy-adoring Katie would have wintered in a leper colony if her preoccupied man-of-medicine suggested it.

So, being indispensable, the school had to put up with its social pariah who slept out in motor trucks. It also kept that outcast lady busy enough to forget about her own petty problems. Scarlet fever, I found, was not an easy thing to fight.

But even in her illness that domineering principal of ours made her influence felt. She reminded me of a half-starved black spider at the center of its web, watching for every faintest vibration that visited every faraway thread of her floating net of animosity. And even between her fits of coughing she devised ingenious ways of keeping the flame of hostility from dying down. Any peace that work and weariness brought me was, I knew, only an armistice. I felt less at sea after Doctor Ruddock had me write to the Territorial Commissioner (following up, I discovered, a secret dispatch of his own) asking for a teacher's position in the Matanuska Valley.

When I heard, by that grapevine circuit which seems to operate in all frontier countries, that John Trumbull had visited the valley and that Barbara Trumbull had flown in to Anchorage, it seemed like echoes out of another world. Even when I heard that Lander had taken over the management of the Happy Day Mine and that he and Trumbull had fought a wordy battle on the open platform of Matanuska station, I failed to be as excited as when Katie told me that the little Indian girl from Iliamna, up in our improvised pest ward, wasn't going to die, after all. I had, I remembered, my own canoe to paddle. And as the days shortened and the snows deepened, I kept waiting for my Commissioner's report.

That report was neither prompt nor encouraging. It acknowledged they were in need of a teacher for Matanuska but that conditions were not suitable there for a young and inexperienced outsider.

I wrote back admitting my youth but pointing out it was a defect which time would undoubtedly correct. I also alluded to my physical sturdiness and my eagerness to work in the new field, with an underlined postscript announcing I was Alaska born. And in the meantime both the calendar and the excitement of our little redskinned wards reminded us that Christmas was close at hand.

Then came the second blow. For Katie and I, with Miss Teetzel still weak and crabby, did what we could to make the children's holiday a happy one. We sent to Anchorage for hard candy and sugar-canes and colored candles and glitter-paper and powdered mica. With my own hand I cut down a spruce tree and dragged it in over the hills. This, when duly installed in the schoolroom, we draped with strung popcorn and emblazoned with bits of ribbon and spangled with tin stars cut out of empty tomato cans, adding copious streamers of wrapping cord dyed red with beet juice and snowy handfuls of absorbent purloined from the surgery. And over everything we sprinkled a generous glitter of powdered mica.

It was all pathetically meager and make-believe. But the raptness of the children's eyes, as they stood and watched that tree, brought a lump to my throat. It paid for the long hours when Katie and I sat up wrapping oranges in red tissue paper, one for each child, and labeling the mitts and stockings and sweaters out of the community gift boxes from Seattle and Juneau.

But my little Injins loved it all. On Christmas morning, in fact, when I appeared in pillow-stuffed Turkey red, as Santa Claus, they got so excited we had to drape the schoolroom doors with blankets, to keep the noise from Miss Teetzel's disapproving ears. They put on paper hats and sang "Rock-a-bye,

My Little Owlet" and "Jingle Bells" and even had a try at Handel's, "While Shepherds Watched Their Flocks," which Katie and I found it expedient to finish out by ourselves. Then they made the rafters ring with "Alouette."

But their little Indian souls eventually got so drunk on music and excitement that we had to ease them down with a square dance. And the easing down would have been less dire if a little Copper River brave hadn't chased a still smaller Innuit blubber-eater from the Kuskokwim right into our twinkling and glittering Christmas tree. That collision overturned one of the lighted candles.

I heard a crackle of flames and a dozen shrill cries from a dozen little throats. Then I saw, to my horror, that our tree was a tower of fire.

I snatched one of the blankets draping the doors and tried to smother the flames. But it was too late. The blanket took fire. Even my Santa Claus gown started to burn, and I tore it off in the nick of time. I knew, as I did so, just what would happen to that old tinderbox of a building if it ever got going. And I remembered there were six or seven helpless children up in the infirmary.

Katie must have remembered the same thing, for she shouted for me to get up to those children while she got the milling and wailing schoolroom group safely out of the building. The walls in the Christmas-tree corner were already ablaze. And something told me our school was doomed.

Even in the outer hall the smoke was thick as I raced for the infirmary. There I caught up a wailing little redskin from the first bed, calling back for the others not to move as I ran for the door and hurried down the stairs to the west-end door, where Miss Teetzel, unexpectedly active and efficient, was commanding the bigger boys to clear out the building known as the Warehouse and spread blankets on the floor. Then I raced back for my second patient.

The smoke was thicker along the hall and stairway, and I found it harder to see. But I knew a surge of relief when Katie passed me, carrying a child in her arms.

Two minutes later I was safely down the stairs with the third helpless tot in my arms. Miss Teetzel, as she took the patient from me, looked sharply into my sooty and reddened face. For the first time in my life I failed to see hate in her eyes. But I hadn't time to give it much thought.

A village Indian who'd been wasting water and energy as one of a bucket brigade tried to stop me as I started in through the door. He shouted that the stairs were on fire. But I pushed him to one side and raced up through the smoke.

I found what was left of the children out of bed and huddled in one corner of the infirmary. There were four of them. They shrieked when they saw me, for Katie had given me a wet sheet with which to cover my head. That seemed to keep some of the smoke away and made it easier to breathe as I groped my way down with a little Nitchie in my arms. And again Miss Teetzel eyed me as I handed over another patient.

"No go back," a ragged half-breed bellowed at me as I faced the burning building. He stood there, blocking my way, with one hand clamped to either side of the door. It was Katie's vigorous kick, coming down with a child in her arms, that sent him sprawling out on the ground and gave me gangway.

I could hear the crackle of timber and see flames licking through the stair boards as I fought my way back to the infirmary. It would, I knew, be my last visit to that room. So I caught up the two remaining children, covering their heads with my wet sheet, and felt my way toward the hall. Their weight, when I was so in want of breath, made me stagger. But they helped me, in their terror, by hanging on like leeches. I could see flames along the floor boards and I wasn't always sure of my footing. I had to feel for the stairhead with my feet, like a horse feeling for footage on a slough bank. And I thought, for a moment, that I was going to faint, my throat felt so scalded with smoke. But at the bottom of those stairs, I knew, was fresh air and safety.

So I clutched the two small bodies closer and staggered down that runway of licking and dancing flames, with my shoes scorching from the heat and my lungs aching for one whiff of pure air. I had, by this time, no sense of place or direction. But through the murk I could make out the pale oblong of the open door. And out through that open door I stumbled, stumbled straight into the arms of Katie O'Connell, who huskily croaked, "Glory be to God!" as she eased me down on the trodden dooryard snow and started flailing my burning clothes with the wet end of a blanket. Then, for a minute or two, everything went black.

When I opened my eyes Katie was trying to make me swallow a cupful of brandy and water. I managed to smile up at her as she mopped the smoke stains from my face.

"That's the ticket," she said. Then she busied herself rubbing olive oil on my scorched hands and cheeks. I didn't know it at the time, but my eyelashes were missing and a goodly part of my front hair had gone glimmering.

"Did I get them all?" I asked, thinking of the children. It hurt me to talk, for my throat was sore from the smoke.

"You did, old-timer," affirmed Katie. "But it nearly got *you*."

And with that she picked me up in her arms and carried me to the improvised barracks that had once been our Warehouse, where a stove had been put up and floor bunks were being arranged for the children. There she tucked me up in a blanket and took a hand in the general hubbub of organizing shelter for the little waifs all about us.

It wasn't long before Doctor Ruddock arrived on the scene. He refused to laugh as he looked down at my oily and heat-reddened face.

"Hello, stoker," he said, blinking down at me. Then he stooped for a moment to take my pulse. "You've got the stuff this country needs."

"I'm all right," I told him. "You must look after the children."

He nodded.

"I'll fix you up later," he said as he put the blanket back over my scorched clothing. "But stay where you are, young lady, or I'll nail you down."

But I refused to stay put. There was too much to be done. I didn't want to seem a slacker when everybody was so busy. And in looking after the others I could pretty well forget the pain of my own flame-blistered face.

Where the rambling old schoolhouse had been was a stretch of smoldering ashes with the skeletonlike iron bed frames and a stove or two standing there as melancholy as tombstones. And everything I owned lay consumed in those ashes. All I had left were the few scorched clothes that hung about my tired bones.

But I hadn't time to feel sorry for myself. A special train, I was told, was already on its way from Anchorage, to pick up our homeless school waifs and carry them on to the Indian orphanage at Fairbanks. From the pile of emergency clothing Katie commandeered for me an oversized pair of corduroy trousers, a patched plaid Mackinaw, and a caribou parka that had seen better days. To these Doctor Ruddock (who'd given up his little wooden-fronted office as sleeping-quarters for Katie and me) added socks and pacs and an old bearskin cap that made me look like a lady-huzzar in a busby.

"It's time to change the guard!" cried Katie as she studied me in my new get-up.

"We don't seem to look very regal, do we?" I said as I surveyed myself.

"Handsome is as handsome does," Katie retorted with a fraternal pat on the shoulder. And I detected in that honest Irish face a beauty which before had escaped me.

"What are we going to do?" I asked the ever-hurrying Doctor Ruddock when he dropped in, next day, to anoint my scorched epidermis with amber-sine.

"We're going to get some eyebrows and the skin you like to touch back again," he said as he finished his veneering job.

"But how about Toklutna?" I asked.

"Toklutna's off the map," he proclaimed. "Katie will stay on here, probably until the breakup, to look after the old folks."

"Then where do I fit in?" I questioned with a sudden feeling of homelessness.

"You fit in very neatly," he said as he listened to my heart action. "I'd the Commissioner on the wire this morning and he agrees with me this country owes you a berth. So you get the school job at Matanuska."

It took some time for this to sink in.

"When?" I asked.

"As soon as you get sense enough to take care of yourself," he said with a barricading sort of curtness. "I told you to rest up, after your fire shock, and you didn't do it. So roll up in that bunk and stay there until you get a release from me."

He stopped in the doorway, with his dog-eared old medicine case in his hand, as I none too willingly shook out the blankets of my floor bunk.

"And there's a long-legged engineer waiting outside to see you," he added as he watched me dutifully crawl into my bunk. "But ten minutes is his limit, remember."

I had my second shock to digest. For the waiting visitor was Sidney Lander.

He stood very tall in that small office-surgery. And my appearance must have startled him a little, since he stared down at me, for a full half-minute, without speaking.

"Are you all right?" he finally asked. I had to laugh a little at his solemnity.

"Just a little scorched around the edges," I said with an effort at levity. But my heart was beating a trifle faster than it should have been.

"I flew over, as soon as I heard," he rather clumsily explained. He looked out the window and then back at me. "That was good work, saving those children."

"But I lost my eyebrows," I reminded him. My smile was a restricted one, for the stiffened skin along my cheekbone still hurt when it moved.

He didn't, apparently, regard the loss of an eyebrow as important.

"How about your things?" he asked as his eye wandered over my old plaid Mackinaw.

"Not a rag of them saved," I had to acknowledge. The memory of their loss made me feel rather rootless and alone in the world. Then I remembered about Matanuska. "But an old-timer never gives up."

Lander walked to the window and back.

"We've at least saved those citizenship papers," he announced.

"What are you doing with them?" I asked.

His jaw hardened.

"I've shown them to John Trumbull," he explained, "and Trumbull claims they're not backed up by the records. That led to an argument that ended in a split-up. The Chakitana Development Company has lost its field engineer."

"What are you going to do?" I asked.

His laugh was curt.

"I was tying up with the Happy Day outfit," he explained. "But Trumbull's just trumped my ace by buying up the Happy Day."

"Why should he do that?"

"To put me where I belong," was the slightly embittered reply. "To chasten a renegade for trying to buck anything as big as him and his company."

"Does that mean you're going outside?" I asked, trying to make the question a casual one.

"Not on your life," was his prompt reply. "We've got to wait until the records show who's right in this."

"But that's *my* problem," I objected.

"I happen to have made it mine," he retorted with an unexpected light of battle in his eyes.

"But what are you going to do?" I repeated.

"The important thing," he countered, "is what *you're* going to do."

"I'm not of much importance," I said, remembering things which he seemed to have forgotten.

"You are to me," he averred with altogether unheralded recklessness. "And if you're moving about this frostbitten map I'd rather like to be in the same neighborhood."

"That's very gallant," I acknowledged. "But it won't quite work out?"

"Why not?" he demanded, stooping over my browless and ambersined face. "What *are* you going to do?"

It wasn't easy, under that coating of ambersine and with my front hair gone, to be as dignified as I wanted to be. But I was still free, white and twenty-one. And I had my own canoe to paddle.

"I'm going to Matanuska," I announced with much the same vigor with which Caesar must have announced he was going to cross the Rubicon.

CHAPTER VII

I BEGAN TO UNDERSTAND the meaning of what they call "the deep cold" before I set out for Matanuska. For the snows of midwinter soon buried the ruins of our lost school, piled high along the trails between the hills, and left it no easy matter for even Katie and her Ruddy to make their rounds. The storms along Alaska's one stretch of railway also brought slides and broken snowsheds enough to block the line and keep trains from moving for over a week.

That cloud had the silver lining of giving me a chance to make over my nondescript wardrobe, to which big-hearted Katie added a sweater of Scotch wool and a pair of wolfskin gauntlets, a trifle oversized. She said I'd need 'em in that valley of jerry-built wickyups where I'd probably have to rustle my own stovewood. She was, I think, genuinely sorry to see me go. But in the North Country, she proclaimed, trails had the habit of crossing. And when the going got better, she further proclaimed, she'd drive through with her dog-team and dig me out of the valley drifts of the Chugacs.

So when traffic moved again and I mounted my day coach I found it crowded to the doors with leather-faced old sourdoughs and cud-chewing trappers and Mackinaw-clad loggers, along with a homesteader's wife who carried an undersized pig in a slatted crate and a commercial traveler from Ketchikan who couldn't understand my lack of interest in his advances, which were as annoying to my already depressed spirits as the all-pervading tobacco smoke was to my throat.

I wasn't sorry when the conductor, pushing his way through that overcrowded day coach, blinked down at my still heat-blistered face and said: "Next stop Matanuska, lady."

I refused to feel depressed as I alighted at the desolate little station where a scattering of fur-clad loungers stood between the soiled snow piles. I saw two silent and stolid-faced Indians, and a blue-eyed Swede boy in a ragged bearskin coat that was too big for him, and a surly-eyed man in a stained Mackinaw beside a wolfish-looking dog-team hitched to a sleigh. I saw a hurrying and blue-jowled youth load parcels and boxes into an absurdly modern-looking truck with icicles decorating its radiator front, and plow off through the drifts into the blue-white silence of the valley. But there was no one there to betray any interest in me or my advent.

I began to wonder, as I stood beside my tumbled-out sprawl of baggage, just where to go or what to do. I ventured into the waiting room, where the warm air was thick with the smell of tobacco and spruce wood, but all I saw was the broad back of the station agent busy over his telegraph key. So I went outside, feeling very homeless in a hostile and empty world. There I finally found the courage to address the surly-eyed misanthrope who was concentrating his attention on piling meal sacks along his narrow-bodied dog sleigh.

"Could you tell me," I asked, "where I'd find Mr. Bryson, Mr. Sam Bryson?"

His face, when he peered up at me, impressed me as both sour and sardonic. It had the seamed and shrunken and slightly scorbutic look of the true old-timer. It remained impassive as he once more inspected me and spat in the snow.

"I'm Sam Bryson," he said as he reached for another meal sack. And any deliverance that reposed in an apparent streak of luck lost its glamour as I awaited the return of his averted face.

"The school superintendent for this district?" I persisted.

"I be," he retorted, plainly resenting my incredulous stare. "And ain't it fit and proper, seein' I happen to *own* that doggoned schoolhouse over there?"

I meekly acknowledged that it was. And with equal meekness I told him that I was the new teacher sent on from Toklutna.

"But you wasn't to turn up here till Easter," he said testily. "We ain't got nothin' ready for you."

I showed him the Territorial Commissioner's letter, which he held close to his seamed old face, his lips moving as he labored through the undisputable message therein contained.

"Well, you should've got off at Wasilla," he complained, "where you could've found lodgin' until things was ready."

And this, I told myself, was the valley I was giving up my young life to redeem!

"But I'm here," I said with a smile that was entirely forced. And as he pushed back his wolfskin cap and stood scratching an attenuated forelock I quietly inquired: "Just where is my school?"

He studied me with a lack-luster eye.

"You ain't got no school," he proclaimed.

"But I was sent here to teach," I contended, trying to keep my temper. At Toklutna, I remembered, I'd had a persistent feeling of being penned up. But I wasn't finding much joy in the valley of my newly acquired liberty.

"Sure you was sent here to teach," acknowledged the old-timer. "But it ain't our fault we wasn't rigged out with a noo schoolhouse this winter. Gover'ment's so danged busy with a heap o' highfalutin' plans for this valley it ain't got time to look after our needs. Spends a half-million on that noo Injin school at Juneau and lets us hillbillies scramble for our book-larnin' as best we can!"

"Then what am I to do?" I asked, feeling more interested in my own immediate future than in the mistakes of governmental expenditure.

He looked at his line of sleigh-huskies lying so patiently in the snow. The lean and wolfish bodies impressed me as fit emblems of Northland fortitude.

"I guess you'll just have to siwash it," he said, "the same as us old-timers did when we hit this valley."

"Just how will I siwash it?" I demanded.

"By froggin' through as best you can, the same as our circuit-ridin' sky-pilot does, without a meetin'-place. We was figgerin' on you circulatin' round the valley homesteads and ladlin' out the book-larnin' where it was most needed. Instead o' them comin' to you, you'll have to go to them."

"Why can't that old schoolhouse be used?"

"She needs a noo roof and noo floor sills," was the listless answer. "And I'm danged if *I'm* goin' to dig down for 'em."

"Are you trying to tell me," I quavered, "that I'll have to go from farm to farm, like a mail carrier, and give my lessons in a kitchen?"

"You've guessed it," he wearily acceded. "Only you'll be plumb lucky to be stretchin' your legs out in a warm kitchen. I've got a girl over home right now, rarin' to git polished up a spell on her readin' and writin'. And if you ain't willin' to do your teachin' on the wing that-away, until this valley gits a real schoolhouse rastled together, I guess, lady, you're mushin' up the wrong trail."

There was no mistaking the finality of that statement.

"But where am I to *live*?" I asked as I stared at the snow that stood so white between the gloomy green of the sprucelands.

"We was figgerin'," he explained, "on settin' you up in the old Jansen shack. That's just over the hill there behind that tangle o' spruce. But you'd sure have some tidyin' up to do afore you got set there." He looked with a frown of disapproval at my sprawl of luggage. " 'Bout the best thing for you to do, lady, is to leg it over to the Eckstrom farm and see if they'd take you in for a day or two."

I had, however, no desire to go wandering about that snowy world asking strangers to take me in. I wanted my own roof over my head. And I so informed the morose Mr. Bryson.

"Well, that's your affair, lady, and not mine," he observed. "I've got to be gittin' home with this stock feed right pronto."

I watched him as he corded a tarpaulin over his sleigh load and started off, his iron-shod runners whining on the dry snow. I was on the point of going back to the red-faced station agent when I became conscious of a strange figure making its way down the opposing hillside. It looked like neither man nor beast as it moved toward me in the slanting sunlight. It suggested some humped and horned monstrosity out of the mists of time, something Pleistocenic and malformed.

Then, as it came closer, I saw that it was a man carrying the carcass of a deer, a ragged and shambling man with a rifle and a tined head above his stooping shoulders. And when he came still closer I saw that it was Sock-Eye Schlupp.

He failed to recognize me, with the sun in his eyes, until he was close beside me. He eased himself of his burden and blinked first at my face and then at my scattering of luggage. There was rime on his rough coat front and tobacco stains on his grizzled chin.

"I'll be hornswizzled if it ain't Klondike Coburn's gal," he said as the sourness went out of his seamed old face. "What're you doin' back in these parts?"

I told him why I was there.

"Where you goin' to bunk?" he demanded.

That question made me feel like a steerage immigrant on an alien wharf end. But I decided to keep my chin up.

"They tell me I'm to live in the Jansen shack," I explained.

"They're plumb locoed," said Sock-Eye. "You sure can't den up in that pigsty."

"I'm north born," I reminded him.

"Mebbe you are," he retorted. "But this is a plumb lonesome valley for a chalk-wrangler t' take root in. I reckon you'd better come along t' my wickyup until things is ready for you."

That, I told him, would be out of the question.

"I s'pose you know young Lander's swingin' in with me?" he said with the air of an angler adjusting a gaudier fly.

That, I knew, made it more than ever impossible. "And if that Jansen shack's not ready, I'll have to make it ready."

"Quite a fighter, ain't you?" he observed. But his head-wag wasn't altogether one of disapproval.

"A woman wants a home of her own," was my foolishly stubborn rejoinder.

He prodded the furred carcass with his rifle butt.

"I've been up in the hills, gittin' me some deer meat," he casually observed. Then still again he turned and inspected me. "I don't believe you savvy jus' what you're bitin' off, girlie."

"I don't believe in turning back," I quietly informed him.

"Okay," said Sock-Eye, after a moment's silence. "I'll give you a hand over t' that lordly abode o' yours."

He left me standing there, to return, a few minutes later, with a hand sleigh borrowed from the station agent. On this, with altogether unexpected dispatch, he piled my belongings. Over them he draped the deer carcass, thonging the load together with a strand of buckskin.

"Let's mush," he said.

I took a hand at the towing line, and, side by side, we made our way along the trodden snow, as crisp as charcoal under our feet. The valley seemed strangely silent. But I felt less alone in the world with that morose old figure beside me.

"Why is Lander swinging in with you?" I asked.

"Seein' this valley ain't bristlin' with hotels," answered Sock-Eye, "he deemed my wickyup good enough for a college dood until they could build him up-to-date livin' quarters at the Happy Day."

"But I thought outsiders bought up the Happy Day," I ventured.

Sock-Eye stopped to gnaw a corner from his chewing plug.

"They sure did," he admitted. "And left young Lander out on the limb. But, as far as I kin make out, that *hombre* ain't no squealer. And I reckon Big John Trumbull'll find him as full o' fight as a bunch o' matin' copperheads."

"Why," I ventured, "should there be hard feeling between him and John Trumbull?"

Sock-Eye squinted at me from under his shaggy brows and then spat into a snowbank.

"That's something, girlie, I was jus' goin' t' ask *you*," he observed.

When he saw I had nothing to say on the matter he rejoined me at the towing line and we trudged on again. We went on in silence until we came to a solitary small figure standing knee-deep in the roadside snow. It proved to be a Swede boy in an incredibly ragged Mackinaw, with a blue woolen scarf wrapped around his waist as high as his armpits. His eyes, I noticed as Sock-Eye asked him about a short cut to the Jansen shack, were even bluer than his encircling sash. And those eyes of Amalfi azure continued to blink at me as he pointed out the side-path for us.

"But ol' Yansen ban dead," he announced. "He ban dead of the flu over three months ago."

"Which same makes room for you, little cheechako," snorted my grim-eyed trail breaker.

But I stopped to ask the sash-wrapped youth his name. I liked the feeling of warmth he carried under that cocoon of wool and rags.

"Ah ban Olie Eckstrom," he said with the friendliest of smiles. And that greeting seemed to take a little of the solitude out of the snow-clad wilderness about me. He stood looking after us as we swung off the road and headed into a winding lane between the alder and spruce. The drifts here were deeper than ever. Our struggles through the unruptured snow left a lonely furrow in our wake.

It wasn't until we came to the edge of a clearing that Sock-Eye stopped for breath. A snowshoe rabbit, moving white against white, lost itself in a tangle of underbrush. I felt equally lost.

"There be your wickyup," said Sock-Eye, with a wave of his mittened hand. And as he spat his contempt for the same I stood studying the little cabin in the clearing.

It was not, I could see, a very appealing abode. It looked, with its sagging and snow-mattressed roof and its time-weathered timbers, about as inviting as a mausoleum. It looked gloomy and dejected and abandoned, for all its air of sturdiness. Even its windows looked unfriendly. And it seemed like an intrusion when we waded up to the sullen and low-framed door, beside which a rusty galvanized tub still hung on the wall logs. Nor did it add to my joy when I saw Sock-Eye, kicking away the snow, disclose the flattened-out body of a dead coyote lying there, its teeth grinning malevolently up from the uncovered jawbones. For that grin, in some way, impressed me as one of derision.

My companion, with a prompt sweep of his foot, brushed the frozen carcass to one side and swung open the door. Doors in Alaska, I remembered, were very seldom locked.

He stood there, with his breath showing white as he stared about the gloomy interior.

I had to shut my teeth tight so the trembling of my chin wouldn't betray me. For about all that musty-smelling and deep-shadowed room held was an untidy wall bunk, a table and two wooden chairs with roughly spliced legs. I could see where the smoke pipe had fallen from a rust-stained stove and where rodents had been attacking a grub-box imperfectly armored with a Joseph's coat of flattened-out tobacco tins. Above it was a dish shelf with a few rusty pans and a showing of sadly chipped crockery. At the foot of the bunk lay the dead body of a parka-squirrel, half buried in a scattering of lint from a much-chewed quilt. Along the wall directly above the bunk were tacked, to remind me Alaska was still a man's country, irregular rows of equally irregular movie-queens, interspersed with dancing houris. Each and every one of them, I observed, was in an arresting state of dishabille.

But even more revolting was the filth that covered the floor, the litter of rags and ashes and mouse-dirt that scarcely needed the sepulchral smell of the place to make my gorge rise a little.

Sock-Eye's questioning glance must have detected some shadow of hopelessness on my face.

"You a-goin' t' stick it?" he challenged.

"I've got to," I said. "There's no other way."

My companion, as he turned and swept that room with a saturnine eye, proclaimed that an old skinflint like Sam Bryson should have two inches of lead in his gizzard. "But since he's put you here, I'm a-goin' t' give you a hand t' git planted."

I had thought of Sock-Eye as a maundering old man. But as he threw off his coat and got busy I realized I had altogether misjudged both his skill and his strength. It was a pretty lousy layout for a female, he acknowledged, but many a time he'd made camp in a damned sight worse dump.

His first act was to force open the windows. A breath of the wintry hills, cold and sweet, swept through that little chamber of neglect. Then he restored the fallen smoke pipe and examined the stove and shook a dead mouse out of the water pail and tore the pornographic ladies from above the wall bunk.

Then, grunting with indignation, he went at the place like a cyclone. He tumbled the greasy table and chairs out into the snow and scraped the litter from the floor. Then he left me alone with my worn-down stub of a broom. He reappeared with a rusted axhead, into which he fitted a rough handle of birch wood. When he started to shovel the ashes from the stove-box I told him to save them, as they'd come in handy for scrubbing. I could hear him, as I tackled cobwebs and dust drifts, chopping firewood back of the cabin. It was a comfortable homelike sound.

By the time he had a fire going and snowwater melting in our galvanized tub I'd unearthed a shriveled cake of yellow soap and a lopsided scrub brush. While I scoured the grease-blackened table and chairs with hot water and wood ashes he dragged the bunk mattress out into the snow, emptied it, pounded the last of the dust from it, and refilled it with wild hay which he commandeered from a pole-stack at the back of the clearing. When he refused to let me scrub the floor I surrendered the brush and busied myself with the pans and chipped crockery. And as the whitened floor boards dried out in the stove heat we washed the grime from the window glass and lifted in our table.

It made me think of a brunette from a beauty parlor, peroxided into a sudden blondeness. But it smelled clean.

Everything smelled clean, and seemed different, and the singing of the old iron kettle on the drum stove was almost homelike. But my spirits declined to rise as they should. I not only felt tired, but I had a fixed feeling of emptiness just under my belt. My back ached, my fingers were wrinkled with lye water, and there was a suspicion of moisture on my half-grown eyelashes.

Sock-Eye, after spitting into the rusty stove front, reached for his coat and crossed to the door.

"I'm a-goin' over t' the village," he offhandedly announced. "We've a one-hoss store there. I'll see if I kin rustle a pair o' blankets and pack in a mite o' grub for you."

He was off with his sleigh before I could call him back.

The shack, as I sat staring at the glow from the stove front, seemed of a sudden very empty and silent. I had the feeling of being lost there, on the lonely last frontier of a spruce-stippled and snow-muffled world. And, to help fight back the waves of desolation that washed over me as I stood contemplating the lone white peaks of the Talkeetnas through the window, I grimly turned to finish my unpacking.

By the time I'd explored what I could of the dooryard and the out sheds and carried in more wood for the fire and brushed the snow from my knees, my ragged old helper was swinging back to the clearing edge.

I stood blinking at the size of his sleigh load.

"Git in out o' the cold," he commanded. "I reckon I purty well know what a cheechako needs."

I felt my throat tighten.

"You can't do this for me," I contended as Sock-Eye piled things on the table end.

"I ain't a-doin' it for you," he retorted. "I'm a-doin' it for your ol' pappy. He rustled many a mess o' grub for me."

That didn't take the lump from my throat. I watched him in silence as he disinterred two candles from his store supplies and lighted them.

"Evenin' 'pears to be comin' on," he said. "I reckon I may as well stay an' have chow with you."

I started to thank him, but he cut me short.

"When you git settled," he said. "You'll have t' have a gas lamp. And I'll tote over a hunk of sourdough for your bread-makin'. And, meanwhile, I'll leave you a slab o' deer meat that'll help tide over the week end."

I laid the table, using a newspaper for a cloth, while the old-timer beside the stove cooked bacon and eggs and put coffee on to boil and punched two holes in the top of a milk tin with his hunting knife. He was surprisingly adroit and quick-handed about it all. When he sharpened a stick and on it speared a slice of bread, which he began toasting at the stove front, I found the aroma of that browning bread mixing with the aroma that came from the coffeepot. And I realized there were times when food was more important than philosophy.

"Things is goin' t' come easier," explained Sock-Eye as we ate together with the honest and unabashed appetite of the hungry, "once you've took root here."

"And made friends with my neighbors," I added.

"You ain't got no neighbors within a mile," countered Sock-Eye. "And the valley folks nacher'ly ain't goin' t' fall over themselves t' welcome you, seein' you was sent in here by them Juneau bureaucrats."

"But I'm here to work for them and help them," I announced with the bravery born of a good supper under my belt. Yet I quailed a little as I looked about at the rough walls surrounding me, and then at the glooming peaks of the Talkeetnas through the window.

Sock-Eye seemed to read my thoughts as my gaze went to the red-rusted stove.

"Yep; you'll have t' stoke that ol' firebox yourself. And rustle your own grub and wood and water. I s'pose you've got a shootin' iron?"

I didn't see, I told him, how a shooting iron could solve any of my problems.

"It kin ease your mind consider'ble," argued Sock-Eye. "There's no satis-faction like knowin' you've got a six-gun in reach. Kind o' perks you up when you're alone. And I reckon I got an ol' blunderbuss or two I kin be bringin' over t' you."

I sat staring at my barbaric wall bunk. I had to fight back the temptation to cry out that I'd come there as a teacher and not as a backwoods squaw to sleep on a pile of hay.

"I reckon you want t' turn in," observed Sock-Eye after a blink or two into my troubled face.

I watched him as he crossed the room and writhed into his ragged old coat. Alaska, I remembered, was called a man's country. And it was self-reliant old fighters like that, I also remembered, who belonged to the North, who derived their strength from its hardness, and found in it some latent glamour to make up for the loneliness.

"I'll be all right," I proclaimed, trying to keep the tremor out of my voice.

I was afraid to thank him for what he had done. It didn't seem to be the valley way. I merely stood in the doorway watching him as he trudged off in the snow and was lost in the blue-tinted darkness. And I felt more than ever like a castaway as I made fast the shack door by wedging the heaviest piece of stovewood I could find under the rusty iron knob.

It seemed very quiet there as I stacked my dishes and stoked my stove for the night. Once or twice I thought I heard a wolf howl. But it may have been merely a distant farm dog. Then I undressed and made a pillow by folding my sweater up in my one and only silk slip. Then I put out the candles.

The only thing I could see, in the darkness, was the valiant glow from the front of the old iron stove. That rose-colored glow seemed like a little flag of courage, a lonely banner of invincibility. But weariness, I found, had rewards all its own. For neither the solitude nor the frost-creaks in the shack roof could keep me from eventually falling asleep.

CHAPTER VIII

THOSE FIRST DAYS IN my Matanuska wickyup always remained a clouded memory of discomfort shot through with incongruous moods of exaltation. But Sock-Eye had been right. One took root, in some way, and fibre by fibre time wove one back to the soil of one's birth.

For day by day I felt more like an old-timer. That earlier sense of unreality which made me feel like a ghost in a world of ghosts soon slipped away. I was, I told myself, a lamp sent there to shed light in the darkness. I had a job to do and a family name to redeem. And, though the nights were long and fanged with frost, the morning light that flooded over the Chugacs showed my shack side so glittering with rime that it made me think of a Christmas card, leaving me teased with the impression that something stirring was just around the next corner.

I also learned more about the valley of the Muddied Waters—for that, in the language of the local Indians, was what the word "Matanuska" meant. It revealed itself as a deep-soiled and lightly timbered valley of almost two hundred square miles, with a friendly huddle of mountain shoulders that cut off the Arctic winds and framed the lowlands in eternal white. Diagonally across the valley ran the Matanuska River, and up that river, in the open season, the salmon came in swarms. Here and there, along the lower benches, little patches of land had been cleared, mostly as subsistence farms for hill trappers and disheartened gold-seekers, like old Sock-Eye and Sam Bryson. On those farms they grew two-pound potatoes and thirty-pound cabbages and oats and rye and hay as high as a horse's back. For the growth from that black soil, once played on by its bath of twenty-hour sunshine, was prodigious.

But the little homestead shacks, I found, were scattered and far apart, and life, apparently, was still precarious, with no fixed market for the settlers' produce and no final reward for a short season of industry after a long season of hibernation.

Yet the valley was rich. It could, according to Sidney Lander, prove itself the grub bag of the North. Its soil was droughtless and inexhaustible. And under that soil it had coal in abundance. And through all its outer hills it had game enough for an ever-enduring backlog on the fires of hunger.

It had, of course, its hardships of frontier life. But hardship and I had never been strangers. And though my rough-and-tumble days left me tired in body and mind, they also left me with the feeling of being strangely alive. For there was a bigness, I told myself, about life in a big country. And I was no longer afraid of the cold. There was even something tonic about it, prompting me to face my daily trip to Palmer as casually as a husky-dog faces an open trail. I became reconciled to rabbit wool next to my skin and my nose no longer turned up at the smell of native-tanned furs.

But I looked a good deal like an Eskimo. Katie's old caribou parka had a dickey-hood fringed with wolverine fur, and along with that, to be worn only in the deep cold, I had a pair of dogskin trousers that advertised their presence by a most creosotic and animal-like smell, to blend with the aroma of my wolf-hide gauntlets. And my Eskimo mukluks, to complete the menagerie, were of sealskin and equally aromatic. But they were both warm and water-proof. And inside that array of animal skins I could face any wind or sleep in any snowbank, and emerge as warm as a ptarmigan from its sub-zero drifts.

I came to Matanuska as a teacher, but it was the valley, I found, that was teaching me things. Its first lesson seemed to be that frontier life was the mother of invention and the father of resourcefulness. For I learned how to attach a wire handle to a discarded gasoline can and turn it into a water pail, and how to cover an empty packing case with chintz and convert it into a dressing table. I learned how to stuff duck feathers into a sugar bag—with the lettering boiled off in lye water—and call it a pillow, and how to make sheets out of factory cotton and dish towels out of flour sacks, and even a Dutch oven out of two boxes interlined with chopped oat straw. I relearned how to whittle shavings from a spruce-stick and start a fire, and chop wood without standing in a tub to protect my feet, to say nothing of the discovery that birch logs split easiest when frozen.

I might have forgotten about Amalfi and Fiesole, but I found that butter froze harder than lard, that stenciled wrapping paper could make window curtains, and that an active-bodied lady could scramble into her clothes, of a cold and frosty morning, as quickly as a parka-squirrel could scramble into its burrow. I learned how to light a gas lamp without taking it apart, and how to melt snow and bathe in a wash tub and get along without running water and fresh lettuce and movies and oranges and telephones and a morning paper.

I got along, in fact, about the same as all my frontier friends did. We managed with what we had. I knew how a baking-powder tin could be turned into a biscuit-cutter, how bag burlap with a design crocheted on its ends made a passable door mat, how a broom handle fastened across a room corner curtained off with calico converted the same into a clothes closet, and how life, after all, was mostly what you made of it.

But the inanimate things, I discovered, were more easily managed than the animate. I'd never liked that red-rusted old stove of mine, standing as it did a monument of neglect at the center of my new family circle. So on a sufficiently mild afternoon when I could afford to let the fire go down I decided to sandpaper off some of the rust and replace it with a bright and shining coat of black lead.

It wasn't easy work. And the old potato sack I'd pinned around my waist didn't leave me looking any too regal. My hair came down and my hands took on a distinctly negroid tint. On my face, too, I must have smudged a good deal of the black lead that should have gone elsewhere. And just as I was wielding my polishing brush on the last rough-surfaced old stove leg a visitor walked into my humble abode and stood regarding me with a quietly bewildered eye.

"Where will I find Carol Coburn?" an unexpectedly well-modulated voice inquired of me.

I saw, when I glanced up, a tall and queenly-looking young woman in a wide-collared mink coat that partly covered a blue and orange snow suit. She impressed me as being very sophisticated and urbanized. And I saw, as she took off her sunglasses, that she had a cool-eyed and incontestably beautiful face.

I knew who it was, even before she told me. And it didn't add to my happiness to remember that I must have impressed her as an impoverished pinch-hitter for a scullery maid.

"*I'm* Carol Coburn," I told her, as quietly as I could. "Won't you sit down?"

She blinked at me, for an incredulous moment or two, and seated herself on my rickety old chair with the spliced leg. Then she began to laugh. It was a musical laugh. But I couldn't escape the feeling it was edged with ice and at my expense.

"So you're Carol Coburn," she said as I took off the potato sack and busied myself stoking the dwindled stove fire. I tried to forget the nose smudge that kept tempting me to stand cross-eyed before her.

"I'm sorry it's so cold in here," I heard myself saying as my visitor's disdainful eye wandered about the shack, from the wall bunk to the tin-armored grub-box.

"I'm Barbara Trumbull," she announced. She was quite serious by this time.

"I know," I murmured as I poured water into my tin basin and engaged in a hasty struggle to remove some of the black lead. "Can't I make you a cup of tea?"

"No thank you," she said, with a second study of my partially cleansed face. She pulled up her sleeve and looked at a jeweled wrist watch. "I'm flying back to Anchorage in a few minutes."

"I'm sorry," I said in the silence that ensued. And that brought her cool and queenly glance back to my black-leaded person again.

"You know Sidney Lander," she observed. She said it softly. But it was like the softness of velvet with a razor blade wrapped up in its folds.

"And?" I prompted, feeling that all the frostiness wasn't to be on one side.

"And you know, of course, that we're to be married next summer?" she continued, making it half a question and half a challenge.

"Yes, he told me about that," I acknowledged.

And again I heard the musical laugh edged with ice.

"You and Sidney, I understand, had a very adventurous trip together a few weeks ago."

"We got storm bound on the trail," I explained. "But he survived it, quite unscathed."

"That's what I wanted to make sure of," said the lady in the mink coat, ignoring the touch of acid in my voice. But her eyes narrowed a little. Then, with great deliberation, she drew off the luxurious gauntlet that covered her left hand. It was a very white hand. And on the third slender finger I could see the glitter of a diamond.

"That's his ring," she quietly but conclusively announced.

"Long may it wave!" I rather foolishly responded.

My visitor refused to smile.

"Then you know what it stands for?"

"Naturally," I acknowledged.

For just a moment she sat silent again, looking at my black-leaded stove front. Then she turned back to me.

"Do you want to stop my marriage?"

It impressed me as rather primitive. But I was at least compelled to respect the lady's directness.

"What makes you think I could?" I asked.

She, apparently, both suspected and resented my air of guilelessness.

"My convictions in that quarter seem to be weakening," she said with a languid sort of asperity.

"Then why bother about the source of them?" I countered, a little tired of being accepted as merely an Audrey of the backwoods.

"Why are you fighting my father?" John Trumbull's daughter rather abruptly demanded. "And making Sidney break with the one man who could have him amount to something?"

"I have no control over Sidney Lander's actions," I said.

"Then why is he backing your father's claim?"

"I never asked him to do that," was my honest enough answer.

"It won't, of course, do any good," quietly averred my visitor.

I met her gaze without flinching.

"Are you saying that for your own sake," I asked, "or for your father's?"

Barbara Trumbull laughed a little.

"My father's big enough to fight for himself," she announced, "as you'll find out before you get through with him."

"Then what are you worrying about?" I found the courage to inquire.

"About the change in Sidney," was the unexpectedly frank response. "He's a man of his word. And he's a good mining engineer. Yet he's willing to throw up his chances by hanging about this God-forsaken valley."

I resented that slur on the land of my adoption just as I resented the implications behind it.

"I have no intention," I said, "of interfering with Sidney Lander's career."

Her studious eye still again seemed to find something reassuring in my rough and humble appearance.

"That's what I wanted to find out," she said as she got up from her splice-legged chair.

"I happen to have a career of my own to look after," I proclaimed, resenting the way my interlocutor was making me feel like Cinderella in the presence of visiting royalty.

"I understand you're to be a teacher here," she said with a commiserative small smile.

"I am," I replied. "And my work will keep me too busy to think of wrecking other people's happiness."

Her gaze, at that declaration, locked with mine.

"May I tell Sidney that?" she asked as she buttoned her queenly cloak of mink.

"Of course," I retorted with more vigor that I had intended.

She stood silent a moment, and I could see the hardness go out of her eyes.

"Thanks," she said, rather quietly.

Before I knew it, in fact, I found myself taking the hand which she held out to me. Her imperiousness made me feel awkward and ill at ease. I was glad to break away and check the draught of the stove, which was beginning to show a cherry-red along its black-leaded side.

"I hope you're very happy," I ventured, for want of something better to say.

"I intend to be," she said as she crossed to the shack door. Then she turned in the open doorway, silhouetted against the strong light. "I'm glad to know how you feel about this," she announced in her softly-modulated voice of assurance. "And something tells me you're a woman of your word."

"I am," I proclaimed as the door swung to and shut out the light. But I'm not sure that she even heard me.

CHAPTER IX

IT DIDN'T COME TO me as a surprise when I learned that Sidney Lander was no longer concerned with the management of the Willow Creek Mine. What perplexed me was the discovery that he didn't go to Seward when Barbara Trumbull sailed for the States.

But it wasn't mine to question why. All I cared to remember was that, for reasons entirely his own, he somewhat sedulously kept his trail from crossing mine. His days, apparently, were troubled enough. He hurried up to Fairbanks, I learned, and then down to Juneau, and then in to the Chakitana again. And I knew that when he had something definite to tell me, he would come and tell it. Even Sock-Eye maintained a somewhat exasperating silence in regard to that unstable shack-partner of his, though once or twice, when the bearlike old eyes blinked into my face I garnered a suspicion or two that my cud-chewing old friend knew a little more than he pretended to.

So, in that interim of suspended action, I lost myself in action enough of my own. I trimmed the wick of the lamp of learning and came a little closer to my valley neighbors. And even Sam Bryson, I began to feel, was no longer an open enemy. He thawed out sufficiently around the edges to come and inspect my shack and declare the school board would have to keep me in firewood. A couple of days later he appeared with two dozen new-laid eggs packed in sawdust, two dozen prizes which I kept from freezing at night by stowing them under the mattress where I slept. And before he left he even made me an old-fashioned crossbar with which to barricade my shack door when I slumbered on his eggs.

But the new valley teacher had other favors bestowed upon her. One Sunday, as I was shoveling the drifts from my doorstep, Sock-Eye arrived with a home-manufactured hand sleigh, which same, he dourly explained, would make it easier for me to mush supplies from the village. On that sleigh, however, reposed a war-scarred old rifle and an equally worn revolver, to say nothing of a Morris chair which he had fashioned with his own hands and upholstered with the hide of a moose brought down by his own trusty forty-five.

When he took me out to practice marksmanship on the side hill back of the shack, the rifle made my shoulder sore and the six-gun did things to my wrist. But I soon found I could hit a spruce plank at twenty paces. Sock-Eye, watching me, eventually admitted I handled a shooting iron like an old-timer.

"I'll bet it was your pappy first showed you how t' handle them peace-makers," he chucklingly observed.

"It was," I admitted as I took a final pot shot and made the bark fly from a hemlock trunk.

"Then he gave you eddication that meant something," conceded Sock-Eye. "I've seen a heap o' changes in this cock-eyed country. But she's still raw around the edges. And there's times when slappin' leather's still the short cut t' a square deal."

I couldn't, of course, agree with him. But I was, after all, living next door to the open wilderness. And it gave me an odd sense of security, especially at night, to know that old rifle was on its wall pegs above my bunk.

It all went to remind me that friendly help was still a tradition of the frontier. And my left-handed efforts as a frontier teacher, I found, were slowly but surely bringing me a little closer to the valley settlers. They no longer regarded me as either a feather head or a Federal spy. To most of them, indeed, I was a welcome break in the monotony of life, a bringer of news from the outside world, a carrier of messages and matching-yarns from farm to farm, with so many of the men out on their trap lines or off in the hills after the game that largely took the place of pork and beef in the scattered settlement.

And my teaching was an odd sort of teaching. For morning by morning, in parka and mukluks, I set out for one or another of the lonely homesteads, and there, beside a stove crackling with spruce wood and birch, I held my classes, sometimes with the Monday's washing or the Tuesday's ironing being done on the other side of the room, sometimes with the sourdough sponge being worked into loaves on the far end of the table at which my solemn-eyed little scholars were at work with paper and pencils. I was asked, as a rule, to have dinner with the family. Sometimes, when I started for home, I'd be given a jar of blueberry jam or a bowl of sauerkraut, sometimes even a slab of deer meat.

But very few of them, I found, were able to be givers. Most of them were shockingly destitute. One family, I suspected, lived largely on turnips, since turnips, last summer, were their only crop. The children in that home were terribly ill-clad. To one of them, bare-legged except for the shredded remains of a pair of cotton stockings, I surrendered my new wool skiing socks. It was the bright-colored tops, I imagine, that most thrilled that little frost-shriveled body. For life, to these people, was very bald and empty. It was pathetic to see their joy when I brought them a few pictures cut out of old magazines.

The doll of the smallest girl was a double-rooted carrot, slightly shriveled and dressed in rags.

But the valley couldn't be blamed for such destitution. For there was one thrifty German housewife whose home stood a triumph of competence. Even her window sills were lined with geraniums, potted in tomato cans corseted with red tissue paper. She had two cows and made her own butter and cheese. She had a well-lighted hennery, with the double walls packed with oat straw for warmth, and was never without fresh eggs. Since her good man could harvest four hundred bushels of potatoes to the acre in the valley's rich soil, she had a cellar stocked with vegetables. Besides that she had pickled salmon and salted meat and sauerkraut and rows of preserves and cranberry jelly. And all were the product of those tireless hands which, even in what she regarded as her interims of rest, were darning and knitting for her children. I always knew, when my classwork took me under Mrs. Wiebel's roof, that I'd have fresh butter on my raisin bread and a little mountain of whipped cream on my rhubarb pie.

But I did considerably more than teach the three R's and correct papers and pass out assignments. Sometimes I looked after a baby or two, and took the bread out of the oven, and airily prescribed for an earache or frostbite, and tried my hand at cutting a pupil's hair, and attached much-needed buttons and even more urgently needed patches to the garments of my not ungrateful little scholars. They no longer laughed at Sock-Eye's old revolver, which I carried in a belt holster around my waist and from which I derived a somewhat foolish sense of protection. For I felt more self-reliant, with that old firearm swinging against my hip. And it wasn't as absurd as it sounds. The fact was brought home to me that this was still the fringe of the wilderness when a huge bear came shambling down into Matanuska Village. It wandered about, sending women and children screaming into their shacks. It may have been a torpid and lazy old fellow lured out of his den by a three-day thaw, more bent on curiosity than carnage. But a bear is a bear. And some unknown Paul Revere carried news of the invasion into the remotest corners of the valley.

I felt rather sorry when I saw the men going out after it. But it was Sock-Eye who brought the wanderer down, with a rifle bullet through its heart. And its great hide was soon stretched out on a drying frame, while Sock-Eye, leaning nonchalantly on his long rifle, dilated on the size of the varmints he used to kill in the old days.

"And some o' them two-legged," snorted Sam Bryson, who was cutting up the carcass for meat. Old Sam believed in wasting nothing.

"Mebbe they was," agreed Sock-Eye, with his mordant and one-sided smile. "And I could spot one or two in petticoats I'd like t' keep in practice on."

When Sam Bryson first told me he had a girl in need of schooling I pictured a frail and frostbitten child in pigtails. But Salaria Bryson—universally spoken of as "S'lary"—turned out to be something quite different. I found myself confronted by a dusky and wide-shouldered Boadicea who towered several inches above me. She wore her hair close-cropped, dressed like a man, and could swear like a trooper. She was hard-muscled and strongly-knit and could swing an ax or drive a team or carry a deer carcass over her shoulder. She proved herself fonder of hunting, in fact, than she was of housework. And taken all in all she seemed about the most perfect specimen of physical womanhood I ever clapped eyes on.

But it was plain that S'lary's education had been neglected. She was a true daughter of the wilderness, scarcely able to write her own name and quite unable to spell out anything in words of more than four letters. She had never been outside, in spite of the fact that her miserly old dad was a mine-owner and a man of property. She was, I imagine, a little afraid of that outer world about which she knew so little. She shielded that timidity in a sort of rough-spoken truculence, spiced with a mannish profanity derived from earlier years in hill camps and the company of bushrats, with a temper that was both quick and uncontrolled. But she protested she could take care of herself with any God-forsaken bohunk who ever drew the breath of life.

Her attitude toward me as a chalk-wrangler was openly hostile, until she discovered I was Alaska born and had once lived in a hill camp. She was willing, after that, to overlook my unhappy dower of book learning. But there remained something pathetic about S'lary. She had missed so much of life, without quite knowing it. She was as strong as an ox and as tireless as a sleigh husky and as fearless, in one way, as a wildcat. She knew her woodcraft and could keep herself alive, I suppose, in any corner of Alaska. But she was afraid of that side of life which a schoolteacher stands for. The sweat came out on her face when I gave her a list of third-grade words to spell.

S'lary, however, was seldom meek. She shared her father's resentment against the outsider in general and all invaders of the valley in particular. And certain newcomers, she intimated, would live longer if they talked less about that raft of broken-winded cheechakos the government was shipping up north in the spring.

"For what," she challenged, "would a lousy bunch o' sun-bleached corn-rustlers know about livin' off the land up here in Alaska? What dam' good'll they be when they git here? And who's goin' to spoon-feed 'em until they git their land cleared and their crops in?"

They were to be families, rumor had it, taken off relief in the Middle West, hard-working farmers who had failed in their old homes and were looking for a new Land of Hope.

"But if they was failures there," contended Salaria, "they'll sure fail here. All we'll git, Pop says, is another moth-eaten lot o' misfits like the weaklin's who ambled in on the ol' Klondike rush. And all they'll do, after the first freeze-up, is amble out and give the valley a bad name."

"But they're to bring their women and children," I pointed out, "and the government is to stand behind them and build their houses and supply them with seed and stock."

I could see Salaria's eyes flash.

"And it's a hell of a lot the gover'ment did for the old-timer," she exploded. "They fixed it so we couldn't even land a salmon or kill a deer without havin' a warden at our heels. They put the bush-rat out o' business by playin' into the hands o' the big minin' companies. They kept us with the Indjins and Eskimos and squealed like a stuck pig when we asked for a school allowance. And they wouldn't even build a road for us. And now they're sendin' in an army o' sorg'um-fed Swedes t' show us how t' farm this valley."

I had, of course, heard that song before.

"Perhaps," I suggested, "they'll bring along some of the things we seem to need."

"What t' hell do we need we ain't got now?" was Salaria's prompt challenge.

I meekly suggested to the indignant daughter of the North that hospitals and schools and churches and good roads and telephones and a radio station might help a little.

Salaria's smoldering eyes viewed me askance.

"I reckon you've been powwowin' with that long-legged college dood who's dennin' up with ol' Sock-Eye for the winter. He sure burns my pappy up hot-airin' about what's goin' to happen to this valley. That *hombre* seems t' feel they're goin' to turn this muskeg into a second Garden of Eden with 'lectric lights and steam-heated sunrooms. And mebbe a swimmin' pool and an orange grove!"

Salaria's opulent bosom grew big with anger.

"But any silk-shirt swamp-drainer needn't look for too many lovin' words from the old-timers who came in here with a skillet and ax and hacked their homes out o' the wilderness. Them was men with the bark on. They cleared their own land and built their own wickyups and didn't ask an agent in brass buttons t' slice their sowbelly for 'em."

It was at this point I loosened an arrow in the dark.

"Then you don't approve of Sidney Lander?"

Salaria's smoldering eyes grew perceptibly softer.

"He don't approve o' me," she finally proclaimed. "He goes dumb ev'ry time I git within rifle-range o' Sock-Eye's shack. When I ran into him up at Willow Creek he seemed t' regard me as something broke loose from a leprosy colony. And when I freed his dog from a fox trap, down beyond the river flats, all he gave me was an absent-minded 'thank you', the frozen face!"

"What did you expect?"

Salaria's face became sullen.

"I didn't expect him t' turn cart wheels up and down the valley. But I looked for something better 'n bein' told booklore was more important 'n bushlore, and bein' presented with a secondhand 'rithmetic and a mild-mannered suggestion that I mush off home and improve my mind."

CHAPTER X

SOCK-EYE APPEARED AT MY door and presented me with a bearskin, fresh off the stretching frame. It was still a bit stiff and ragged around the edges, but once spread out, it looked prodigiously big on my shack floor. And it proved itself so full of electricity, on cold nights, that if I crossed over it, to reach the stove, I could see a spark flash from my fingertips to the metal.

Yet that bearskin, I suspected was merely an excuse for a man-to-man talk that didn't seem to get us anywhere.

Sid Lander, my caller casually explained, had just blown in after a week out on the trail. As I had no answer for that announcement Sock-Eye sat morosely and meditatively chewing his cud.

"I reckon you think quite a lot o' Sid?" he finally ventured.

I felt the need of picking my way with care.

"He was very kind to me once," I acknowledged.

"There's too many females think a lot o' that *hombre*," proclaimed my saturnine old friend. "It's sure gettin' him roped and hog-tied before his time."

"What's the trouble?" I asked with an effort at lightness.

Sock-Eye spat in my stove front.

"The immejit trouble is that outlaw offspring of ol' Sam Bryson's," he announced. "S'lary's hit so hard she ain't got no shame left. She's borrowin' readin' books from him and carryin' home his socks t' darn. And that ain't good for no *hombre* who has obligations elsewhere."

"What obligations?" I inquired.

"I reckon he's told you he's goin' t' marry Big John Trumbull's daughter?"

I could feel the bearlike old eyes studying my face.

"Yes, he told me that," I said as quietly as I could.

"Then where's it goin' to git S'lary, messin' round after somebody else's man?"

I could have said, of course, that it might have proved good for that primitive girl's soul, since it is always more blessed to give than to receive. I might have said, too, that men had been known to change their minds. But that was thin ice over which I had no inclination to venture.

"Salaria's a wonderful woman," I merely observed.

"And about as untamed as a she-grizzly," qualified my visitor.

But I couldn't forget what Sock-Eye had said when I was giving Sam Bryson's daughter her next lesson. She surprised me by her new determination "to better herself" as they express it in this neck of the woods. She at last seemed willing to improve her mind. She no longer growled and grouched about the assignments I gave her. She pored over her word lists and learned to wield a pen without sympathetic side-movements of her outthrust tongue. For the first time in her life, apparently, she was studying the mail-order catalogues and giving some thought as to how other women adorn their persons.

She even asked me about cosmetics and how they were used, though those rich and ruddy lips of hers were in need of no chemical kalsomining. Then she inquired about cold cream and other emollients.

"All I've had along that line," she confessed, "was a pot o' bear grease. And that don't make you no bed o' roses in a warm room."

I could see a faraway look come into her eye.

"D' you ever git a sniff o' Sid Lander after he's had a shave?" she hungrily inquired. "He smells better 'n that drugstore down t' Anchorage."

"I prefer men without perfume," I said as I shrank back into the shell of the pedagogue.

But Salaria, plainly, wanted no aspersions on her new idol.

"Scent or no scent," she proclaimed, "that *hombre's* made o' he-man timber. He ain't no weaklin'."

"But a mining man should be running a mine," I objected.

"That's what I can't figger out," ruminated the cloudy-eyed Salaria. "I can't savvy why he doubles up with an ol' has-been like Sock-Eye Schlupp, why he's willin' to batch it with a run-down bush-rat when he ought t' have a woman doin' a woman's work for him."

"Have you ever told him so?" I asked.

Salaria's wide shoulders drooped a little.

"It wouldn't do no good," she listlessly proclaimed. "He ain't interested in females that-away."

"But he's a man," I reminded her.

"I s'pose he is," Salaria retorted with a heightening flame of indignation. "But I'll bet my bottom dollar that lousy four-flushing pie-eatin' Trumbull blonde back in the States is sourin' that *hombre* on women for life. I seen 'em when she flew in here. And he wasn't turnin' no handsprings when she hunted him up."

"She's a very beautiful woman," I observed, wondering whether Salaria's words should make me happy or unhappy.

"P'raps she is, the lily-fingered pink-face," conceded my pupil. "But if I had a claim on a *hombre* like that I'd stick a damned sight closer to him."

As I stood staring into Salaria's flashing eyes I began to realize that she was of the same statuesque mold as Lander. She had the same love for open trails. She had the same ruggedness of body and the same wide jaw and the same brown tone to her skin. And I fell to wondering, with a ghostly twinge of envy, if there mightn't eventually be some kinship of spirit between them.

"Perhaps the lady knows that a claim is a claim," I reminded my deep-bosomed daughter of the North.

"Mebbe it is," was the reckless-noted reply. "But that fact wouldn't keep me awake nights if I found him lookin' for a female t' rustle grub for him."

"I'm afraid, Salaria, we'll have to extend our studies to something more abstruse than reading and writing."

But that suggestion was promptly brushed aside.

"I could work for a guy like that until the glacier worms turned green," Salaria averred with a new look of humility in her eyes.

I studied her as she threw back her shoulders in a way that revealed the superbness of her young breast.

"I'll respect your secret, Salaria," I said with what dignity I could command.

"Secret? It ain't no secret," was the prompt and primitive reply. "Even ol' Sock-Eye knows Sid Lander could do what he likes with me. And the fire-eatin' ol' killer piped up and said he'd put a bullet through any short-horn female who made a pass at that shack-pard o' his."

"What's Sock-Eye saving him for?" I found myself questioning.

"For that sap-headed Trumbull blonde that's got him hog-tied, I s'pose," was the sadly intoned answer. "He's willin' t' play ball with her even after her yellow-bellied old man came and bought up the Happy Day outfit jus' t' give Sid his walkin' ticket and grind his nose in the dirt."

I sat down to think this over. And my thoughts, at the moment, didn't add to my happiness.

"Isn't there some reason," I inquired, "why Trumbull and Lander are no longer friends?"

"Search me," said Salaria. "Folks say he was Trumbull's pet until he tried to buck the Big Boss."

"Because of whom?" I probed, wondering how much or how little Salaria knew.

"I'm damned if I can figger it out," was Salaria's morose-noted reply. "But if I know my onions a square-jaw like Sid Lander ain't goin' t' take a fadeout like that with his hands folded."

"Why do you say that?"

"Because," answered Salaria, "I've a feelin' he's waitin' for somethin'. And when the cards fall right he'll be back in the game. For a *hombre* like that ain't roostin' around this frostbitten valley jus' for the sake o' the mountain scen'ry!"

CHAPTER XI

LIFE IS LIKE A husky-dog that refuses to be entirely tamed. We imagine we've mastered it and made it into something decent and docile. Then quite unexpectedly the old wolf strain breaks out.

Several weeks ago I'd arranged to have young Olie Eckstrom bring me a quart of milk every morning. And I looked forward to Olie's daily visits. For I liked Olie and Olie liked me. I liked the flash of his boyish wide smile and the friendly warmth in those sky-blue Scandinavian eyes of his. He was always glad to fill my water pail and do some trivial little chore for me. More than one snowshoe rabbit came to my stewpot from his hand. And his loyalty, I found, was good for my morale.

But one day, instead of the towheaded Olie, it was his little sister Frieda who proudly toddled to my door. She made a funny figure as she stood there in her patched old corduroy trousers (plainly inherited from Olie) and an equally abraded old wolfskin coat that was much too big for her and was held in at the waist by a turn or two of sled rope. She couldn't have been more than six years old but she showed an active interest in my school crayons and building blocks. After she'd pored over a picture book or two I tied her up in her wolfskin coat, gave her an apple, and started her off for home.

I stood in the doorway watching her as she toddled away in the slanting sunlight. There was a feeling of Spring in the air. I noticed that my shack eaves were dripping and my dooryard drifts were diminishing. But the Talkeetnas were still white to their base and there was no sign as yet of any softening buds along the birch groves. And it occurred to me, as I turned back to my work, that these north-born children who could push blithely along a mile of woodland road were a sturdy lot. Little Frieda, I remembered, was of the race that had once given Vikings to the world.

But about midafternoon Olie appeared at my door. He stood there with his wide smile, bathing my somewhat puzzled face in his adoring blue glance.

"I ban come for Frieda," he announced.

"But Frieda went home hours ago," I explained with a faint chilling of the blood.

His face, as he stood frowning over that, became suddenly mature. She had not come home, he said, and his mother had thought that maybe I had kept her for dinner.

"Then where is she?" I demanded, feeling my heart go down in my boots.

Olie, however, showed no undue alarm. She might, he ventured, be playing in the spruce woods somewhere. Or she might have been picked up by a homesteader and carried on to Palmer, for the sake of the ride. "She ban glad to talk to men like that."

"But she must be found," I proclaimed as I reached for my parka and shoepacks. The valley with its surrounding pinnacles of snow, glinting white in the afternoon sunlight, suddenly became a very stern and inhospitable country. It was no place for a child to be lost. And I, in a way, was responsible for that child's safety.

"We ban find her," said Olie, beginning to be disturbed by the alarm on my face.

"Of course we'll find her," I argued. And we began the search by first looking through the outbuildings and skirting the clearing edges where the shadows were growing longer. It was foolish, I suppose, but I kept calling out, "Frieda! Frieda!" as I went. And there was, of course, no childish answer to that call.

Then we went back to the road and examined the muddy ruts and the sun-softened snow for any betrayingly small footprints. But there was nothing there we could be sure of. In our indecision we made circling excursions into the spruce and alder thickets, calling as we went. We explored a still-frozen cranberry bog and quartered back and forth through a tangle of roadside underbrush.

"Perhaps," I told the solemn-eyed Olie, "she's home by this time."

I pinned my faith on that hope. But it proved to be a hollow one. And the stricken look in Mrs. Eckstrom's eyes did not add to my happiness. She called her husband, who came from the stable with a hay fork in his hand. The smile faded from his wide blond face as Olie explained the situation. The sun, I could see, was already low over the mountain tops. And every hour counted, with night coming on.

"We've got to have help," I told them. "We've simply got to find that child."

"I can find my little Frieda," proclaimed the father as he started off down the road. His face was grim. But he would be covering ground, I knew, where we'd already searched. And I still felt we'd be better with help, expert help.

That took my thoughts back to Katie's Indian baby, the abandoned little papoose who'd been found in the valley birch grove. And the god from the machine, on that occasion, had been Sidney Lander's sheep dog.

"Olie," I said, "could you get on a horse and hurry over to Sock-Eye Schlupp's? There's a man there named Lander, who has a dog called Sandy. And something tells me Sandy might find Frieda."

It wasn't Sandy I wanted, I'm afraid, as much as Sandy's master. And I felt sure, as I helped Olie up on his horse, Lander would respond to that call. It would be inhuman not to.

"But stop at every house on the way over," I said as Olie tightened the reins, "and tell them to come and join in the hunt."

He was off like the wind. I helped Mrs. Eckstrom fill and trim two kerosene lanterns. I saw Frieda's father return to the dooryard and stand there gazing helplessly about the darkening valley. Twice Mrs. Eckstrom went to the edge of their cleared land and called out through the twilight for her daughter. I could hear her loud and prolonged "Frieda" echo across the valley slopes. And there was something indescribably pathetic in that cry of a mother for her lost child.

Lander arrived more promptly than I had expected, with Sandy at his heels. I noticed, as he swung down from his horse, that he had a flashlight in his hand. His face, as he hurried over to us, was stern but not excited. And he didn't stop to ask many questions.

"I'm having Sock-Eye notify the settlers," he said. "When they get here, tell them to strike north and south of the trail at fifty paces apart. Let 'em work a half mile each way. And when they've finished their trip in and out have 'em report at the Jansen shack."

He turned for a moment to the lost child's mother, who was quietly weeping in the doorway. "That's all right, Mrs. Eckstrom. We'll find your girl for you."

There was such assurance in that deep-timbred voice of his that I half-believed him. I found myself, without quite knowing it, moving a little closer to his side in the uncertain light, as chilled children move closer to an open fire.

Then, for the first time, he looked squarely into my eyes.

"It's only trouble," he said in a lowered voice, "that seems to bring us together."

"We haven't seen much of each other," I answered, resenting the quaver in my voice.

"Isn't that what you asked for?" he demanded, almost sharply.

"Was it?" I temporized, arrested by the deeper lines in his face.

But Mrs. Eckstrom's wailing call for someone to find her Frieda cut short the answer he seemed about to make.

"What shall I do?" I asked, trying to stand matter-of-factly before him.

"You'd better come with me," he said after a second brief study of my face. And my heart, at that command, gave an absurd little leap of relief.

"Let's go," I said, matching curtness with curtness.

"And you, Eckstrom," Lander called back over his shoulder, "line up the men when they get here. And you, Olie, ride straight over to the station and tell the agent there to get the marshal. Tell him to wire up and down the line for any men he can get here. This calls for fast work. So come on!"

I didn't resent the brusqueness of that order. I was glad to swing along beside him, with Sandy close behind.

"How old is that child?" he asked as we reached the open road.

"About six," I answered. And that struck me as such a pitiably small figure that I was prompted to add: "She seemed quite a sturdy little tyke."

"How was she dressed?" was his next question.

I told him about the old wolfskin coat. It was not easy, I found, to keep up with his long strides.

"That's in her favor," he said as he hurried on. "And a child of six wouldn't go far in country like this. She couldn't." He glanced about the darkening bowl between the lavender-tinted hills. "She's somewhere within a mile of us."

"Then why haven't we found her?" I asked. I thought of the river, where the rising water was making the ice unsafe. I thought of the bear that had shambled down into Matanuska Village. And I thought of the whiteness of the coyote's teeth that had once grinned up at me from my own doorstep.

"We will," asserted Lander. And I was foolish enough to find comfort in the quiet assurance of his voice.

"Won't Sandy help us?" I asked. For I was still thinking of Sandy as a small-sized Saint Bernard from an Alpine hospice, pushing unerringly through the snow to where some fallen wanderer might be lying.

"He hasn't enough to work on," Lander explained. "Or, rather, he has too much, here on the road. He wouldn't know what's expected of him. A hundred different feet have passed along this trail."

Lander switched on his flashlight and studied the oft-trodden ruts. He even dropped to his knees and inspected the stained snow and moved back along the road again and once more studied what to me was merely a series of meaningless marks.

He said nothing, but I was conscious of a new tenseness about him.

"What is it?" I asked.

"I don't know yet," he answered. But he straightened up and studied the valley, point by point, as though he was making sure of his position in those darkening slopes of spruceland. Far off, in the chilly night air, we could hear the voices of men. Now and then we could see the moving light of a distant lantern. I tried to keep from picturing a little dead body with a tear-washed face and a rope tied about its waist.

Lander left me and pushed his way in through a tangle of berry canes, with Sandy whimpering at his heels. That, for some reason gave me a flicker of hope. But it resulted in nothing. Man and dog worked their way back to the road again and once more Lander sidled along the ruts, step by step, studying the broken surface. I saw him rather abruptly leave the road, push through a mat of last year's fireweed, and drift away across a flattened meadow of wild hay. I thought, for a while, that I was both deserted and forgotten. But he circled back to me, in the end, a little breathless from running.

"Come on," he said. "I've struck a trail."

It was easy to follow him, since the meadow, for all its roughness, sloped downward. But I remembered, with a gulp, where that slope ended.

"Aren't we going toward the river?" I asked.

"Yes," he answered. "But that doesn't mean anything."

I wanted to believe him. But I couldn't. All I could think of was treacherous float-ice and a little fur-clad body wedged between green blocks where water boiled black. But Lander turned, when a scattering of white birches barred our path, and veered off to the left, penciling the ground with the ray of his flashlight as he went. He stood in doubt, when we came to a spruce wood, but pushed on again, skirting the gloom of the close-serried trees. Then he suddenly stopped and showed me a mark on a mounded snowdrift. It didn't mean much to me. But the excitement in his voice was unmistakable.

"That," he said, "is a child's footprint."

He called Sandy to his side and talked to him. He pushed the dog's nose down in the snow and patted him and started him off with the cry of, "Find her, Sandy!"

But Sandy disappointed us. He struck off in the darkness, quivering with excitement, only to circle back to us and whimper at his master's heels. "Find her, Sandy," I implored as we moved uncertainly on again.

Then a cry came from Lander. The beam of his flashlight had fallen on an empty tin pail, lying beside a fallen spruce bole. One glance at it told me it was the pail in which the Eckstrom milk was daily carried to my door. That sent Lander running about in an ever-widening circle, sweeping his flashlight from side to side as he went. I could hear, for the first time, the sullen roaring of the river under its tangle of ice. And I didn't like the sound of it.

He rejoined me, as I stood there with a new chill in my blood, and thrust the flashlight in my hands.

"We've got to have help here," he said. "You keep Sandy and the flashlight when I go back for the men. And blink the light from time to time, so we can place you."

"All right," I agreed, as quietly as I could.

It was no time, I knew, to show the white feather, much as I disliked being left alone there.

"Can't you find her, Sandy?" I said as I stood with my fingers hooked through his collar. For it would be natural, I knew, for the dog to follow his owner. I let him sniff at the pail as I held him trembling against my knee. Then he suddenly whimpered and broke loose. And I realized, as I staggered after him in the darkness, that I had failed to keep a part of my promise. He was off, I knew, to join his master.

I could hear his bell-like barks in the cold night air as he quartered off from the woodland and crossed a treeless slope that led to a hayfield as level as a floor. It was a stretch of open land, I could see, where some homesteader the summer before had cut wild hay for his stock. But Sandy, instead of racing after his master, seemed to be crisscrossing about this open floor windrowed with its sun-shrunken snowdrifts. He came back to me, barked twice in my face, and was off again.

I followed him, as best I could, wondering if his excitement was due to a fox or even some larger animal prowling about in the gloom. But I found him, at the meadow edge, with his nose buried in the tumble of loose hay at the base of a poled stack covered with a faded tarpaulin. His bobbed tail, I noticed, was going from side to side like a metronome.

I dropped down on my knees beside him, pawing away the loose hay. Then I suddenly stopped. I shrank back, with a quick little curdle of nerve ends. For my bare hand, pushing deeper, had come in contact with warm fur.

I was sure of that. And I was equally sure that Sandy had smelled out a sleeping bear.

My one and only aim in life was to get away from that stack and hear the comfortable voices of armed men about me again. I ran stumbling across the drifted hayfield, wondering as I went why I could see no moving lights in the distance. I felt alone and defenseless in a wilderness not meant for women.

Then my flight came to an end. For I realized that Sandy, who was following me, did not approve of that retreat. His sharp barks were plainly meant for sounds of protest. He even came and tugged at my parka end, as though to drag me back.

I stood there, in my weakness, and hesitated. I must have stood in the darkness for a full minute, without moving. Then a second wind of courage took me slowly back toward the stack.

It wasn't easy to go back. I could even feel a little needling of nerve ends eddy up and down my spine as the dark mass of the stack disclosed itself in the starlight. And I had to take a second grip on myself before moving forward again, for in the excitement, I found, I'd dropped my flashlight somewhere in the loose hay.

But I shut my jaw and crept gingerly forward, wondering how I should defend myself if an aroused wild animal lumbered out at me. My hand, I'm afraid, wasn't a very steady one as I thrust an exploring arm into the little cave under the stack shoulder, the cave where some stray deer or perhaps a moose had been feeding during the deep cold.

It was quite a deep hollow. My arm, in fact, went in up to the elbow. Then it went still deeper. It went until I could feel the warm fur again. But, a moment later, I could feel something else. About it, strangely enough, was wrapped a coil or two of rope. And then I realized the truth.

It wasn't a sleeping bear: it was the body of a child in a worn wolfskin jacket. It was our lost Frieda.

She roused a little and emitted a sleepy whimper or two as I caught her up and held her to my breast. And my heart beat faster when I felt the responsive tug of her small arms. It took me only a moment to get off her mitten and find her pulse. That pulse was not only beating as it should, but the little hand itself was warm.

"Frieda, speak to me," I cried as I once more took her up in my arms. And a great surge of relief swept through me as I heard the sleepy small voice complain: "Ah ban so hongry!"

"Of course you're hungry," I said, a little drunk with excitement. And both Sandy and the half-awakened child must have thought that I'd suddenly gone mad, for I managed, in some way, to clamber to the top of the stack and there, standing up in the darkness, I shouted with all my strength. I called and called again, until an answering shout came back to me. I heard it repeated, farther down the valley, where it was followed by a series of signal shots.

"They're coming, Frieda," I said as Sandy's voice belled out on the cold night air. It wasn't long before I could see lanterns moving across the drifted meadow floor.

Lander came first, a little out of breath, pushing Sandy away from him as he stooped over me.

"I've found her," I said as I struggled to my feet in the loose hay. "She's all right." But, with Frieda in my arms, I wasn't sure of my footing. And a sudden sense of security went through me as I felt Lander's long arm encircle my waist and hold me up. He held me close in under his wide shoulder, for just a moment, in what I accepted as a silent gesture of gratitude.

"She's all right," he shouted back over his shoulder. And he took the child from my arms as the twinkling lanterns drew nearer. I could hear a cheer go up from the crowd and a moment later I could hear the tremulous voice of Mrs. Eckstrom saying over and over again: "My leedle Frieda! My leedle Frieda!"

I was, for a minute or two, quite forgotten in the tumult of those crowding figures. Then I was startled by Sock-Eye Schlupp, who cried out as he accosted me with an approving thump on the back: "You're good leather, girl! You're good leather!" And I was equally startled when Olie, without saying a word, crept rather shyly up to me and tightened his arms about my waist. I simply pressed his head against my breast, in my happiness, and held it there for a silent moment or two.

I realized, as I heard them talking of all going back to the Eckstrom house for hot coffee and schnapps, that I was very tired.

"I've a horse for you here, teacher, if you want to ride," Sam Bryson suggested with an unexpected absence of truculence.

"I'd rather go home," I said from some mysterious trough of depression following after my wave of exaltation.

Lander pushed through the crowd and stood beside me.

"That's good work you did," he quietly acknowledged. And the trough of depression, as I heard him, didn't seem so deep.

"It wasn't me," I contended. "It was Sandy."

"Then Sandy and I'll see you get home safe," he said as he linked his arm in mine.

Neither of us, for some reason, had much to say, once we were off by ourselves. But I was glad of that strong arm to lean on as I made my way homeward under the steel-bright Alaskan stars with just a quiver of the northern lights showing above the ice-fanged sky line. And in that silent partnership of a peril confronted and conquered I felt unexpectedly close to the man at my side.

"Why are you so afraid of my help?" he asked out of the silence.

"I'm not," I said, clinging a little closer to him as we turned into the clearing. The world of men and women, at that moment, seemed very far away. And Lander must have shared with me that feeling of barriers tumbled down, for he suddenly turned and confronted me in the starlight. Just beyond him, in the darkness, I could make out the gloomy square of my shack front. It looked forlorn and empty and infinitely lonely under the stars.

"Can I come in?" my companion quietly inquired.

A wave of recklessness went through me as I stood looking up at him.

"Of course," I said, conscious of something portentous in the midnight quietness about us. We only live once, I told myself as I stared up at the star-strewn sky. We grope blindly along open trails that fail to bring us to any final Inn of Happiness. And it's only human to hunger for a little warmth along those cold and tangled roads of misadventure.

"You're tired," said Lander, with his face just above my upturned face.

I had to fight back the impulse to let my two reckless arms creep up about his stooping shoulders. I could even feel surge through me a secret hope that he himself would be ruthless and reckless, that those two strong arms of his would reach out and draw me so close all thought of our yesterdays and our tomorrows might be forgotten.

Lander must have been conscious of the shiver that went through my body. For this time he said: "You're cold," and relinked his arm fraternally through mine. I wasn't disappointed as we moved in silence toward the shack door. It seemed merely a great moment deferred. And I wondered why all the clocks in the world had stopped.

Then I drew up, abruptly, with a little gasp of surprise. For plainly, in the midnight quietness, I heard the nicker of a horse.

A moment later, in the shadow of the shack front, I could make out the uncertain figure of a man. Equally vague, beside him, was the dejected figure of a four-footed animal which, for all his weariness, might have belonged to one of the Four Horsemen of the Apocalypse.

"That you, Sid?" challenged the man standing beside the horse with an empty saddle.

"Yes," answered Lander in an oddly flattened voice. The intruder, I could see, was Sock-Eye. And for all the darkness I could feel something accusatory in his stare as he confronted us.

"You forgot your horse," Sock-Eye explained.

That was all he said. But to me it seemed to carry a hint, as I realized we weren't so alone in the world as I'd imagined, that even more important things might have been forgotten.

CHAPTER XII

THE BREAKUP, THIS YEAR, meant more than the coming of spring to Matanuska. It brought us longer days and a deeper glow to the sunlight that filled the wide bowl between the Chugacs and Talkeetnas. It turned the valley's rich black loam into a batter of mud. It lured the scattered settlers into the open, like denned-up bears emerging to blink at skies once more a robin's-egg blue.

But it brought the valley another sort of awakening. One detected a new stir in the air. Along the railway siding at Palmer great piles of lumber were being unloaded. Train after train brought in a mountain of machinery and supplies. Federal engineers in khaki and high-tops went about consulting blueprints and driving stakes and squinting through theodolites. Then a little colony of tents began to dot the roadside, and two or three trim cabins of peeled spruce logs appeared out of nowhere.

That meant, I was told, the ground was being laid out for the two hundred families to be brought in from the Middle West, the new settlers who were to show the outside world that Alaska was something more than "Seward's Icebox."

But nothing seemed ready for that incoming army. Not one-tenth of the land was cleared and fit for cropping. There was no shelter for livestock, no homes for women and children. The only solid habitations appeared to be a string of old bunk cars which had been pushed down the valley siding. In these the CCC workers were to sleep and eat, like navvies, until a tent colony could be established. And three days later the toilers themselves put in an appearance, a whole trainload of them, promptly making the quietness of the valley a thing of the past.

They were like children turned loose on a holiday, romping and singing and ki-yiing, quarreling and drinking. They commandeered timbers from along the track, as night came on, and made bonfires that lit up the countryside. About these fires they squatted and to banjo and accordion accompaniment let loose those blithely plaintive old words of

"Oh, then Susanna,
Don't you cry for me;
For I'm off to Louisiana
With a banjo on my knee."

Sock-Eye, viewing them with a morose eye, reported that they'd been rais-ing hell all the way up from Frisco and Seattle. He further announced that the first banjo-strumming cheechako who made a crack about his shooting irons would get three ounces of lead in his larynx.

"They won't listen to us," snorted Sam Bryson as his S'lary and I dined on yak meat after a two-hour school lesson. "But before summer's over they'll be bellyachin' about everythin' goin' wrong."

"I tell you, Pop, they're just a bunch o' half-wits," averred Salaria. "They're yappin' about not usin' any old-timers. But before freeze-up next fall they'll find swingin' in a hammock don't git no houses built. They're hot-airin' about town halls and administration buildin's when they ain't even a road built or a well dug or shack logs ready for a wickyup."

"What," demanded her father, "kin you expect from fruit-tramps and dock-bums? And what'll we git from that shipload o' broken-down sod-busters when they're dumped in this valley? From a lot o' silk-shirt cake-eaters who'll be askin' the gover'ment to drop around ev'ry mornin' to do their milkin' for 'em?"

It was the familiar old song of the disgruntled sourdough.

"But won't it mean something," I ventured, "to start a settlement that's really going to take root here? Isn't that what Alaska needs, settlers who bring in their women and children and stay on the land?"

"They won't take root," contended Salaria's father. "They'll jus' whimper around for more relief and then head for outside agin. And down in the States they'll be sayin' Alaska's only fit for Eskimos."

It was then that Salaria presented me with a surprise.

"I can't see," she said, "why a squarehead like Sid Lander should be wantin' to swing in with them."

"To swing in with them?" I echoed, trying to make the query seem a casual one.

"As sure as sundown," proclaimed Salaria. "That misguided *hombre* seems t' feel this is the biggest thing that's happened since the Children o' Israel hit out for the Promised Land. He thinks it's as doggoned stirrin' as the Pilgrim Fathers' landin' on Plymouth Rock. And he reckons it ain't too late for the right man t' step in and git things organized."

"What can he do?" I asked, wondering at the small thrill that went through my body.

"He can't do nothin'," retorted Sam Bryson. "He's got a fool idee that if them Federal bureaucrats make him field manager up here he kin straighten out a tangle that was started wrong from the first. He contends the whole scheme should be took out o' the hands o' the War Department and give to a practical-minded worker. But while they keep on passin' the buck and squabblin' about who's the real boss here he'll jus' curl up and die of a broken heart."

"He's the type of man who doesn't believe in turning back," I found myself asserting.

"He'll never even git started," protested Sam Bryson. "And nobody but a damn fool'd ever wade into that mess."

I thought over this on my way home. I was still thinking over it as I swung through Palmer and stopped for a moment to watch three CCC workers languidly throwing baggage into a truck backed up to the railway siding. Their hearts, plainly enough, were not in their work.

One of the trio suddenly stopped and stared at me.

"Look who's here," I heard a slightly mocking voice observe.

I detected, in that voice, an unpleasant ring of familiarity. And even before I glanced about I knew it was my soapbox orator known as Eric the Red.

"So you've swung in with the cattle," he said as he dropped to the ground. Then he laughed. "Matanuska's no longer the mudhole it was!"

I was able, even though it took an effort, to look him squarely in the eye.

"The last time you addressed me," I told him, "you were put where you belong. And history sometimes repeats itself."

His laugh had the familiar old ring of audacity.

"This is a free country, teacher-lady. And there's no law I know of against talking to a good-looker like you."

The oldest of the trio, who knew an indignant woman when he saw one, gave Ericson a side glance of disapproval.

"Lay off the rib," he had the decency to say.

But my tormentor ignored that suggestion.

"This," he announced, "is an old friend of mine. And we've a thing or two to talk over before I'm through."

It was anger more than fear that made me resent that announcement.

"I'm afraid," I told him, "you're already through."

"Oh, no, I'm not," he said with his repeated reckless laugh. "We've got some old scores to even up."

I declined to answer him. I merely turned away, with what dignity I could command, and moved off between the scattered dunnage piles. What I resented most, I think, was his power to translate life into something cheap and ugly. I felt sorry, in fact, that in the last few weeks I'd given up the habit of going about with Sock-Eye's old six-gun swinging at my hip. But Eric the Red was right and I was wrong. He wasn't through. He swung out from the truck and came striding along beside me.

"I don't think you're going to like this valley," he had the effrontery to proclaim. "Something tells me you're likely to get what I got on the *Yukon*."

"Is that a threat?" I demanded.

"No, it's just a reminder," he said with a venomous sort of bitterness. "You had your innings, and I'm going to have mine. And d'you know what's going to happen to you?"

I essayed no answer to that challenge. But I felt less defenseless as I noticed an open car pounding and lurching along the deep-rutted roadway. In it I could see a man, a wide-shouldered man, wearing a leather coat and a leather-vizored cap.

I realized, as he came closer, that his face was strange to me. But there was strength in that heavy-jowled face slightly spattered with mud. And I lost no time in wrenching my arm away from Ericson's clasp and signaling the stern-eyed traveler.

"Will you help me?" I called out.

The car stopped beside us. It was, I discerned, a new car. But the mud of Matanuska made it look old.

"What's wrong here?" asked the driver, without getting down from his seat. It was my embattled face, I suppose, that made him smile a little.

"This coward," I cried, "is threatening me."

"Threatening you with what?" inquired the stranger, still impartial. But he swung down from his seat, after a quick inspection of Eric the Red, and stood beside me. I saw then that he was tall and grizzled, but without the earmarks of the old-timer. He looked purposeful and well-bred. His voice, too, was crisp and cool yet singularly deep-chested.

"I don't know what," I had to admit. "But it's not the first time he's annoyed me."

The eye in that stranger's wide-jawed face, I noticed as he once more inspected my unabashed enemy, was as cold and clear as glacier ice.

"Who is he?" was the newcomer's curtly impersonal query.

"He's a transient called Ericson," I said, trying to keep my voice steady.

"Has he any claim on you?" inquired the still noncommittal stranger.

"Of course not," was my quick retort.

Then he turned back to Ericson, who was advertising his composure by lighting a cigarette. But in doing so, I noticed, my enemy quietly backed a step or two off the road.

"I think, son, you'd better be on your way," the tall and grizzled stranger announced in a disappointingly casual voice. Then he turned to me and once more looked me over. I didn't like the assessing way that glacial eye inspected my person. He was, I could see, very sure of himself.

"Where are you going?" he asked.

"To my home," I answered. "That's in the Jansen shack down the valley."

"Get in," he said, "and I'll take you there."

He promptly rounded the car and waited for me to climb into the seat beside him. He threw in his clutch and plowed forward through the mud, entirely ignoring my meek-noted, "Thank you!"

"You've rotten roads up here," he said as we swung away, leaving the narrow-eyed Eric the Red looking after us from the ditch side.

"They'll be better from now on," I announced, wondering why his voice made me think of the voice of big business.

"Do you belong in the valley?" he asked as he picked his way along the puddled ruts.

"I'm the teacher here," I explained. That brought his eye quickly back to my face.

"What's your name?" he questioned, in a voice too well modulated to be called curt.

"I'm Carol Coburn," I answered.

My companion, for the next minute or two, seemed to be giving the road all his attention.

"So you're Carol Coburn," he said with meditative quietness. Then he laughed. But it was a laugh without much mirth in it. "I rather thought we'd be coming together soon."

"Why?" I asked.

He let me wait a moment or two for his answer.

"Because I'm the new owner of the Happy Day Mine," he said. "My name's John Trumbull."

He laughed a second time as he felt my quick glance go over him.

"But I'm not quite what your friend Lander is trying to make me out to be," he added. "I've never tried to steamroller orphans out of their rights."

I felt, all things considered, the need of caution.

"Then you acknowledge I have rights?" I asked.

"Where?" he inquired, obviously fencing for time.

"In the Chakitana," I answered.

"Have you ever been there?" he questioned.

I told him that I hadn't.

"Then you don't and can't understand the situation," he said with a fatherly sort of deliberateness. "There may be mineral in that claim. But what good is a claim when it's out on the edge of nowhere and road-building costs more than your mine could produce?"

"Whose mine?" I asked in a slightly sharpened voice.

His cool and not unkindly eye considered me for a moment.

"That's a decision, apparently, neither you nor I can make. It all goes back to vested rights and the records. And since we've come together in this friendly way, I don't even want to talk about it."

"But it will *have* to be talked about," I reminded him. There was, I suspected, a strain of contempt in his casualness.

"There's been too much of that," he announced, "especially from Lander. Are you in love with that man?"

It was plain that he didn't believe in beating about the bush.

"I'm quite heart free," I said, meeting his side glance without a flicker. He was compelled, for a moment, to give his attention to the road ruts.

"You know my daughter's going to marry Lander?" he finally observed.

"So she told me," I retorted. And that seemed to give him something to think about.

"This whole mix-up is something we've both inherited," he asserted, after another moment of silence. His tone, I thought, was more friendly. "Neither of us asked for it. And there ought to be some reasonable way out of it."

"What would you suggest?" I quietly inquired.

I had the feeling of being weighed on a pair of invisible scales.

"I'd suggest that we leave Lander out of it," he said, "and go at the thing without rancor or prejudice. Lander's bullheadedness hasn't got you anywhere. And it won't get him anywhere."

"I've never had any cause to question his loyalty," I asserted.

"Well, *I* have," was the prompt response. "And if you'd fly out to the Chakitana and actually look over the ground you'd understand the situation a little better."

"With whom?" I questioned.

"With me," he answered.

I laughed a little. For I pictured him, in my mind's eye, burying me in one of his test pits, or emulating the Wicked Uncle of the Babes in the Wood and leaving me to die in the unmapped wilderness.

I could see his frown at my prompt, "No, thank you!"

But his voice, when he spoke, was both suave and controlled.

"Don't run away with the idea this Chakitana claim is my only trouble," he said. "I've got mine interests that take me from the Circle right down to Mexico. And I like to clear things up as I go along."

Once again I recognized the deep rumble of big business. But the thought of my father's lone grave somewhere out along the tangled trails of the Chakitana confirmed me in my own blind course of opposition.

"We turn in here," I explained, indicating the oozy path that led to my shack front. "Lander," I said as we came to a stop in the dooryard, "seems to feel the fight has only begun."

But John Trumbull, apparently, was giving his attention to my small and lonely wickyup.

"You shouldn't be living like that," he asserted.

He must have seen, from the flush on my face, that his commiseration was misplaced.

"It won't always be like that," I retorted. "This valley has a future. And I want to be a part of it."

His face hardened. He plainly wasn't used to opposition.

"It's a hopeless mess," he curtly proclaimed. "And it will end up a worse one."

"Perhaps some of us," I said, with my shoulders squared, "can keep it from ending up that way."

It sounded foolish, I suppose. But it plainly puzzled him.

"You've been outside?" he questioned.

I told him that I had, though I was Alaska born.

"Do you mean you're satisfied with this sort of thing?" he demanded, his contemptuous gaze on my littered dooryard, left so unlovely by the spring thaw.

"I'd like it better if I had a school," I said as I looked out over the spruce-stippled valley between its towering peaks.

John Trumbull sat watching me as I climbed down from the car seat. I couldn't have made a very impressive figure in my old trail togs.

"What would you say if I put a few thousand into a school for you," he said with what impressed me as a purely achieved matter-of-factness, "as good a school as they've got anywhere in this Territory?"

It was my turn to remain silent as I looked up into those glacier-ice eyes of his. They were cold and calculating and without any glow of generosity. And I remembered my old school maxim about fearing the Greeks when they come bearing gifts.

"Does my claim impress you as worth that much?" I found the courage to demand.

His color deepened, apparently with the embarrassment of a contestant who has underestimated the power of his opponent.

"What it's worth won't be decided by either you or me," he said in an unexpectedly sharpened voice. "But I was hoping we could get together on it in some friendlier way."

I realized from what quarter his daughter Barbara had inherited that lordly manner of hers.

"I happen to be Klondike Coburn's daughter," I reminded him.

That brought a steelier look into his averted eyes.

"I was trying to forget that," he retorted, almost in a bark. "But hate and stupidity, you'll find, won't get you far."

"I'll get along," I said, forcing a smile of assurance. And as I stood confronting him I began to nurse a new and sharper fellow feeling for Sidney Lander. He too had refused to be crushed by that human car of Juggernaut.

John Trumbull started his engine and threw in his clutch.

"You may not last here as long as you imagine," he asserted as he swung about my dooryard and headed for the road.

And as I stood watching him as he lurched along that rutted highway between the towering and pink-tinted Talkeetnas, I realized that his words constituted the second threat which I had heard in one day.

CHAPTER XIII

SATURDAY, OF COURSE, MEANT a day off for the valley chalk-wrangler. That weekend escape from the three R's always made me feel like a whale come up to breathe. And the Saturday Sidney Lander interrupted my breathing broke bright and happy over the mountain tops. By the time I was up and astir the yellow sunlight was spilling over into our dusky bowl between the Talkeetnas, with a flash of turquoise where Knik Glacier shone sometimes apple-green and sometimes blue-white in the shifting beams. It made me feel that life was good and the mere going on could still be a matter of high adventure.

But a day off didn't mean idleness. I had my mending and darning to do, my sourdough sponge to work into loaves, and my house to put in order after six days of neglect. I'd baked my bread, and finished my washing and ironing, and with the fortitude of the true frontiersman was just filling my big woodbox with neatly split spruce boles when a truck rumbled up to my door.

It was a rather official-looking truck of battleship-grey, similar to those I'd seen of late about the Administration Camp at Palmer. And it startled me a little when Lander swung down from the driver's seat. He looked tired and a trifle solemn.

"I suppose you know what that means?" he said as I continued to stare at the truck. He laughed, rather curtly, when I told him I was entirely in the dark. "It means I'm field manager for the Matanuska Valley Project."

From my silence he seemed to reap some final impression of disappointment. He stood, for a moment, studying my face.

"I suppose you think I've failed you?" he said, more solemn than ever.

"In what?" I asked, resenting his power to interfere with my heart action.

"In marking time this way about your Chakitana claim," he observed as he followed me into the shack and once more stood watching me while I quietly proceeded to make tea for him.

"I can live without that mine," I found myself saying.

"But nobody likes to be robbed," Lander observed as he thrust some papers into my hand. One of those papers, I noticed, was my father's dog-eared certificate of citizenship. And as I glanced down at the faded portrait appended to it I realized I was looking at the face of a fighter. It made me stiffen my shoulders.

"We can't, of course, pick our ground for this particular fight," Lander was saying. "We have to know our enemy's line of attack. And in this case he seems to be playing safe and turning to court procedure and trying to make everything look legal."

"Then what can *we* do?" I asked.

"I have Canby working for us at Juneau," Lander explained. "He's both dependable and resourceful. But you can't, of course, hurry those Record Office chair-warmers. And we'll have to depend on Canby."

"While I have to depend on you," I ventured.

"Why not?" asked Lander. And I remembered, as I met that somberly steady gaze of his, how I'd schooled myself to think of him as "Lander," since the blunter surname had seemed to stand for a casual announcement of camaraderie and at the same time tended to keep everything more impersonal.

"But don't you see what this is doing?" I pointed out. "It's doing for me what Federal help's doing for these colonists. It's making me lean on others."

He laughed as he stood before me, so disturbingly rugged and strong and self-reliant.

"That's what I'm here for," he said. And I was tempted, for a moment, to let my crazy hunger for independence curl up and die in the ashes of a burnt-out pride. But I remembered the girl in the raincoat on a wind-swept Seattle wharf. And reason came back to her throne.

"Trumbull's going to lose out, remember, on his first round," Lander was explaining. "That report shows your father's naturalization papers can be confirmed. It'll leave the issue hinging on the question of clear or clouded title definition. And that issue may have to be decided out on the Chakitana."

I didn't want to question his judgment or dampen his interest. But I couldn't help feeling that the glacier of time was disappointingly slow in giving up its bones of uncertainty. And Lander, studying my face, seemed to read some sign of indecision there.

"I understand," he said, "that Trumbull's been talking to you."

"It didn't do much good," I acknowledged.

"Fine!" he exclaimed, as though a load had been lifted from his mind. "And we've our valley work, remember."

"Why have you swung in with it?" I asked.

"Perhaps it's to be near you," he answered, compelling his gaze to meet mine.

"I haven't asked for any such sacrifice," I protested. But I was conscious, a moment later, of some fleeting disappointment in my lukewarm reception of that answer.

"It's not a sacrifice," he contended. "There's something big going to break here, and I want to be in on it. And I want to see *you* in on it. We're going to be needed here, both of us."

I couldn't help thinking, even while that speech bracketed us together so neatly, that his sojourn in the valley had failed to bring our trails much closer. There were ghostlier things than geography, I remembered, to keep people apart.

"I wonder if we *are* needed?" I questioned out of my momentary mood of misgiving.

"You know you are," said Lander with a glance about my wickyup, "or you wouldn't be standing for this hardship."

"It isn't the hardship I mind," I confessed, realizing for the first time just how wrapped up in one's work one could become.

"I know," he said, though his next words showed that he didn't know at all. "But time, remember, is working for us on that other problem."

I wasn't, of course, quite sure of the problem he was referring to. But there could be no doubt as to his earnestness when he began talking about the valley changes confronting us.

"Things are going to be different around here," he confidently affirmed. "They've got to, or there'll be hell to pay. And it'll be a man's size job, making this muddle ready for those two hundred families."

"Isn't it a trifle late for that?" I asked as I filled my two crockery cups with hot tea.

Lander admitted that it was. But that, he contended, was just why we had to pitch in and help.

"You'll get a school, of course," he went on as he abstractedly stirred his tea. "And we'll have to have a hospital of some sort. And a Red Cross nurse. And a marshal to keep order in those transient-camps. And someone to speed up the building-gangs and stop all this bungling about supplies and the eternal buck-passing that's mainly responsible for the mess they're in."

"I want to help," I said. Something in my voice brought an approving smile from the man across the bald pine table.

"But there'll be times," he said, "when you'll be needing help yourself. And that, remember, is why I'm here."

It was said, I suppose, with the best intentions in the world. But, for some reason, it made me feel abysmally alone in the world, as remote from companionship as a mud hen lost in the middle of the Dismal Swamp. It was a field manager's duty, of course, to help the weaklings who faltered along the way. But my biggest and most personal problem didn't, apparently, swing within the orbit of his official duties.

"I'll get along," I said, trying to make the words sound big and brave.

"Of course you will," remarked Lander, intercepting me as I moved over to stoke the stove. He looked up, with a spruce-stick in his hand. "And in two weeks we'll have a radio station here, to link us up with the outside world. That'll take us out of the wilderness, at one jump. And before winter we'll have electric lights and telephones and cold storage and a cannery and snug homes for every one of those two hundred families."

I thought of the undug wells and the unfinished roads and the carloads of cement that had been left to harden along the railway siding.

"It will take a bit of doing," I said, mistily envious of his he-man initiative. But he, apparently, was thinking of other things.

"You know, of course, that your friend Ericson is in the transient-camp here?"

I disclaimed any friendship between Eric the Red and myself.

"That's just the point," proceeded my visitor. "He's as yellow as they make them. And two days ago he had a talk with John Trumbull up at the Happy Day."

"What's that to me?" I asked with what was only a pretense at indifference.

Lander hesitated.

"Trumbull," he explained, "is pretty ruthless. There are mighty few road rules left when he starts steamrolling toward his own selfish ends."

"Shouldn't you be a little more loyal to the Trumbull family?" I said with unexpected sharpness.

He stiffened at that and his color deepened just a trifle.

"I've tried to be loyal to you," he finally observed, his voice both quiet and controlled as his gaze wavered about the shack. "And I know you can't keep on living like this."

"What can you do about it?" I said with more of a note of challenge than I had intended.

He laughed a little as he pushed his chair back and stood up.

"I've been talking with Colonel Hart," he casually announced. "And he agrees with me we've got to have a medical man here. There's a chance he'll bring Doctor Ruddock over from Toklutna. And I've put in a word for your friend Katie O'Connell. There's no reason she couldn't swing in as a Red Cross nurse."

A wave of joy went through me. Katie, I realized, would be an answer to prayer.

"How soon?" I gasped. It must have been the happiness in my face that made Lander smile, rather wistfully.

"That depends," he said, "on how much red tape can be cut between here and Washington. All they send us, these days, is a clash of orders."

Before I could answer him Salaria appeared at my door, brown and wind-blown. In the crook of her arm she carried a rifle and over one shoulder swung a full game bag. Her jacket was open at the throat, showing a triangle of smooth dark skin that made me think of a wood duck's breast. She declined to come in for a cup of tea. But her dusky eyes rested rather hungrily on the silent Lander.

"You goin' my way, old-timer?" she inquired, indicating the truck in the dooryard.

Lander's gaze met mine for a moment. I could see the heat-lightning smile that hovered about his lips.

"That means the tired Artemis wants a lift," he said as he reached for his coat and hat.

"Will you give me one?" exacted the Artemis in question. I could see Lander's gaze rest for a moment or two on the brown triangle between the jacket flaps. It reminded me that she was still a woman, under all the roughness of her hunting togs. And she was a woman, I remembered, who wouldn't beat about the bush in getting her man.

"Right to your door, S'lary," Lander answered her, with a hand wave toward his truck.

It was while the Artemis with the rifle was still frowning over some faint tinge of mockery in his voice that Lander turned back to me.

"How about coming to Wasilla tonight?" he asked.

"Why to Wasilla?" I questioned.

"They have a roadhouse dance there, every Saturday night, for our relief-roll toilers. And I want to get a line on the bad actors in that bunch."

I could see Salaria's face fall. I suspected, in fact, that Lander's question was meant as an announcement of his aloofness from the urgent-eyed Artemis.

"I'll be seeing you," I acquiesced in the offhanded note of the frontier.

"Fine," said Lander as he waited for Salaria to climb into the truck.

Yet as I stood watching them while they went riding away, two stalwart figures in the slanting northern sunlight, kindred in their vigor and courage and love of the open, I knew a faint twinge or two of envy. A speech of Sock-Eye's came back to me as I saw the spruce slopes swallow up the truck and the two shadows swaying so companionably together. "Gold may be where you find it, girlie, but don't forget it's the first finder usually absorbs the metal!"

Lander called for me that night, much later than I'd expected, and carried me on to the Wasilla dance. It was many a year since I'd seen an Alaska jamboree of that kind, and it left me wondering if life hadn't rather spoiled me for such affairs. For along with the dancing was much brawling and love-making and the imbibing of a local brand of hooch known as moose-milk. The orchestra was merely a tinny old piano helped out by a fiddle and accordion. Even as we pushed our way into that crowded roadhouse with its open bar I wondered if the natives weren't doing the best to revive the old Klondike days. For the air was thick with smoke and dust, the drinking was continuous, the music was aboriginal in its raucous shrillness, and the dancing was altogether ursine in its roughness. Men in flannel shirts and high-tops gyrated about with gum-chewing white women in slacks or held well-rouged and sloe-eyed half-breed girls in calico close to their Mackinawed bosoms. The stag line was long, the moose-milk was obviously potent, and the participating ladies, since there were ten men to every woman, expressed their temporary importance by a rough and strident pertness not exactly suggestive of an evening with Junior Leaguers. Some of them, in fact, were quite drunk.

I looked into Lander's face as we began to dance. Its grimness dispelled some vague sense of disappointment which his readiness to relapse into frivolity had brought me.

"I never thought of you," I told him, "as a dancing man."

"I'm not," he admitted. "But it's not often I have a partner like you."

For just a moment his arm tightened about me and I had to fight down a little surge of joy in womanly power. Then he caught sight of a painted squaw, swinging past us in the still closer clasp of a Mackinaw-clad mine-worker, and his arm relaxed.

But he danced much better than I had expected. He danced, in fact, with a smooth sedateness that left us almost conspicuous in that swarm of jigging bodies and flying heels. And I felt oddly small and passive in that strong arm of his. The sense of his nearness, I suppose, should have made me happy. But it failed, for some reason, to fill my cup of joy. Life, I knew, couldn't be all toil and hardship. People were entitled to their human share of happiness. My own existence, of late, hadn't been marked by too much laughter and lightness. And we only live once.

But everything, that night, was wrong. I couldn't drum up any enthusiasm for that falsetto and loose-jointed hilarity born of bad music and worse whisky, for air thick with floor dust and tobacco smoke, for rowdy love-making and the aroma of overheated bodies.

I tried to tell my partner that there was something pathetic in such childlike efforts to escape the isolation of wilderness life. But Lander only laughed.

"This is easy," he said. "There'll be a broken head or two before the night's over." There'd even been a stabbing, the week before, with the stabber packed off to the calaboose at Seward.

But I had no craving to see fist-fights and knife-play.

"I want to go home," I said at the end of our dance. For along the line that crowded the bar I'd caught sight of Eric the Red, surrounded by a circle of transients. He was too busy drinking and talking to give any thought to dancing. But his sardonic smile as we passed within six paces of him confirmed my distaste for the place.

"All right," said Lander. Yet I knew by the way his gaze lingered on the flushed and bleary-eyed faces all about him that he would have preferred to stay.

"They've already made life cheap enough," I contended as we escaped to the open.

There the air was sweet with a small wind that blew down from the Talkeetnas. About us lay a world that looked ghostly in the long sub-Arctic twilight where the hours of darkness were so brief.

"I guess this is better," he said as he tucked a blanket about my knees and climbed in beside me. He was silent for a while, tooling the truck along the spectral ribbon of a road.

"I'm afraid I took you away from your work," I ventured.

Lander laughed as that none-too-even road kept our swaying bodies in rough but friendly contact.

"That's about the best I can ask of life," he said. "To be next to you like this."

My answering laugh, I suppose, was largely defensive.

"While we both remember to keep to the center of the road," I suggested.

"It'll be a better road before we're through with it," the resonant low voice beside me announced. He was speaking in riddles, of course. Yet I knew well enough what he meant.

"But where will it lead to?" I asked.

"I don't know, yet," he answered after a moment's silence. "But I don't want it to lead me from you."

"Hasn't it already done that?" I questioned.

It may have sounded a bit cruel. But I was depressed by a feeling of moving alone through an empty world. It was the ghostly Alaskan half-light, I suppose, that made the spruce and birch groves look like long and misty waves of gloom fallen asleep in their tracks.

"I'm strong for the straight-shooter," I heard Lander's voice saying. "But I've a hankering, on the other hand, for not shooting in the dark."

"Then let's make sure of what we're aiming at," I quietly suggested.

He turned and made an effort to study my face in the none-too-certain light.

"I thought we meant something to each other," he said with a quick and boylike candor that was more disarming than all the earlier riddles. "I rather thought you liked me."

"I *do*," I said in an effort to match casualness with casualness.

But that, plainly, didn't solve his problem. He drove on in silence until he came to the narrower trail that led in to my shack.

"I suppose there's somebody else?" he finally ventured, coming to a stop in the cabin clearing.

"There's nobody else," I was honest enough to acknowledge.

"That's all I wanted to know," he said with a new resoluteness in his voice.

I was more afraid of myself, I think, than I was of him. I didn't like the way my heart was pounding as he got down from his seat and crossed to my side of the truck.

"With *me* there is nobody else," I compelled myself to say.

I knew, by the way he stiffened, that my shot had not missed its mark. I had the feeling, as he folded his blanket and tossed it up on the empty seat, that one of life's bigger moments was in some way failing to live up to its expectations.

"You're right," he quietly acknowledged. Then he laughed his curt laugh. "I guess I'm running a little ahead of the game."

I felt like calling after him, as he backed and turned and went lurching out to the highway. I felt that life was cheating me, that we were cheating each other. And I stood on my doorstep, looking after him until the valley shadows finally swallowed him up.

The silence of my cabin, when I went inside and lighted the lamp, struck me as tomblike. It seemed a dolorously lonely place for a woman to live. I saw it, for the first time, in all its cold and meager baldness. And I remembered, as I undressed and went to bed in the bunk little wider than a coffin, how it was only an empty heart that made life seem empty.

CHAPTER XIV

MATANUSKA WAS NOW ON the map. The colonists had arrived. Our pilgrims from the Midwest, perplexed and travel-worn, had at last reached their Promised Land.

But that Promised Land, apparently, didn't live up to their expectations. For all they found were unfinished roads and harried officials and lumber piles and an impromptu city of tents along the valley flats, army tents in rows as regular as a military cantonment, each with a wooden floor and boarded side walls and a smoke pipe going up from its roof.

There was no teaching for the chalk-wrangler yesterday when word went round that the first trainload of the colonists was on its way up from Seward, and Katie O'Connell was hurried over from Toklutna to look after the women and children. And since I was detailed to stand right-hand man to Katie, I was there to help make boilers of coffee and watch the disembarking of the disheveled and sea-worn army.

They weren't very impressive to the eye, as they came tumbling out of their day coaches, like range cattle out of a corral. But I wanted to believe in them. I kept telling myself that these inlanders who'd fared so far from the hills of their birth were really a fine and valorous band of frontier-seekers. They stood, I felt, for something glamorous and invincible in the race. They'd set out to conquer a new world, as their fathers' fathers had done with the ox teams and whitetops of an earlier generation. I refused to think of them as a collection of nondescript clodhoppers luxuriating in army-transport cabins and red-plush car seats and free meals on the way. I tried to look on them as an army of heroes, pioneering into the unknown North, making ready to face and tame a new wilderness. As Lander had expressed it, something big was about to break in the valley.

But the note they struck was not always epic. Some of them looked like refugees from a far-East rice famine, and some like survivors of a pier-end dance marathon. And after them came their belongings, boxes and bales, bags and carryalls, bedding and house pets, baby carriages and bird cages. From one of these cages, crowning a pile of baggage as high as my head, I could hear a Hartz Mountain canary burst into song. From another I could hear a parrot squawking out language plainly not learned from a Lutheran rector.

But the general tenor wasn't one of blitheness. I could see women still petulant over their weeks of homelessness, surrounded like ship-wrecked sailors by what they could salvage from their long-traveled belongings. I doled out coffee and sandwiches to toil-hardened tillers of the plains and drought-wizened cattle-raisers from valley farms and Mackinawed ax-wielders from wooded slopes. I tried to give them a welcoming word or two as they stared gloomily about at their Arctic El Dorado and herded their children up to the grub tables. The fact they were to live in tents, it was plain, didn't appeal to them.

"Them damn' flimflammers said there'd be a house waitin' for every family," raged a Wisconsin mother with a sick baby in her arms.

She looked tired and worried and showed no interest in the cameramen taking press-shots of their discomfort. It was the young people, to whom Alaska meant excitement and Matanuska spelled romance, who crowded about the cameras—lanky youths and laughing girls, not in the slatted sun-bonnets of earlier free-soilers, but in the sweaters and slacks of their own blithe generation. And there were children, slathers of children, with tousled heads and toys in their hands, staring wide-eyed at the white peaks of the Talkeetnas and lustily proclaiming to the world they were hungry. Some of them were even more lustily crying for parents lost in the crowd.

For it was mostly confusion and tumult and bickering, with loud complaints about tent assignments and arguments over the ownership of baskets and bales. It kept Katie on the jump, consoling wives who couldn't find their husbands and rescuing toddlers who kept losing themselves between the tent rows and lumber piles.

"You belong in these parts?" a petulant voice inquired of me as I refilled the coffeepots. I found myself confronted by a rotund matriarch with a terrace of chins and eight obstreperous children.

I said that Matanuska was now my home.

"Can't say you look like a girl who'd been brought up on whale blubber," observed my new friend, who asserted that her name was Betsy Sebeck and that she'd be glad when she could rest her fanny in a rocking chair of her own. "But them cock-eyed bureaucrats, of course, ain't got anything ready. There ain't even water, they tell me, in them two-by-four tents. And they ain't got lamps—when they told us we was to be steam-heated and lit by electricity!"

"Things will straighten out," I said as I caught sight of Lander haranguing a group of grumbling free-soilers.

"But there ain't even blankets enough to go round," persisted Betsy. "And if I don't get at a washtub before the week's out them kids o' mine will have to go naked."

The bureaucrats, I discovered, had declined to bring in a piano for her, had lost two of her trunks, and were now trying to stow her away in a back-row tent which her man wouldn't accept. They'd even failed to stock the Commissary up properly, she lamented, and that'd mean, of course, going without grapefruit and ice cream.

But even in the midst of all that confusion and complaining I wanted to cling to the claim there was something epic about the migration. It might, as yet, have little dignity. But it stirred one, in spite of mistakes and misunderstandings, to think of a thousand souls being carried thousands of miles to seek their fortunes in a new country. Some of them might be ill-chosen, and some ingrates, but few of them could fail to be touched by some ghostly spirit of adventure. They were making history.

That fact came home to me more than ever when I stood under an azure Alaskan sky that arched above the blue-ravined slopes of mountains towering up to stately peaks of white and watched the two hundred family heads draw lots for their farm plots. For fate, of course, reposed in that little wooden box that held the plot numbers, since a few of the farmsites were already cleared and fenced and blessed with cabins, while others were nothing but swampy niggerheads and unbroken forest. And as the lucky and the unlucky crowded about a big map of the valley, to determine the position and state of their tracts, there was much cheering and grumbling and groaning.

It disheartened me a little, though, to see so many of those Argonauts light-heartedly swapping their claims. And I wished the newsreel men had left the settlers alone. Even the triple-chinned Mrs. Sebeck, I noticed, was developing a hero-complex, having been thrice photographed in the midst of her large and clamorous brood. And the old-timers, watching from the side lines, seemed to find their darkest fears fulfilled.

Salaria, deep-bosomed and Indian-brown, drifted up to my table, and viewed the scene with a lip curl of contempt. There she was joined by Sock-Eye, waiting and watchful for the first open jeer from one of those preoccupied cheechakos. He impressed me, with his huge sheath-knife and his six-gun swinging from his belt, as oddly like a shadow out of the past.

"Looks like a potlatch t' me," observed Salaria. "A potlatch with Uncle Sam passin' out forty-acre farms instead o' two-bit knives. And most o' these poor coots don't even know what they're gittin'."

Sock-Eye spat dourly into the road dust.

"They think they're gittin' something for nothing," he averred. "But them giloots'll be about as happy in this valley as a blacksnake on an ice block."

"They're sure off to a grand start," the old-timer's daughter mordantly agreed, "tentin' out and livin' off a Commissary and raisin' Cain 'cause their electric washin' machines is slow in gittin' here."

"And growlin' at Washington," added Sock-Eye, "instead o' gittin' out and grubbin' the spruce roots out o' their land."

"Lander says there's a shortage of axes and work tools," I was prompted to explain.

"Of course there is," exulted Salaria. "They've got grand electric coffee-grinders but no power t' run 'em. They've got a string o' threshin' machines, but no crops in t' thresh."

"And stoves over there rustin' in the rain," added Sock-Eye, "but nowheres t' put 'em. And a mountain o' them new-fangled enamel sinks and no kitchens t' set 'em up in. And a carload o' harness, by gad, and no workhorses t' buckle it on."

"And ten miles o' the richest soil in all Alaska yellin' for a plow-point," said Salaria, adding a final note to that song of woe, "yet instead o' havin' gumption enough to git out and hustle for a crop they're raisin' a holler because they can't all be on the road front and have cream for breakfast and a fiddle-orchestry t' play for 'em when the evenin' shadows grow long!"

Salaria's charge, I knew, was not without some shadow of reason. There had been mistakes and much changing of plans. There even had been waste and confusion, and a tragic loss of time when time was so precious. But someone had to carry on. And it was too late to complain and quibble.

The tumult had subsided and the shadows were growing longer and I could see smoke going up from the unbroken line of smoke pipes before Katie was able to join me at my alfresco coffee table. I knew just how tired she was by the way she sat down on one of the bench boards and nodded toward a coffee pot.

I gave her a steaming cup, fresh from the fire, and three sandwiches from my shrunken mountain of beef and bread.

"They're pretty well settled," she said as she munched a sandwich between her strong white teeth. "But I wish Ruddy was here."

I asked her why. She postponed her answer until she had polished off her sandwich and reached for her second cup of coffee.

"There's a baby over there I don't like the looks of," she finally announced.

"What's wrong with it?" I questioned.

"I don't know, yet," she said as she bit into a sandwich. Then her eyes became ruminative. "Wouldn't it be sweet if measles got into this little family circle. Or scarletina! Or even whooping cough." Her tired-looking eyes surveyed the row of white-walled tents. "There's six hundred kids in that camp, in one mad huddle, and not a roof over their head if a bug or two got into their blood!"

I asked if they all hadn't had medical inspection.

"They're supposed to," admitted Katie. "But if I know my onions there's a father of seven over in that line-up who won't last long. He's plainly tubercular. And there's a Michigan woman who's been having labor pains all the way up from Seward."

"What does that mean?" I asked with a qualm of dismay.

"It means," said the weary-eyed Katie, "that we can't sit here enjoying the scenery. You'll have to scrub up, old-timer, and help me with the delivery."

Two hours later I heard the first faint wail of the first baby born in the Matanuska Colony. To me it looked like a pink rabbit with an oversized head. But Katie, bare-armed between two flaring gas lamps, announced it was as fine a boy as you could clap your eyes on.

And as I looked out at the quietened cluster of tents, under that high-arching sky so spangled with stars, a touch of mystery seemed to fall across those travel-worn exiles lost in sleep. I felt, in a way, at the center of life. I felt foolishly important and dignified with some new task of guardianship. I saw myself as a part in a movement much bigger than my own petty interests.

CHAPTER XV

IF I'M THE LAMP in the valley I've got to burn with a brighter wick. Colonel Hart called me into Headquarters and told me I was to have a schoolhouse as soon as they could find a building that would suit the purpose. The real school, he explained, couldn't go up until next year. But if the Colony children could be grouped into classes of some sort, and a teacher rotated among them, there might be less grumbling from the parents and less hell-raising by the youngsters.

So for two or three weeks, he proceeded, I'd have to do the best I could as a circuit-rider teacher. The first call on the workers, of course, was to get homes built. But with the help of the Territorial School Commission and the elimination of that old illiterate known as Sam Bryson I'd soon have textbooks and supplies and four walls in which to house my pupils.

"But in the meantime," he continued, "we'll have to keep that rabble of kids tied down to classwork. And your circuit, after this, will have to take in our different camps. It won't be easy. But nothing's easy up here. It's a matter of facing pioneer conditions. And it's the job of the pioneer to get through with what he has at hand."

I affirmed that I would do the best I could. Then I suggested that a portable blackboard would be a help, since a blackboard was to a teacher what a throne was to a king, the seat and symbol of his power.

"All right," the man at the desk answered across his mountain of blue-prints. "Tell that bunch of transient workers out there to make your board and make it pronto. Tell them I said so."

He turned to other problems and left me remembering that pioneers were not to be pikers. So I sallied forth to where six flannel-shirted CCC workers were languidly piling lumber at the track side. I ignored a quite audible, "Pipe the peach!" as I approached them. Even their overfamiliar, "Hello, Toots!" failed to shake my dignity. I merely informed them of the Administrator's order for the concoction of a four-by-six portable blackboard.

"So you're the dry-nurse of this God-forsaken hole," said the boldest of the sextette. "Some chalk-wrangler," he observed as he blinked at my hunting boots and whipcord riding breeches. They didn't seem to gibe with his ideas of pedagogy.

"You can have anything we've got, baby-eyes," said another. And still another coyly observed that his own schooling wasn't all it should have been and it seemed about time to be starting over. A fourth Casanova of the North announced he was plumb ready to learn anything a rosebud of the frozen North could teach him.

It wasn't, of course, as bad as it sounded, being carried on with that half-respectful and heavy-jointed jocularity peculiar to the regions where life is rough and chivalry is apt to stay in its shirt-sleeves. And, for all their banter, they assured me I'd have my board, neatly nailed together and ebonized with a flat coat of lampblack. They even promised to have it at my cabin the next day.

I rather overlooked their eagerness to know just where that cabin was. And it would all have worked out better, I imagine, if they hadn't first gone over to Wasilla where flourishes the valley's only open bar, and where they were joined by a dozen or two other transients. There, at any rate, they plainly drank more moose-milk than was good for them. I could hear them as they came in a body toward my cabin clearing, singing as they came:

> "Oh, then, my Booska,
> Don't you cry for me,
> For I'm off to Matanuska
> With the teacher on my knee."

Someone with an accordion was leading them in that familiar old pioneer tune. But I didn't find the newer wording altogether to my liking. And by the time they came swarming in from the road they were a shouting and irresponsible band of adventurers, set on giving their lone chalk-wrangler a housewarming and a "shivaree" all in one.

I closed and fastened my door, in fact, when I caught sight of them charging across the clearing. They rather frightened me, yelling as they were, like Pawnees on the warpath. I couldn't, of course, believe they were as bad as they sounded. But I got an inkling of how the Indian-harried women of the overland trail must have felt, in the old days, when I found that band of tipsy roisterers swarming about my windows and pounding on my door.

I had no intention of hiding away under the bunk mattress. I pretended, instead, to be writing at my table end, sitting there, rather anxiously, as they worked pole ends under the sill logs and tried to impart a ship-at-sea motion to my small cabin. But they soon tired of that, finding the shack too heavy to be converted into a rocking chair. So they proceeded to serenade me, more noisily than ever. And to the general din they added a salvo or two of revolver shots.

It sounded like the capture of the stagecoach in a wild and woolly western. And even that I endured without protest. But when I realized that one of the faces peering in at the window was that of the fire-eating Eric Ericson I found the last of my patience ebbing away.

I didn't, even then, altogether surrender to panic. I didn't, on the other hand, propose to sit there and shiver like a white mouse. When they started to pound on the door again, this time with one of their heavier poles, I could see that it would soon go down under their blows. And that not only brought the light of battle into my eye but prompted me to cross to the dish shelf and reach for Sock-Eye's old revolver. Then I lifted away the crossbar and swung the door open. I felt very much of a pioneer woman as I stood there facing them.

But instead of shrinking back, as they should have done, they began to laugh at me and my threatening firearm. They even crowded in closer, pushing about me like a group of sled huskies about a grub bag. They could see hesitation, I suppose, in the very way I held that old six-gun.

It was Eric the Red who swayed closest to me, with a hand wave toward my equally swaying revolver.

"Mightn't it go off, angel-eyes?" he taunted.

"It will," I warned him, "unless you stand back."

His laugh reminded me of his power to make life both ugly and cheap.

"It would be a joy, sweet lady, to receive lead from a hand so fair."

I hated him more than ever for that. I could even feel an impulse to resent his mockery stiffen my finger on the trigger. And I could, without much trouble, have given him what he asked for. But he was too quick for me.

With an unexpected upsweep of his hand he knocked my arm above my head. The shock of that blow made the revolver go off, high in the air, and before the smoke cleared away they were crowding in closer, pretending to be fighting for its possession. But I could see it was only a pretense. They refused to be afraid of me. They were merely mauling me and circling their arms about me in an offhand sort of intimacy that was all the worse for its casualness. I could see, by their laughing faces, that they rather liked my struggles. But they made it a point to keep my right hand pinioned above my head.

"It mustn't lose its temper," said Ericson, with his face close to mine. He even passed mockingly admiring fingers across my tumbled forelock. And as

I shrank back from that odious touch a motor truck of battleship-gray came clattering across the clearing. I could see a tall figure swing down from its seat.

It wasn't until I saw him pushing in through the crowd that I realized the newcomer was Lander. He scattered the startled transients right and left as he came. A heavier-bodied man, who tried to block his way, went suddenly flat on the dooryard soil as my rescuer's fist thudded against his jaw. The crowd was no longer laughing.

Ericson, close to me in the doorway, half-turned to fathom the reason for the sudden silence. And I could see Lander's mouth harden into a grimmer line as he saw and recognized that half-turned face. The mallet-like fist, swinging for the second time, sent my tormentor sprawling in across the cabin floor. He lay there, face-down, as Lander turned on the resentful group behind him.

They fell back a little, milling and shouting as they went. But they at least fell back. Lander, stooping down from his towering height, lifted Ericson from the floor and flung him out through the open door. Then he reached for the revolver still clutched in my hand and took it away from me. I stood watching him as he stepped out through the door, swinging it shut behind him.

I expected to hear the sound of shots, for more than one of those transients, I knew, carried firearms. And it seemed rather craven and cowardly for me to be hidden away there behind a barricade of heavy timbers. But instead of the sound of shooting I merely heard Lander's voice, diminishing in volume as he stepped away from my doorsill.

What he said to them I didn't quite know. But I could hear that deep and indignant voice above the mutterings and catcalls of the others. I could hear a final ringing challenge that brought no reply from their ranks. And by the time I could think a little straighter and stand a little steadier on my feet the door opened again and Lander stepped into the cabin. He looked at me with a quietly questioning eye.

"Are you all right?" he asked.

"I'm all right," I told him. And I attempted to prove it by going out and bringing in the mud-smeared and forgotten blackboard.

He stood watching me as I wiped the mud, and then what was unmistakably a bloodstain, from that ignobly acquired symbol of authority. Then, still without speaking, we stood rather foolishly looking into each other's eyes.

"This won't happen again," he said with a steely sort of quietness. He glanced down at his bruised knuckles. "You know, of course, what that rabble-rouser wants to do? He wants to throw a scare into you, to frighten you out of your job, to make this valley intolerable."

"Why should he?" I asked.

"I think," answered Lander, "it's because he has Trumbull behind him. There's more than one way, remember, of fighting a mine claim."

"But it's all so unfair," I cried. "It's been unfair from the beginning."

"Of course, it is," he agreed. Then he turned and let his gaze lock with mine. "But it at least brought us together."

"Has it?" I parried, with a feeling that we were edging out on perilously thin ice. And I felt his quick glance searching my face for second meanings.

"We're not through yet," he affirmed. His laugh was brief and edged with bitterness. But that proffered strength of his seemed to give me strength of my own. And it was pent-up gratitude, I suppose, that brought a dangerous little glow somewhere under my floating ribs. A ghostly voice was telling me that it would be sweet to lean against a wide shoulder like that, whatever the outcome, until life lost a little of its uncertainty. It would be infinitely soothing to nest in that enfolding strength and preen smooth the ruffled feathers of pride.

But all I did was to back into a chair and look at Lander's bruised knuckles. Yet life's final battles, I remembered, weren't decided by brawn. And the shadow of a far-off figure fell between me and the man who was offering to make life safe for me.

"This can't go on," I said with an unlooked-for note of desperation. "You simply can't go on helping me like this."

A car horn sounded outside the shack, as he stood studying my face. But he continued to study it as though he were inspecting a roadmap that didn't work out right.

I could see the ghost of a smile soften the hard lines of his mouth.

"You're pretty easy to help," he said. He even took a slow step or two toward me as he said it. Then he swung on his heel, as the door opened, and stared at the rough and mannish figure of Katie O'Connell, who inspected me with an indifferent eye and promptly turned to my visitor.

"You're the bozo I want," was her grim-noted announcement. "We've got to get action here or there'll be hell to pay."

"What's wrong?" asked Lander as he leaned my blackboard against the bunk edge.

"There's three clear cases of measles in that tent colony," was her answer, "and about two hundred kids who've been exposed to it. Colonel Hart's gone over for the Anchorage doctor, but that doesn't solve our problem."

"What is it you want?" asked Lander.

"I want Doctor Ruddock here," was Katie's prompt proclamation. "And inside of twenty-four hours I've got to have a hospital of some kind."

"Then you'll get it," Lander said with reassuring curtness. "We've got the material and we've got two hundred workers. And we'll turn 'em loose on it without waiting for Washington's okay."

"What workers?" challenged Katie. "Those bindle stiffs in the CCC camp have just told me they're walking out. They say they're on strike. And the building-gangs claim they have orders to stick to houses."

"To hell with orders," barked Lander, "at a time like this. I say you'll get that hospital. And you'll get it, lady, before I take these boots off."

CHAPTER XVI

ACTION IS ELOQUENCE, AS Shakespeare once said. And in frontier life like ours the hero seems to be the man who can get things done, no matter how difficult the doing.

Lander didn't fail the valley in its time of need. He bluntly kept his bluntly made promise. And Katie got her hospital.

All she got was a board shed interlined with plywood and roofed with tar paper, a bald-looking building with square windows and a row of army cots along one wall. But it was shelter for Katie's patients.

It didn't come easy. When Lander put his pride in his pocket and talked to the transient workers he got nothing but jeers. For Eric the Red, obviously, had been working on them. They declared they were already imposed on and underpaid, and announced they had no intention of losing sleep for a bunch of slave-driving autocrats who ought to be in Russia.

Then Katie talked to them. She told them it was a mission of mercy and appealed to their manhood. She begged them to forget past differences and get busy, for the sake of the colony and the good name of the Project.

They merely laughed at her mannish figure and started singing one of their bindle-stiff road songs. Then most of them, to the sound of banjo music, marched off to Wasilla and got good and drunk.

But Lander didn't give up. He hurriedly canvassed the colony tents and unearthed three men who had once done carpenter work. Then he went after the old-timers. He got Hans Wiebel, the frugal German farmer of the upper valley. Then he got Sock-Eye, and the quick-handed father of Olie Eckstrom, and a stalwart ex-cabinetmaker who knew the meaning of edged tools. The acid-spirited Sam Bryson, it's true, flatly refused to come to our help. But Salaria just as flatly defied all paternal injunctions and joined up with the group.

Then the dirt began to fly. Half an hour after the site and size of the building had been decided the pillars were bedded and the sills laid. While I helped to lug two-by-fours from the track side lumber piles the wide-shouldered Salaria strode back and forth with twelve-foot boards on her back. She gloried in dumping her gigantic loads at the feet of the busy Lander. And almost as fast as we could carry the allotted timbers they were caught up and measured and shaped while the sound of hammer and saw filled the valley.

Northern nights, at this time of the year, are not long. But, when darkness came on, fires were lighted and lanterns were swung above the busy workers. They neither grumbled nor rested. They made me think of gnomes in a mine pit, determined to finish some ghostly task before daybreak drove them back to some deeper underworld. And they restored, in some way, my belief in humanity.

It wasn't until the sun began to show over the peaks of the Talkeetnas that Katie and I took time off to serve them with coffee and hardtack. But by then the floor had been laid and the walls were up and the roof was ready and waiting for its covering of tarpaper. While some of the workers swept the shavings from the floor boards and fitted doors and windows, army cots were carried in, followed by blankets and sheets and pillows, and a stove was put up, and in it was started a fire from the waiting shavings and blocks and board ends.

By noon the roof was finished and Katie's brand-new Red Cross flag was flying from its peak. Then the windows were screened, and the drugs and dressings and towels and instruments and enamelware were carried in from the emergency tent. Everything looked so shipshape that Katie hurriedly donned a uniform, as brand new as her Red Cross flag, and gave instructions for the carrying in of the sick children. There were seven of them by this time. And just as the last of them was being tucked into bed Doctor Ruddock appeared in our midst and promptly announced that from that day forward he was to be recognized as the official man-of-medicine for the valley project.

I could see the glow that came into Katie's Celtic eye as she caught the significance of that announcement. She reached out for her Ruddy's hand and held it for a moment in her own capable big paw.

"That's great," she said, with a quaver in her voice.

But the new Project doctor, it seemed to me, didn't give much attention to his nurse. He ran his eye down the row of cots and said they must have blinds for the windows, to keep the light from the children's eyes. He inspected the building and lamented the absence of running water and laughed at the electric sterilizer, which couldn't be used, of course, until the completion of the Project's generating plant.

"They're throwing money away on the wrong things," he said after a quick appraisal of the supplies.

And that seemed confirmed, two days later, when a motor ambulance was unloaded from a flat car, a highly varnished and urban-looking ambulance designed for the use of the new Red Cross nurse. But Katie promptly cottoned to that vehicle, which because of its sable paint scheme, she christened "Black Maria." Without loss of time, in fact, she tried it out on the new highway between Palmer and Matanuska Village, and confided to me, on her return, that the old boat was good for seventy miles an hour.

But Katie soon had other things to think of. Two cases of scarlet fever developed in our little tent city. And that stirred her Ruddy into still more frantic action. He bundled his nurse off to an isolation tent in a clearing at the edge of the Wiebel farm and commanded her to carry on as best she could.

"This is like stamping out a prairie fire," he announced. "We've got to check it before it starts."

Katie went without a murmur. I think she would have gone to the north pole if her abstracted man-of-medicine had ordered it. But all he thought about, apparently, was his medicine and the fact that new patients were trickling into his field hospital. He boiled with indignation at the carelessness of the colony mothers, at his lack of help, at the non-existence of officials to enforce his quarantine regulations. One neglected child, in spite of his warnings, developed pneumonia. And that brought a hurry call to me.

"We've got to have help here," he said when I confronted him in his crowded little tent office. "And as I'm stopping all public assemblage, your school-work peters out and leaves you free."

"I'm not a nurse," I reminded him.

"I know it," he agreed. "But you've got nerve and initiative. And I want you to take charge of the measles shed here."

I told him I'd do the best I could.

"Of course you will," he said as he started to stow compressors and bottles into his dog-eared old handbag. "But don't let 'em ride you too hard. Club the head off any colony parent who pokes a nose into that shed. And keep every kid in bed until I order otherwise."

So I was not only a day-nurse and scrubwoman and deputy-marshal but also a human laundry and a stove-stoker and milk-distributor and oiler of desquamating little bodies. I took temperatures and changed sheets and doled out a gallon of cathartics. I kept the shed warm at night and the sunny side screened by day. I patted soda solutions on itchy little torsos and swabbed out spotted little mouths and baked sheets and played checkers with the convalescents and shooed over-inquisitive urchins away from the door and went to bed so dog-tired that seven hours' sleep seemed nothing more than seven ticks of my alarm clock. For work, I found, was a sort of anesthetic. It seemed to wipe out, at one sponge stroke, all my own little problems and perplexities.

But work like that, I also found, wasn't without its compensations. For it brought me a lover. He was a very young and inarticulate one, but there was no mistaking his adoration. Little Olie Eckstrom, I think, has been my most grateful patient. When I showed him his blotched and swollen face in a hand mirror he laughed and said: "Ah ban like a bull moose!" And when I was trying to make him more comfortable by oiling his scaly pelvis-skin he quietly lifted my hand up to his lips, and, with a native courtliness all his own, as quietly kissed it. As soon as he was able to be up and about he stood almost too eager to help. He kept my woodbox filled and my floor swept and saved my weary feet many a step.

But behind my back, all the while, life was going on as life has the habit of doing. The valley seemed as busy as ever. It was filled with the sound of hammer and saw, of trucks roaring back and forth between Palmer and Matanuska, of the clatter of tractors where the Road Commission workers cut and graded new highways. Most of these roads looked like black gashes through stretches of silver-blue spruce, with a night's rain turning them into mire that could swallow up a truckload of gravel at a gulp. Along those black lanes I could hear the thump and hiss of the well-diggers' engines. In the clearings I could see the gleam of peeled spruce logs, showing where a new home was going up. At the top of a pole between the new Administration Building and the equally new wireless station I could see a flag bravely flying. But it seemed no braver than the family wash that fluttered between many a tent along the valley flats.

For the colony wasn't without a valor all its own. Every mass migration, I felt, must have had its casual mishaps and touches of misery. Even the Children of Israel weren't any too happy on their big trek. And Matanuska's interim of discontent and enforced idleness, of sickness and strife, of being cooped up in tents while homes were being built and land was being cleared, was really a testing-time during which the good grain was being separated from the chaff, the real workers from the idlers.

The misfits might rail at Ruddy and his health rules and the malcontents might squat about the Commissary porch and orate at the bureaucrats who were turning Matanuska into something worse than Soviet Russia, just as the CCC trouble-makers could think up ingenious ways of hamstringing Lander's plans for a well by every door and a roof over every head before the freeze-up. But the serious-minded workers, the real home-seekers, were already out on their plots getting a bit of land ready for belated seeding or lending a hand at building shelter for their belated stock. They were the hope of the Project.

And among the women, I found, there was the same division between the misery-mongers and the homemakers. The winners were intent on winning out. I could tell, as soon as I invaded a tent home to investigate an ailing child, whether it was ruled over by an adept or an indifferent housewife. For in one case I'd be confronted by a forlorn sort of neatness and order; and in the other I'd find myself surrounded by dirty bedding and dishes, smoky stove pipes and littered floors and shrewish voices and the oft-repeated claim that honest folks had been dishonestly beguiled into a wilderness of rain and mud and mosquitoes. While the triple-chinned Betsy Sebeck sat on a chopping-block and railed at the Commissary for ladling out coffee that wasn't dated and butter that smelt cheesy, a more energetic group of housewives were down at the salmon stream, with pitchforks, ladling out half a ton of fresh fish, where the water was almost solid with red-meated bodies, which were promptly dressed and salted, or processed and canned and stowed away against a rainy day. Some of them, I noticed, had already planted sweet peas along the black-earthed terraces in front of their still unfinished shacks. But I shouldn't have said "shacks." Lander explained to me one day that these were to be a group of the best-built houses in all the Territory.

They made my own humble wickyup, when Ruddy's prairie fire was finally stamped out and I moved back to my home on the Jansen clearing, seem a very small and antiquated affair. The quietness oppressed me.

I was glad when Katie dropped in, on her way from dressing a crushed finger, and for half an hour filled my room with the companionable smoke of her cigarettes. But her spirits, for once, seemed anything but light and airy.

"Isn't it grand," I said in an effort to dispel the gloom, "to have Ruddy back with us."

"Is it?" said Katie, quite without enthusiasm.

"What's on your mind?" I demanded.

"A couple of snapshots," was Katie's rather cryptic answer.

"Snapshots of what?" I asked.

"Of a snip of a surgical nurse down in that Seattle hospital," the gloomy-eyed Katie replied. "Ruddy just showed 'em to me. He seems to think she's the last word in womanhood."

"What did she look like?" I questioned, with a prompt and sympathetic heart sag.

"Like a movie-queen in white," barked Katie. "And I had to say so. And I don't like the way he stowed 'em away in his breast pocket."

Life, I felt when Katie went on her way again, was a dolorously muddled-up affair.

It didn't make a good beginning for my first night back in the wickyup. And, a little later, it was crowned by a still more unpleasant thing, a rather nightmarish thing that I'd still prefer not to accept as reality, if it weren't for the bullet hole in my spruce-log wall, about a foot away from the door frame.

For most unmistakably, on that first midnight of my new loneliness, some-body came to my cabin and tried to force the door open.

I could distinctly hear the sound of prying and a small crunching of wood. I wasn't sure just how much pressure my crossbar would stand. So I groped about in the darkness, after slipping out of my bunk, and made a search for Sock-Eye's revolver.

I waited, with the big six-gun in my hand, until the sounds began again. Then I deliberately fired a shot at the wall, as a gentle reminder of what that would-be intruder might expect.

The warning, apparently, wasn't wasted. For nothing but silence, after that awful roar of sound, came to my ears.

I waited, for quite a long time, with my glance doubling back between window and door. Yet nothing happened. I was merely left there, with a foolish big revolver in my hand and a feeling of frontierlike defenselessness in my well-chilled body.

But, even though I took Sock-Eye's six-gun to bed with me, it was a long time before I could go to sleep.

CHAPTER XVII

LIFE GOES ON, EVEN when we turn our back to it. Acedia may be one of the seven deadly sins, but Sidney Lander, apparently, didn't believe in letting the grass grow under his feet.

For while I was holed up in my hospital shed he was busy getting my school ready for me. And, according to S'lary, he must have had his troubles.

Long before this colony was thought of there was a small school at Matanuska Village. It was housed in what had once been a wooden-fronted trading post, a relic of earlier times. Its floors had heaved with the frosts of many a long winter, its walls had sagged, and its roof leaked like a sieve. Sam Bryson, its owner, soured by his removal as district superintendent, refused to lift a hand in repairing the old wreck, though, according to certain old-timers, he was wringing a left-handed sort of consolation out of the situation by exacting an annual rental three times what it ought to have been. The CCC workers were equally recalcitrant. So Lander marshaled a corps of volunteers and tackled the job. The undulating floor was made level once more; the side walls were patched and straightened; two new windows were put in, and the roof was made waterproof. They also built a double row of rough little desks and replaced the rusty old drum stove with a new and shining air-tight heater, to say nothing of four equally bright and shining gas lamps.

The Project officials may have been short on labor but they proved prodigal enough with supplies. For they promptly shipped in six gross of blackboard wipers and a half truckload of chalk boxes and enough paper and pencils to run a state university. They also, ironically enough, sent a nickel and enamel water-cooler and an electric fan, both of them, of course, quite useless. But all shipments of textbooks apparently, must have fallen by the wayside.

S'lary, openly defying her acidulous old dad, helped me sandpaper the rough little chair desks and sweep up shavings and brighten the windows with chintz. A magnificent big map of the world, beside striking the pedagogic note, also served to cover the cracks in the side wall.

When I asked S'lary, as we worked there side by side, if it wouldn't be easier to pursue her studies in such surroundings, she startled me by the vigor of her revolt.

"Me plant my carcass in one o' them kid seats?" she indignantly demanded. "Me squat here and do sums with a bunch of undersized cheechakos who ain't able t' wipe their own noses? Not by a long shot!"

She was conscious of my frown of disapproval as I watched those full and rose-red lips framing language so unsuited to the seeker of culture.

"Excuse me for talkin' rough, big girl. But I guess I'm too much of a malamute ever t' git house-broke."

"What's discouraged you?" I asked, puzzled by that new spirit of defeatism.

"Learnin' don't seem t' git me nowhere," she lugubriously acknowledged.

"It's a long trail," I pointed out. "But you seemed to be off to a good start."

She stood silent for a minute or two.

"Pop's been wonderin'," she observed with a new meekness in her smoldering eyes, "if you couldn't come and teach me private. And once I got t' handlin' a pen as easy as I handle a rifle, he allows, I'd be ready t' go outside and have a winter in the States."

She said it without enthusiasm.

"Don't you want to do that?" I asked.

Salaria shook her Juno-like head.

"I reckon I'll stick t' the valley," she quietly affirmed.

"Why?" I inquired, puzzled by the listlessness that had come into her face.

"I've my reasons," she said with a shrug.

And I, in turn, had my suspicions. She was hungering, not unlike myself, for something beyond the knowledge that comes out of books. What she wanted was the knowledge that came from life lived deeply and womanhood roughly awakened. But women, I remembered, had to wait for that awakening.

"They make it hard for us, don't they?" I ventured as Salaria swung my big box of books up to the table top as lightly as though it were an empty bird cage.

"T' hell with 'em all," said Sam Bryson's daughter, plainly conscious of the target I was shooting at. But I stood wondering why the clean firm lines of her figure, which the fullness of her breast kept from being masculine, and the strain of wildness, which some childlike hunger in the dusky eyes kept from being offensive, should touch me with a vague yet disquieting envy.

"Love is never wasted," I said, reaching for solid ground in that copybook maxim.

Salaria's glowering eyes studied my face.

"Then why," she demanded, "does a silk-wearin' and washed-out she-cat who ain't got the guts t' stick t' his side tie up a real man like Sid Lander? Why should she harpoon him for life and then back-trail t' the States and reckon he's safe among us walrus-eaters?"

I gravely considered that double-barreled question.

"I suppose it's because he's a man of honor," I finally affirmed.

Salaria crossed to the door and looked out at the towering peaks of the Talkeetnas.

"Honor wouldn't cut much ice," she said over her shoulder, "if I was the blubber-eater he was pickin' out."

It was necessary, of course, to reprove Salaria for that anarchy. But my words were plainly wasted on her. When she spoke, in fact, there was a passionate note of wistfulness in her voice that kept it from being altogether grotesque.

"If he wanted a woman around his wickyup as much as he wants this cock-eyed colony on the map," she abandonedly proclaimed, "he'd damned soon see my shoepacks under his bunk rail!"

I kept telling myself, after that talk with Salaria, that there was something dignifying in the job of teaching, in molding the minds of the young, in bringing light into the dark places of the world. I was the lamp in the valley.

But the lamp, plainly, stood in need of some new oil. And full as my days were, I'd a feeling that something important in life was forever slipping around the corner before I could quite catch up with it. Yet all I could do, I argued with myself, was to tighten my belt and carry on. I'd no intention of turning into a grumbler. We had enough of them already. I tried to tell myself there was something moving and mysterious about this northern Project, that it implied hardihood and high adventure and a touch of the heroic. These two hundred families, I maintained, would eventually do for Alaska what the covered wagoners did for the Coast States, seventy long years ago. Or even what the Pilgrim Fathers did for New England. That the newer pilgrims came off relief-rolls and were hauled in by an iron horse instead of oxen shouldn't and couldn't rob them of that final valor which belongs to all frontier-seekers. The great thing was to live valiantly, to avoid inertia.

But there was reason, of course, for some of the grumbling. These people were tired of being penned up in tents. They wanted to get into their homes. Yet construction lagged because wrong material had been sent in and the workers wouldn't work. Some of the misfits and trouble-makers had already been sent back to the States, to spread the news of the colony's collapse. Some of the others imposed on the Commissary and wolfed more than their share of the supplies. Some growled in secret and some drew up a daily round-robin of complaints. Others went to Wasilla and got drunk. And the less illiterate of the women-folk deplored the rawness of the country that had betrayed them.

Even Katie, as I helped her bring her second colony baby into the world, agreed with me that it *was* a raw country. It seemed stripped down to essentials, the struggle to keep warm, to find food, to mate and procreate. The mating was often done in an animal-like way, with mighty little glamour and romance to muffle the primal impulse. In a city of tents, where privacy was unknown, I saw things and heard things that at first touched me with horror: love-making with all the candor of the kennel, family-fights echoing through thin walls of canvas, the moans of child-birth mixed with the strains of a mouth-organ, a loose woman with a canine cluster of idlers about her, stripped men bathing openly in wash-tubs, mothers in sunny corners combing lice from their children's hair, girls jeered at as they slipped into an unscreened outhouse, stained sheets and flimsy underwear flapping on clotheslines, farm-stock surrendering to the biologic urge under one's very nose, profanity and praying side by side, grossness and greediness, empty cans and offal, crying babies and thrumming banjos.

It was all honest and open enough. It was *too* open, from Betsy Sebeck unbuttoning her waist and giving her big breast to a crying baby with a dozen males watching the operation, to the bed-pots which, in a land without plumbing, had to be emptied in the light of day. But that reversion to the primitive, I told Katie, produced both a bluntness of address and a coarseness of fibre. And women, I contended, felt it most.

Katie didn't agree with me. She said modern woman had got a damned sight too refined for this world, that it did her good to get out on the frontier where life could fling her back to first principles.

"We're here," said Katie, "for just one end: to work and reproduce."

"That," I retorted, "leaves us no better than animals."

"Well, that's what we *are*," Katie affirmed, "only the fripperies make us forget it."

"But surely civilization's brought us something worth keeping," I suggested.

Katie laughed.

"We're not as civilized as you imagine," she said as she buttoned her mannish-looking leather coat. "You'll find that out when your first baby's pulling at your breast."

I had no wish to pioneer that far into the future. But it came home to me, after Katie had left, how restricted stood one's circle of safety in the wilderness. A shack in a clearing, ringed about by the eternal ice of Alaska; a lonely shack, flanked by woods where wild animals roamed; a little wooden building with a bunk and a grub-box, but, most important of all, with a stove. For as I shaved my spruce-stick and restarted my fire and heard the whine of the draft and sniffed the hot metal and the warmer air, I remembered how that old stove was the core and center of life for me. Its singing flames, in twenty minutes, had turned a cavern of gloom into a place of comfort, a refuge from the darkness, a haven from the cold. There was even a stubborn sort of joy in knowing that, with a turn of the hand, I myself could bring that miracle about. I could stand up to Nature and tell her to step back before a real fighter.

But a fire of spruce logs, I knew, would never warm the hearts of my fellow colonists. Their unrest went too deep to surrender to stove-stoking. And a touch of this unrest, I noticed, extended even to my pupils. They could boast of a big yellow motor bus to carry them to the school door every morning. But only a sprinkling of them came. Compared with the children of the old-timers, the stolid little Scandinavians and Finns and native Alaskans who were inured to hardship, the A R C newcomers were both harder to manage and more exacting in their demands. They arrived well fed and well clothed, their lunch-boxes stuffed with Commissary food. They were eyed with envy by the native-born children, who probably saw an orange only at Christmas. But these wards of Uncle Sam came carrying two or three oranges, day by day. Sometimes they had grapefruit and chocolate bars and store cake. Since the supply proved unlimited, they liked to have a pitched battle with those comestibles.

After a final overreckless barrage of oranges I had to make it a rule that no Project child was to bring more than one orange into the classroom. Otherwise my dust barrel back of the drum stove would fail to take care of the waste. And it gave me an unpleasant feeling just under the fifth rib to see poor little Olie Eckstrom rummaging through that waste, for a half-eaten orange or two, to carry home to his sister Frieda, who couldn't come to school until her mother was able to get to Anchorage to buy her a pair of shoes. I began to realize that you can hurt people by too much help.

Lander, I knew, was campaigning for less War Department red tape and more self-government. But the chair-warmers, of course, were none too ready to give up their soft berths. And Lander plainly had trouble enough with his construction gangs and with getting the heads of families to help a little with the house building. He refused to let them shake his faith in the Project.

But when the grumbling and selfishness of so many of these Project settlers both dispirited me and rather shook my faith in human nature, I felt better when I thought of Olie, who would trudge to the Arctic Circle at a word from his teacher. And next to him was Katie.

Katie might be a bit arbitrary and aggressive and mannish in appearance, but underneath all that brusqueness of hers was a heart of gold. She might be a bit unkempt herself, but she demanded order and cleanness about her. She scolded and stormed. But she never spared herself. And she loved her work.

And her Ruddy might be a trifle self-absorbed and irascible, but he too was giving every possible ounce of energy to his job here. And there was enough of it, apparently, in this crowded valley. They were on the go, sometimes, for twenty hours out of the twenty-four. They had nothing more than a canvas field-hospital and their hurriedly-built shed with its row of army cots along one wall. They were without the supplies and appliances that make hospital work easier. They hadn't even a shed in which to stable Katie's Black Maria. But she stood ready to start out with her Ruddy, at any hour of the night, and plow through mud and rain and darkness to look after a broken leg or help bring a baby into the world. And if they got ditched on the way she lent a hand to work Black Maria back on the road. If Ruddy overlooked a meal she filled him up on coffee and scrambled eggs. If she found him with a button missing she sewed one on for him. When he came in with wet feet she dried out his shoes for him. And when he got a fat letter with a Seattle postmark on it she scrubbed out the dispensary and sterilized all the instruments, whether they needed it or not. But her wide face lost a little of its earlier carefree audacity.

When I opened my door in the morning, and watched the blue-gray columns of smoke going up from the scattered cabins between the ruffled green of birch and spruce and poplar and willow, I told myself that life wasn't as muddled as it might have been. Those wavering smoke columns went up first blue-gray and then rose-gray against the purple and lavender of the mountain slopes. Above the slopes were the eternal peaks, remote and majestic, each sun-bathed mountain top meringued with a creamy layer of cloudlets that made still deeper the throbbing blue of the high-spanned sky above them. I could hear a dog bark, and the valorous sound of an ax in some echoing woodland, followed by the sound of a cow calling to her calf. The valley seemed like a cup, waiting for its wine of twenty hours of sunlight. There was even something seminal in the smell of the air, where every living thing seemed to open its arms to the awakening warmth and reach up for the sun and drink in its blessed rays. It suggested fullness and fecundity. Growth became almost audible.

I was singing as I went to the road with my water pail. With one lobe of my brain, as I sang, I was thinking that women never knew the luxury of running water until taps and enamel tubs were taken away from them. With the other lobe I was thinking of Barbara Trumbull, proud and stately in a

casually accepted security brought to her by another's wealth. And as I turned
into the road I came face to face with Eric the Red.

He smiled at my sudden silence, as I made an effort to circle about him. I'd
heard, often enough, there were no snakes in Alaska. But something about
this man made me think of a coiled copperhead.

"Why avoid me, Moon of my Delight?" he said with his habitual and hateful
mockery.

"Why shouldn't I?" I asked. I compelled myself to meet his gaze. For along
the road I could see the approaching figure of Olie Eckstrom, swinging his tin
milk pail as he whistled to the tree tops.

There was something maddening about the cool assurance of Ericson's
smile.

"Why should you, sweet lady, when it's written in the stars we're to come
together?" His laugh was both brief and unpleasant. "I'm still awaiting that
happy hour. And when it arrives I don't intend to be the forgotten man."

I made no response to that. Instead, I turned and called to Olie, who quickened his pace as he caught sight of me. My little Swedish friend was no
Goliath, but even his diminutive figure meant an acceptable ally along that
lonely road.

Ericson, watching that figure in bibbed overalls, essayed an ironic gesture
of farewell and moved on down the road. But even Olie's wide smile of adoration failed to bring the warmth back to the crystalline Alaska sunlight.

" 'E ban a bad man," Olie announced with quiet conviction.

"Why do you say that?" I asked.

Olie's answer, when he gave his reasons, was in English both broken and
bewildering. But in the end it rather took my breath away. For from the
slow-tongued Swede boy I gathered that he had been in the habit of collecting
building blocks for his sister Frieda, small board ends that could be picked
up between the lumber piles along the siding track. The workmen there were
apt to treat him roughly and drive him away with a cuff and a kick. So it
was natural, the night before, that he should promptly hide away when he
heard voices. But he was able to gather the gist of the talk among those
transient soreheads. And their plan, apparently, was to stage a demonstration
in front of the Commissary (where a curb had been put on the open-handed
distribution of Federal supplies) and while the officials were busy with that
riot Ericson and his followers were to start a fire, a purely accidental fire, in
the great piles of timber and equipment that lined the railway track.

"Are you sure of this?" I demanded.

"Ah t'ank so," admitted the half-doubtful boy. Then, disturbed by my ex-
pression, he added, more hopefully: "But maybe dey choost talk."

I couldn't agree with him. And I knew no time was to be lost.

"We must find Lander," I said, remembering I'd made much the same speech in Olie's hearing when another and an earlier emergency had arisen.

CHAPTER XVIII

I HAD TROUBLE IN finding Lander, who was at one of the farther camps where a well drill had broken down. He impressed me as a woefully exasperated and mud-covered man, but he listened, with a quiet enough eye, as I told him what I could of Olie's story.

It didn't, however, make much impression on him. Instead of venturing any comment on the situation he asked me if John Trumbull had been in touch with me during the last few days. When I informed him to the contrary he wiped his hands on some cotton waste and led me over to his truck, saying he'd be glad to drop me at my school door.

"But you can't tell how this will turn out," I argued, "and if it's going to be dangerous I want to be around."

"That's just when I don't want you around," he said. "You've had trouble enough in this valley."

"But it may mean danger for you," I persisted.

Our glances locked, for a moment, and I could see a warmer light well up in his eyes. But his brief laugh was both cool and self-confident.

"That's *my* job," he maintained. "And this colony work's pretty full of false alarms."

But when we stopped at Palmer and he had a quiet look over the towering supply piles along the siding there his face took on a new seriousness. For hidden under a layer of empty hemp bales, between two piles of pine flooring, he found a five-gallon can of gasoline. The contents of this can he quietly emptied into his truck tank. Then, after a moment's thought, he filled the can with water. Making sure his movements were unobserved, he restored the cap to the can and restored the can to its hiding place under the hemp bales.

"I guess you're right," he said, as he climbed back into the driver's seat.

"What'll you do next?" I asked, disturbed by a new grimness that had come into those meditative eyes of his.

"We'll get them redhanded," he announced.

"But you can't tell what will happen," I persisted, chilled by some ghostly foreboding of evil.

"I know what will happen," Lander said. His eye remained stern as he studied my face. "But I want you to keep out of it."

My pupils didn't get the attention they should have that day. There was many a flicker, before the afternoon wore away, in the lamp of learning.

I was still in my classroom, after the big yellow bus had carried away the last of the children, when Sock-Eye appeared in the doorway. He may have struck a note of ferocity, with his big sheath-knife and his two six-guns swinging from his abraded old belt, but he came in rather hesitatingly, plainly repressed by the aroma of higher education that surrounded him. And I could see, as I studied the weather-beaten old face with such deep crow's-feet about the corners of the eyes and so puckered about the leathery jowls with ancient hardships, that Sock-Eye had something on his mind.

"I ain't much of a hand at g'ography," he said as his bearlike eyes blinked up at my wall map, "but I've got me a homemade chart here I'm needin' a mess o' help on."

He produced a soiled and rumpled sheet of paper diversified with many pencil-markings and placed it on the desk top in front of me.

"What's this?" I asked, trying in vain to read some meaning into the roughly penciled lines.

"That," said Sock-Eye, "is a map o' Klondike Coburn's claim on the Chakitana as I kin best work it out."

"What are you going to do with it?" I promptly questioned.

Sock-Eye's stubborn old mouth hardened a little.

"I ain't sayin'," he answered. "But that's the mine, remember, that ought t' be yourn."

"John Trumbull says it shouldn't," I reminded him.

"And Sid Lander says it does," retorted Sock-Eye. "But I ain't goin' into that now, girlie. What I want t' check up on is where them location stakes o' your old pappy ought to stand." His stubby finger pointed to a marking on the map. "Here's the Chakitana, and it ought t' be about here the Big Squaw comes in. But I can't figger out which side o' that crick the Trumbull outfit is anchored to."

"I'm afraid I can't help you much," I said. "You see, Sock-Eye, I've never been there."

"Then why ain't you there now?" demanded the old fire-eater.

"Because I'm needed here in the valley," I answered. "And Sidney Lander's supposed to be looking after my claim."

"Yes," snapped Sock-Eye, "fussin' round with these pie-eatin' pikers and waitin' for a bunch of law sharks t' put in the final word. But court rulin's don't git you nowhere, back on the cricks."

I sat looking at Sock-Eye until he shifted a little uneasily under my gaze. I was thinking, as I studied his seamed old face, that he was so misplaced in time that he was pathetic. He impressed me, for all his bristlings of belligerency, as childishly helpless before the newer forces crowding in on his trail. He made me think of a cumbersomely armored turtle, overconfident of his safety as he ambles along a motor highway between the flashing wheels of change that could so easily crush him.

"What's right or wrong," I finally observed, "isn't decided by gunpowder."

Sock-Eye's laugh was brief and raucous.

"More'n once, girlie, I've seen it blow a short cut t' the seat o' justice," he said as he patted the worn leather of his gun holster. "And this valley wouldn't be where she is if she could rouse up a leather-slapper or two t' straighten her out."

"What's wrong with this valley?" I challenged.

Sock-Eye, after a pitying look at me, shook his head.

"Nothin's wrong with her," was his ironic response, "except them rockin'-chair dirt farmers they brought up here and presented with double-enamel bathtubs, and them CCC bums who hell around night and day, and them hooch hounds off relief who'd rather sit and wait for a weekly handout than git a bit o' land cleared and seeded. Would've been a damn' sight more reasonable, seein' it's a holiday they're lookin' for, t' have packed 'em off on a Dollar Liner and sent 'em on a nice long trip around the world."

"They're not all like that," I contended.

Sock-Eye, at the moment, declined to answer that. His mournful and mordant gaze went out to the distant peaks of the Talkeetnas.

"This valley's spoilt for me," he finally announced. The desolate old figure took a bite of plug tobacco, chewed vigorously, and spat into the stove front. "Filled with a mess o' women and gas cars that ain't needed here."

"The trouble with you," I suggested, "is that you've lived too long alone."

Sock-Eye looked at me with the kingly scorn of the unmated male.

"Because I never got me a woman?" he demanded.

"If you want to put it that way," I acceded.

Still again Sock-Eye spat adroitly into the stove front.

"I ain't had trade nor truck with 'em for forty odd years," he averred. "And I guess I'll git along without 'em to the last roundup. No, ma'am, I ain't succumbed t' the plumb loco idee a shack ain't a home unless there's a female fussin' round the dough-crock."

"What can you do?" I asked.

Sock-Eye chuckled in his leathery old throat.

"I can break trail for the back hills where a he-man's still got breath-in'-room," was his solemn-noted reply. "I can mush on to a valley that ain't overrun with weaklin's and womenfolks."

"Thanks," I said. And the squinting old eyes, the eyes with the narrowed sagacity that always made me think of a bear, slewed about and studied my face.

"I ain't got nothin' against you, girlie," he said. "I've been strong for you from the first crack out o' the box. I savvied, from that snowy day I spotted you on the trail, you was good leather. And later on I savvied you was mixed up with a bunch o' snakes here. That's why I kind o' hate t' mush on and leave you sittin' out on a limb."

"I've always managed to take care of myself," I assured him.

"That's what you think," said Sock-Eye. "But it's time some plain-spoken *hombre* put a bee or two in your bonnet. For I savvy a heap more'n you imagine, girlie. You think Big John Trumbull'll give you a square deal on your claim trial. But he won't. He ain't built that way. And there's a glib-talkin' tarantula right over in that transient-camp who's figgerin' on bustin' you up in this colony, when the chance comes around. And he's got Trumbull behind him."

"Is that Eric the Red?" I demanded, my thoughts suddenly back to more imminent things.

"That's the bird," acknowledged Sock-Eye as a leathery old claw stroked his six-gun holster. "And in the good old days when us sourdoughs cleaned up a camp as she ought to be cleaned up that windjammer'd have swung from a tamarack bough afore he'd passed out his second mess o' pizen-talk. I don't like what he's sayin' about you and Sid Lander. I don't like *anything* he says. And I could take a crack at that reptile myself, any old day, and like as not git me a Carnegie medal for riddin' the valley of a white-skinned Pawnee who's sure showin' himself a trouble-maker."

"What's he got against Lander?" I asked.

"One item worth mentionin'," Sock-Eye said with his not unkindly smile, "is the fact that Lander's ridin' range for *you*."

"Why should he ride range, as you put it, for me?" I inquired with purely defensive obtuseness.

Sock-Eye took another chew before deigning to answer.

"Why, that long-legged giloot's so crazy about you, girlie, he can't see straight."

I could feel the color come up into my face. But I managed to keep control of my voice.

"Did he ever tell you this?" I asked.

"That *hombre*," asserted the frowning Sock-Eye, "ain't given to talkin' much. But when he gits set on doin' a thing he does it in his own way."

"But it would be in an honest way," I proudly proclaimed.

Sock-Eye's shaggy head nodded its dubious assent.

"He's a straight-shooter all right. But that's jus' where the hitch is. He's *too* straight. And considerin' what he's facin' it ain't gittin' him far." Sock-Eye's gaze wavered away and regarded the design I'd embroidered on a gunny sack for a floor mat. "I ain't nosin' into that tie-up with the Trumbull dame. That's something 'twixt him and his Creator. But there's that girl o' Sam Bryson's. S'lary ain't what you'd mebbe call civilized."

"She has her good points," I regretfully admitted.

"Mebbe she has. But when a maverick in petticoats like that gits an idee in her head, when she's set on somethin' she ain't no special right to, she's a-goin' after it like a wildcat after a rabbit."

I began to discern the threatening bush about which my old friend was so artfully beating.

"Lander seems able to take care of himself," I ventured.

"Mebbe he is," retorted Sock-Eye. "And mebbe he ain't. But book learnin' and shadow-boxin' with the Ten Commandments ain't goin' t' help you much when you're competin' against a she-wolf."

"I haven't," I ventured, "seen signs of any conflict."

"You wouldn't," acceded Sock-Eye. "But as I told you once afore, gold's where you find it. And so is a *hombre's* consolation for livin' alone. But it's mebbe worth rememberin' that both the man and the metal is usually corraled by the forager who's first t' hightail it in t' where the strike is."

I took a little time to ponder that double pearl of wisdom.

"Why are you telling me all this?" I asked.

"B'cause I liked your ol' pappy," Sock-Eye said as he reached for his hat, "and b'cause I think a heap o' you, girlie. That's why I'm puttin' a blaze or two on the tamaracks along the trail o' twisted intentions. I ain't no Bible-thumper. But I'm enough of a powder-blistered ol' rock-wrangler t' know what a claim-jumper can git away with when you ain't got your location posts marked plain. And that applies t' both sides o' the fence you're sittin' on."

He crossed to the door and stood looking out over the valley.

"What are you going to do now?" I asked as I studied the desolate old figure that blocked off the light.

"I guess I'll go and git drunk," he said without turning his head. "And then I reckon I'll wrassle my outfit together and mush back t' the cricks again."

I sat, deep in thought, after he had gone. I sat, turning over all he had said, until the lengthening shadows reminded me I had a problem closer at hand. The memory of that took me hurriedly to my shack, where I picked up two letters which had to go to the post office at Palmer and at the same time gave me a ponderable excuse for invading that forbidden territory.

But my letters went unmailed. For as I approached the wooden-fronted Commissary, with the usual evening rabble loitering about the porch rail, I realized that crowd was doing more than loiter. They were all men, a mixture of transient workers and sullen-faced colonists. A few of them had pitchforks in their hands; a few had pick handles and axes. Still others, I noticed, carried heavy clubs of spruce wood. And a broken cheer went up from them as Eric the Red pushed through their ranks and mounted the porch end.

"Are we cattle," he demanded, "or are we freeborn Americans? They tell us to keep our trap shut or go back to the States. But this is the time and place for some plain talk. For every man in this valley knows he was brought here under false promises, that he was lied to from the first, that he hasn't been given a square deal and that he can't expect one from the brass-button bureaucrats in that Administration Building over there."

"You're right, Redney," shouted a shirt-sleeved man from the edge of the crowd.

"Of course I'm right," went on the soapboxer from the porch end. "Instead of coming to a colony of homes you were brought like driven sheep to a hobo city of lousy tents. You were fed on tainted beef and big promises. Your women and children waded through mud and you were told to grub out spruce roots or go without a crop. And when your children fell sick they were taken away from the homes where they belonged and carried off to a jerry-built pesthouse and kept prisoners there while a couple of overfed she-nurses sat around smoking cigarettes and playing checkers with an imported sawbones who lined up your little ones and vaccinated them whether they needed it or not. And now it's about time——"

That was as much as I heard. For a wave of resentment went through my body and rang a little bell somewhere at the back of my brain. Knowing what I did, it was more than I could stand. And that wave of resentment carried me like a cork through the scattering crowd until I found myself clambering up on the porch beside the momentarily silenced Ericson.

"Wait a minute," I heard my own voice shouting above the jeers and the derisive laughter my over-abrupt eruption gave birth to. "I want to tell you the truth about this trouble-maker and what he's doing to this colony. For if you're fools enough to let him poison your minds with his cheap lies and his half-baked Red ideas you don't deserve the chance this Project is giving you.

You've a chance to be nation-builders. You've a chance to be heroes. You've a chance to conquer this last frontier and make happy homes here and——"

But that, in turn, was as far as the envious rabble-rouser at my side would let me get. He had no intention, obviously, of surrendering the stage to an outsider. There was a shout of laughter as I was unceremoniously bumped off the porch end.

"Don't listen to this kid-tamer," I could hear Ericson shouting as I gathered myself up. "She can't pull that kindergarten stuff with men like us who know our own minds. And know, as well, that she's the private pastry of that imported college-dude engineer who's trying——"

And that, still again, was as far as Eric the Red got.

His speech was cut short by a bullet that splintered the porch post within ten inches of his head. Before he could recover from his astonishment at that interruption a second bullet cut through the crown of his hat and buried itself in the woodwork behind him.

I glanced back, at that second shot, and caught sight of Sock-Eye standing just beyond the outer fringe of the crowd. He was standing with his heels well apart, his body weaving slightly back and forth, oddly like the body of a circus elephant chained to a stake. And in each hand he held a leveled six-gun.

"Grab that old fool," someone cried. "He's drunk."

But no one in the immediate vicinity betrayed any intention of interfering with the embattled old figure and his two bristling six-guns.

"Drunk, am I?" he croaked as he advanced slowly toward the porch end, the clustered bodies making way for him as he so threateningly moved forward. "Mebbe I am; but I'm still sober enough t' scotch a two-legged snake."

He mounted the porch and faced the crowd, his two glimmering old revolvers still in front of him.

"Stand back," he commanded. "Stand back, every man jack o' you, or stop lead!"

The only person who didn't fall back was Ericson. I don't know whether it was courage, or whether it was hopelessness. But he remained there at the porch end, white-faced and motionless, with his narrowed eyes on the swaying old-timer.

Sock-Eye took three slow steps toward him.

"Now dance high, tenderfoot," he suddenly barked out. And with equal abruptness the two poised pistols repeated that bark, splintering the porch floor at Ericson's feet.

Ericson didn't exactly dance. His foot-movement, as a third bullet nipped the toe of his foot, must have been largely an involuntary one. But his repeated movement, as another bullet cut into the sole-edge of his other boot, might have been interpreted as a none too happy dance step. And that was repeated until he stood with his back against the porch post. There Sock-Eye confronted him, confronted him for a moment with a venomous sort of quietness.

When he suddenly holstered one of his revolvers and jerked out his sheath knife I thought, for a dreadful second or two, that the old fire-eater was so far forgetting himself as to disembowel a helpless enemy. But I could see, when it was all over, that the flashing knife blade had merely severed Ericson's belt and slashed loose his trouser legs, leaving him standing there bare-kneed below his ridiculous cotton shorts. Then with incredible dexterity the old desert-rat swung the twisted leg cloth about the younger man's startled body, knotting him there a prisoner against the post. His movements were more leisurely as he tied a third strip about Ericson's thin neck.

He turned, at a hoot of protest from the crowd, and regarded them with inebriate solemnity.

"I ain't no Soapy Smith," he announced, "and I ain't garrotin' that fountainhead o' oratory. But there's something on his mind I'm a-goin' to shoo away."

I had no clear suspicion of Sock-Eye's intentions until I saw him stroll down the steps and pick up an empty salmon tin lying in the road dust. There he eyed it with solemn approval.

His steps were distressingly unsteady as he returned to the porch and placed the tin on Ericson's head. A laugh went up from the crowd when Ericson shook the can from its resting place.

Sock-Eye solemnly replaced it.

"Do that again," he croaked, "and I'll sure fan the bump o' veneration off'n your skull."

He backed slowly away, the full length of the porch.

"That gun-fanning old fool's going to pull the William Tell trick," cried someone at the edge of the crowd.

"Better get an apple," cried another guttural voice.

But I couldn't see any excuse for mirth in the situation. I could feel my heart come up in my mouth as I saw Sock-Eye's long arm swing about in an airy half-circle, with the heavy six-gun in the tremulous old hand.

My impulse was to stop such madness. I even called out and started forward. But I was too late.

The shot rang out before I could reach the porch. And at the same time the empty salmon tin went spinning through the evening air.

Sock-Eye, ignoring the shouts of the crowd, went solemnly after it. His intention, apparently, was to repeat that foolish and perilous performance.

But it was cut short when a military-looking car swung in from the highway and Colonel Hart flung out of the seat beside his driver.

"Arrest that man," he called to the Anchorage marshal who stood on the running board.

But with an altogether unexpected nimbleness Sock-Eye rounded the Commissary, dodged out past the stock shed, and disappeared in the spruce scrub, at the same time that Katie and her Black Maria roared closer along the highway that skirted the railway siding. On the seat beside her was Salaria, armed with a rifle, and plainly a self-appointed vigilante.

"Who's hurt?" I heard Colonel Hart call out as the ambulance shuddered to a stop. And for the second time my heart came up in my mouth. For I at once thought of Lander.

Katie, glancing down at my face, smiled obliquely and gave me the high sign.

"Who's hurt?" repeated the Administrator.

"Two transients caught setting a fire," answered Katie. "They showed fight and had to be subdued."

"And it was Sid Lander done the subduin'," proudly announced the self-appointed vigilante at her side.

CHAPTER XIX

WHEN BARBARA TRUMBULL AND her father came in, they came by plane. What prompted that return was, of course, unknown to me. But the stately lady from the States must have talked with Lander. And what passed between them is equally unknown to me. All I could be sure of was that she had installed herself in the superintendent's lodge up at the Happy Day Mine and had made no effort to get in touch with me. This humble chalk-wrangler of the Matanuska, apparently, wasn't of much importance in her arrogantly allotted scheme of life.

But I was more worried, at the time, by Sock-Eye's abrupt disappearance. The facts, as I gathered them, were not reassuring. The bullheaded old gun-fanner had possessed himself of two pack mules, which he hid in the hills beyond Knik Glacier and loaded down with grub and equipment and three cases of dynamite. Rumor had it that S'lary Bryson had not only been his go-between during those preparations but had been his companion and trail mate on his first day's travel out through the hills. And after that the silence had swallowed him up.

When I went to the Bryson shack, to glean a little more light on the matter, I found Sam alone there, alone and singularly acid-spirited. But when I questioned if Sock-Eye wasn't too old and erratic-minded for lone-fire prospecting like that S'lary's father refused to share in my fears.

"That ol' sourdough knows his hills. And he knows how t' mush through 'em, winter or summer."

"But he's alone," I said. "And the freeze-up comes here early in September."

" 'Twon't bother that ol' desert-rat," averred Sam. "He knowed his way about b'fore a plane ever nosed over them Ar'tic niggerheads. For it was when folks started flyin' over them back cricks instead o' battlin' through 'em with pack mule and husky team they sure got considerable spindlier in the shanks. That's why Alaska's gone soft on us. There ain't much o' the ol' manhood left. When me and Sock-Eye was workin' a tommyrocker they didn't pack a *hombre* two thousand miles off t' a hospital sawbones ev'ry time he got a touch o' frostnip."

I refused to believe that the plane wasn't a godsend to those sub-Arctic wastes. But Sam Bryson scoffed at my claim.

"Why, back on the Little Caribou I seen a musher brought into camp with his foot froze and the flesh turned black. I seen 'em give him a half pint o' hootch t' drink and a bullet t' bite on when they took off that foot with a knife made from a sleigh runner filed sharp and heated red hot in the campfire. And, by crickety, he had manhood enough t' survive that sleigh-runner surgery and go stumpin' round the gold fields for another ten years."

I had my doubts about such stories. But Sam was fixed in his faith in the older order.

"O' course in those days," he contended, "these ol' hills still had men with the bark on. They knowed how t' wrassle a blizzard and live off the land as they went. They weren't askin' no Commissary agent t' feed 'em on chocolate bars and bed 'em down on feather ticks."

It was, of course, the familiar old song, the never-ending enmity between the old-timer and the over-coddled cheechako. But I had a problem or two much closer to hand.

"Where's Salaria?" I asked as I made a show of producing the textbooks that motivated my visit.

"Bear shootin'," was Sam's truculent reply.

"I'm sorry," I said, "that she's missing a lesson."

That seemed to give Sam the opening he wanted.

"It ain't wringin' no tears out o' me," he protested. And there was no mistaking the tremor of indignation in his voice. "What's more," he continued, "instead o' all this book-readin' doin' my S'lary a bit o' good, it's fillin' her up with enough loco idees t' founder a pack horse. And I ain't thankin' you or anyone else for pizenin' her mind and makin' her about as easy t' live with as an underfed she-grizzly."

"What has poisoned her mind?" I inquired.

Sam reached to the side table that held a dough-crock and a sheath knife and a box of shells and a kerosene lamp surrounded by a scattering of books. He took up one of the books and thrust it into my hands. I saw, at a glance, that it was a volume of Kipling.

"Where did this come from?" I asked.

"It came from Sid Lander," was the indignant answer. "And I don't thank that long-legged quartz-cracker for polootin' my girl's mind with readin' matter that ain't fit for a barroom."

"What's wrong with Kipling?" I challenged, perplexed by the fierceness of his indignation.

Sam took the book back and squinted through its pages. Then he triumphantly held the open volume up in front of me.

"How about the *Sergeant's Weddin'* there? Would you call that fit readin' for a girl who's never stuck her nose into a dance hall? And this stuff about the liner bein' a lady and all the rest of it!" The ballads of Kipling went through the air and landed in the woodbox. "If that's what you git from a spell o' schoolin' I ruther see S'lary so plumb ignorant she couldn't read the labels on a flour sack!"

I did my best to smother a smile as I glanced through the volume.

"But this," I ventured, "tries to give an honest view of life. And Salaria's old enough to know that life isn't just a bower of roses. What we want is the truth about things. And when a writer gives us truth, even though it's ugly and hurts a little, we're all the stronger for not playing ostrich and running away from facts."

"Well, I've lived long enough t' know there's a heap o' facts it ain't healthy for a girl t' fasten her mind on. And I know what this tripe's doin' t' my S'lary. It's got her moonin' 'round this wickyup as dreamy-eyed as a sick duck. It's made her about as sociable as a timber wolf. She ain't interested in housework. She ain't interested in shootin' irons. She can't eat reg'lar. And for the past few weeks she's been so plumb moody she don't savvy which end she's sittin' on."

I declined to air my suspicion that S'lary's unrest derived from matters far removed from Kipling. And I could have told Sam Bryson that I too, being a woman, was not entirely ignorant of that moodiness which came to the best of us.

"But do you approve of her going off in the hills by herself?" I asked.

"My approvin' or disapprovin' of a thing don't stack so high with S'lary," was the embittered answer. "She does what she's a mind to. And after forty miles o' mountain-mushin' she'll be amblin' back about nightfall as hungry as a malamute and with some o' the meanness worked out o' her system."

But Salaria didn't come back about nightfall, if our brief spell of midnight grayness could indeed be called nightfall. By the following noon, when she failed to put in an appearance, her father became alarmed. He even appeared at the Administration Building and asked for help. And it seemed the most natural thing in the world that Lander and his lean-nosed Sandy should be among those who hurriedly made ready and trailed out into the surrounding hills in search of her. Why Lander headed out past the Happy Day I don't know. But I *do* happen to know that when Barbara Trumbull intercepted him on the outer trail and offered to join him in what she termed his gesture of gallantry, he promptly and firmly declined her companionship. This, apparently, piqued the lady from the superintendent's lodge, for she later visited Katie's tent office and made inquiries as to the character and appearance of the missing Artemis. And it obviously didn't add to her questioner's happiness when Katie informed her visitor that Salaria Bryson was the most superb specimen of vital and lawless womanhood she'd ever clapped eyes on.

It was unfortunate, I suppose, that Lander should have been the searcher who eventually found Salaria. He succeeded in locating her, late the second evening, half way up the slope of Big Indian Mountain, in an impromptu camp behind a windbreak. For she was woodsman enough to take care of herself in the open. When Sandy nosed her out, in fact, she was quietly broiling bear steaks over a campfire. But she had been unable, apparently, to resume her homeward journey because of a hurt ankle, incurred when she had a hand-to-hand encounter with a wounded black bear. There may have been some question as to the extent of her injury, but the bear carcass was there to substantiate her story of the encounter.

So Lander did what he could for the wounded ankle, packed up the scattered camp equipment, and started out with the pain-ridden Salaria on the down trail to the valley.

They had to rest and make camp on the way, which took up a night and a day. The ankle, I gathered, grew worse, and for some of the distance Salaria surrendered her independence of spirit to the extent of permitting her rescuer to carry her. At other times, by clinging to his shoulder, she was able to hobble along at Lander's side. And I could imagine how the forlornly primitive heart of that dusky Artemis went pit-a-pat against her ribs when she felt those sustaining arms about her. But the final portion of that safari wasn't as harmonious as it might have been. For it happened to be John Trumbull's car that picked Salaria up, just beyond the Happy Day, and carried her to her father's door. Lander, for quite discernible reasons, declined to ride in that car with his charge. And Trumbull's openly expressed view of the adventure in no way added to Sam Bryson's peace of mind.

But Salaria, back under the parental roof, impressed me as singularly silent and self-contained. She reminded me of a willfully sullen child who might be hugging her own Mona Lisa secrets to her own tired and dubiously triumphant bosom. But, for reasons of my own, I altogether refused to share in Sam Bryson's misgivings.

"The first thing," I suggested, "is to have Doctor Ruddock look at that ankle of yours."

Salaria, however, promptly declined the services of Doctor Ruddock. She agreed, in the end, to let me bring Katie and her first-aid kit to the shack. And it wasn't long before that expeditious nurse had the ailing member looked over and strapped up.

"Will she be all right?" I asked as Katie's Black Maria went lurching back to Palmer.

Katie's Celtic gray eyes met mine.

"It's not her ankle that needed strapping up," announced the Red Cross nurse. "It's that man-hungry heart of hers that needs attention."

Katie smiled at my small and meditative, "Oh!"

"Isn't it a bad sprain?" I inquired.

"There's something there all right," conceded Katie. "But I've seen girls dance half a night on a foot worse than that."

This gave me something to think about.

"You mean," I suggested, "that Salaria wasn't as helpless as she pretended?"

Katie's laugh was slightly enigmatic.

"Such things," she observed, "have been known to happen. She probably saw him coming and thumped herself with a stone."

"I wonder," I said as my thoughts veered around to Barbara Trumbull, "if that crazy girl knows she's setting her salmon net in closed waters?"

Katie's wide mouth grew grim.

"When you're in love with a man," she retorted, "you don't think much about geography. You don't care what the claims are or where he goes or what he does. You just stick to him through thick or thin."

"We're not," I ventured, "all that primitive."

"Then God pity the people who aren't," declared Katie. "For they're missing a lot out of life."

But Katie's declaration of faith, I found, wasn't as all-embracing as it might have been. When I stopped at the post office for my mail I saw Lander's truck there. A moment later Lander himself came out, with an open letter in his hand. He looked harried and haggard. I could see a somber light in his eyes as he stood silent, for a few seconds, staring rather pointedly into my face.

"You know what's happened?" he questioned.

"About Salaria?" I countered, perplexed by the grimness of his face.

His gesture was almost one of disgust.

"That's not important," he proclaimed.

"It was to Salaria," I reminded him. And I could see his quick glance search my face for second meanings.

"That's over and done with," he said as he stepped closer to me. "We've more important things to face."

But it wasn't over and done with. For, even as he confronted me there, the Trumbull car swerved in and shuddered to a stop close beside the truck of battleship-gray. Alone in the driver's seat was Barbara Trumbull, with her face pale and her eyes flashing fire.

She sat, for a moment, staring at Lander, without speaking. But I noticed that her lips were trembling.

"I see you're back from beyond the Happy Day," she said with a deadly sort of intentness. "You know, of course, that we're thinking of changing that name to the Happy Night."

I could see the color flow slowly up into Lander's face. But his voice, when he spoke, was both quiet and controlled.

"Let's not go into that now," he suggested.

"Why not?" demanded the irate lady in the car. "For I've just seen the heroine of your mountain adventure. She seems less ashamed of the situation than you do. She was, in fact, barbarously frank about it all."

Lander stiffened.

"Then there's nothing much for me to say."

That brought a vibrata of passion and hurt pride into Barbara Trumbull's voice when she spoke.

"I suppose not," she cried. "Especially as it isn't the first time you've indulged your penchant for nocturnal romance." Her angry eyes slewed about to me and her curt laugh was one of contempt. "But the thing that puzzles me is the fact you've shown yourself such a poor picker."

I made no response to that oblique thrust. But Lander's movement as he stepped between us seemed almost a sheltering one.

"That's about enough," he said in a voice as hard as nails.

"I'll say it is," cried the lady to whom life must have brought very few frustrations. And it was all so futile and foolish that I felt vaguely sorry for her. For with a shaking right hand she drew a ring from her finger and with a little gasp of anger flung it at Lander.

She flung it badly. It went past the tight-lipped man and landed in the road dust a dozen paces away. But Lander disregarded it. He merely stood there, rather gray of face, studying the woman in the driver's seat who so abruptly threw in her clutch and roared off down the long-shadowed roadway.

I picked up the ring and held it out to Lander.

"You'd better keep this," I said. "It'll all straighten out in time."

But Lander didn't seem to hear me. His eyes remained on the vanishing car, even when I forced the ring into his hand. Then he looked at me, like a sleepwalker suddenly awakened.

"Do you believe that rot?" he challenged.

I tried, quite without success, to laugh the tragedy out of his face. "I went through much the same thing, without any apparent peril," I reminded him. "I've always rather banked on your honesty."

"Then you trust me?" he asked in a disturbingly lowered voice.

I tried to keep my heartbeats steady under the questioning gaze that rested on my face. The barriers, I felt, were finally down between us. It was only my woman's pride, I suppose, that made me fight back the impulse to comfort him in his unhappiness.

"Of course," I answered. I said it casually. But I was hoping for more than casualness from the man in front of me.

"Then you'll have to keep on at it," he grimly asserted. And the granitic hardness of his jaw-line forewarned me that one of life's big moments might be slipping away between our fingers.

"Why?" I asked with a creeping sense of disappointment.

That sense of disappointment sharpened as he reached for the letter which he had thrust into his coat pocket. There seemed, at the moment, only one thing of importance. And, manlike, he was brushing it aside for second-rate issues.

"Because I've just had word Trumbull's putting through his cancellation of your Chakitana claim. He's to head through to the mines there as soon as a plane can pick him up."

It failed to stir me as it should have. There was a cloud on my heart, I remembered, more important than mine claims. But men, I also remembered, too often preferred facing a hard fight to uttering soft words. And that feeling of a curtain coming down on a scene from which something vital had been omitted must have shown on my face, for Lander's voice, I noticed, became more tolerant.

"It's not easy to understand," he patiently explained. "But your father's patent was granted and recorded. There's no dispute about that. But the Territory has a large area of unsurveyed land, land remote from any center of population. The Chakitana falls under that heading. So the field notes of a survey for any claim there, where the survey is not tied to a corner of the public survey, has to be tied to a location or what they call a mineral monument, something showing definite adjacence to some recognizable landmark, such as a creek or a river or a mountain. Is that clear?"

"I think so," I dubiously responded.

"In the case of the Chakitana claim," he proceeded, "the anchoring land-mark is the Big Squaw Creek. But the Trumbull plat shows the Big Squaw to be where he wants it, and not where your father first found it. And Trumbull's

intention is to fly in with the Registrar of Mines and a couple of official sur-
veyors and have his plat reading confirmed."

"Then what are we to do?" I asked.

"I want you there as owner," was his answer, "when that official survey is
made."

"Why?"

"Because there's been trickery from the first. And this final trickery has to
be stopped in some way."

"Does that mean you'd go too?" I questioned.

"Of course," was his prompt response.

"But how?" I asked, trying to speak calmly.

"We'll go by plane," he explained, "as soon as I can get one in here to pick
us up."

"But that takes you away from your work here," I demurred. "There's the
colony to think of."

Lander looked about at the scattered roofs that showed above the spruce
tops. He saw, apparently, a gratifying number of them.

"That knot's pretty well untied now," he said. "They can shuffle along
without me, from now on. But we've got a tangle of our own to unsnarl."

"Can it be unsnarled?" I asked as sobering afterthought brought me a
qualm or two.

"That's what we've got to find out," was Lander's answer. "How soon can
you be ready? And ready for traveling light?"

I looked into his face, and something there took away the last of my hesitation and a little of my disappointment.

"Anytime you say," I quietly announced.

He smiled, for the first time, as he looked down at me. It was a restricted
smile, not without a note of grimness in it. But he seemed to be thanking me,
without putting his thanks into words, for still having some tatter of faith in
him.

I found something consoling in that discovery, during the tumult of packing and making ready and saying an abrupt good-by to my schoolchildren,
who faced their midsummer vacation a few days earlier than they had expected. Olie, when I told him I had to go away for a time, cried openly. He said,
through his sobs, that life meant nothing to him without me. I could only hold
him in my arms and tell him I'd be back before he knew it.

Then I hurried on to explain to Katie. But Katie, when I found her in Doctor
Ruddock's new surgery surrounded by crates and boxes, didn't seem greatly
interested.

"Why the sudden grandeur?" I asked that tight-lipped lady as I watched her hanging curtains in the wide-windowed living room that still smelled of fresh paint.

"Then you haven't heard?" queried Katie. Her voice was quiet but her color, I noticed, wasn't all it ought to have been. "It's that boss of mine, getting the nest ready for the new ladybird."

It took a little time for the truth to filter through.

"You don't," I demanded, "mean the nurse from Seattle?"

"Of course I mean the nurse from Seattle," was Katie's even-toned reply. "She's sent up her silver and linen. And the lady herself lands at Seward on Friday." Katie adjusted a curtain pin and stepped down from her chair. "They're to be married on Saturday at Anchorage. And Ruddy wants everything shipshape when they swing back to Palmer on Sunday."

Katie endured my stare without flinching.

"Who told you all this?" I asked.

"The big boss himself," said Katie as she turned to hang another curtain. The pins in her wide mouth muffled her speech a little. "Took me into the office yesterday and showed me the radiogram and read me her last three letters." Katie laughed again. "It won't be the sick around here who'll be getting that man's first thought the next few weeks!"

I studied the line of Katie's brawny shoulders, dark against the window light.

"And what did you tell him?" I asked, trying to keep the tremor out of my voice.

"What did I tell him?" repeated Katie as she turned and faced me again. "Why, I shook hands with him, man to man, and told him I hoped they'd be as happy as the day is long."

She smiled a little, at my gasp of protest, but deep in those Celtic gray eyes of hers I could see the light of tragedy. And being afraid to put all I felt into words, I merely reached out and shook hands with that extremely white-faced Red Cross nurse, very much, I suppose, as she must have shaken hands with her blind and blundering Doctor.

"You're a good sport," I said, trying to swallow the lump in my throat. But it refused to go down.

"Am I?" Katie questioned as she let her gaze lock with mine. But her under-lip, I observed, was trembling as she crossed over to where her official blue cloak slashed with red was lying. She put it about her with the deliberation of a knight donning his armor.

"Where are you off to?" I asked as she moved toward the door.

She stood looking out at the valley bathed in sunlight, with the smoke going up from its hundred scattered homes, the homes of happily mated men and women.

"I guess I'll take Black Maria out and break the speed laws for half an hour," she said with a laugh that hadn't much mirth in it. "For if I'm what you call a good sport I've certainly got to learn to consume my own smoke!"

CHAPTER XX

IT'S ODD HOW DESTINY can hinge on small and unforeseen things. In this case it was nothing bigger than a safety pin that proved the god from the machine.

For our flight in to the Chakitana wasn't as prompt as Lander had expected. When he came to look over my equipment, and casually suggested that I include Sock-Eye's six-gun in my carefully sorted outfit, I knew by the hardened lines about his mouth that things were not going to his liking.

"I can't get a plane in today," he explained. "Every ship within flying distance seems either chartered or spoken for."

"But there are plenty of planes in and out of Fairbanks," I protested. "And others at Juneau and Wrangell."

"But everyone of them, apparently, tied up," was Lander's grim rejoinder. "And in that I detect Trumbull's fine Italian hand."

"Then what can we do?" I asked.

"We'll get our plane," Lander said with a ring of iron in his voice. "You may have to wait for a day. But keep ready."

So, having no choice in the matter, I waited. And I wasn't ungrateful for that breathing spell, with its promise of some final adjustment to a new viewpoint. It gave me a chance to consider the valley and the changes that had taken place there. The problems, as Lander had said, seemed to be finally straightening themselves out. The idle and the inefficient were beginning to dribble back to the States. The Project was like a prospector's pan: what seemed like foolish agitation was really a sorting out of the true metal, with the weaklings and the rubbish slowly washed out over the rim of the North. There had been, of course, more rubble than there should have been, the selfish and shiftless who clamored for sporting rifles and radios, who declined to keep their own dooryards clean yet talked volubly enough about dirty politics.

In most cases, I remembered, the frontier made people strong because its trials and perils taught them to be self-reliant. But on this particular frontier there had been no peril and no threat of want. They'd had a benevolent government to think for them and keep their grub-box full, to give them houses and seed and stock, to school their children and doctor their sick. But in doing that, with all but the sturdiest, it had taken the adventure out of life and killed their initiative.

But the vast majority of them, I contended, hadn't been robbed of their birthright, hadn't entirely lost their manhood. The sons of Martha still outnumbered the sons of Mary. For, week by week, the real workers were taking root and making their half-finished homes a little more livable, or building fences and sheds, or clearing and draining and seeding more land—and discovering it to be incredibly rich land, land that could grow thirty-pound cabbageheads and Climax oats that would run sixty-five bushels to the acre. For that northern valley was actually a frost-sealed storehouse of fertility, built up by slow centuries of freezing and thawing, of growth rotting into slime and hardening into soil, loam deepening layer by layer until it could bury a mastodon in its ooze, loam anchored there by the eternal cold, buried away and sealed up for future use, so organic that it had a fœtor all its own, a lush stink of richness, of a million plant-corpses gone bad, piled tier by tier in their decay. And along with that richness was sealed the moisture needed for growth, a base of frozen silt from which the sun released water, inch by inch, as the surface was played on by summer heat. It could know no drought, with that cushion of moisture always to draw on.

But equally important was the factor of sunlight. The twenty-hour summer day breathed warmth into that black bowl, touching the dead silt into life, steaming, abundant, explosive life. It brought growth that one could almost see with the naked eye, hay that could hide a team of horses, a tropical prodigality of growth, rank and arrogant, gargantuan vegetables, grain as high as a man's head, too rank with straw, peas and vetch that smothered themselves in their own luxuriance, sweet-peas that could overrun a cabin and smother it in bloom before frost cut the mad growth short, berry-brambles that became a forest, muskeg-surfaces that turned into a choked tangle of grass and alder and cranberry, tilled gardens where potatoes grew as big as footballs, where carrots were like war-clubs, where one strawberry could fill a teacup.

The tillers of that soil may have wondered where their ultimate markets were to be. But they tapped its richness and were stunned by its rewards. Their two-pound potatoes may have been watery and their overlush hay may have been hard to cure, but they learned that man nor beast need grow hungry in such promise of abundance. And those believers in the soil, I realized, were the true pioneers, forgetting the discomforts of the moment in the promise of tomorrow. And much of the glory, I also knew, went to the women who worked at their side. They hadn't been compelled to run a spinning wheel with one hand and load a squirrel rifle against redskin marauders with the other. But they'd faced the hardships of sea travel and tent life and cared for their young and in their crowded little kitchens canned salmon for the coming winter and cooked and sewed and slaved. They'd even toiled on the land with their mates, shrouded in that strange mosquito net known as a "Matanuska veil."

They had waited so long to get into homes of their own that there was some excuse for the noisy and foolish way they kept celebrating every escape from tent life. Each one of those rough-and-ready housewarmings had meant an all-night party, with mouth organs and accordions and much to eat and drink. It had meant a boisterous gathering of the clan, with a dozen or two babies parked sardinelike on one saturated bed, and music and dancing and drinking and much yodeling to the morning mountain tops. Yet now and then a more gracious note had struck through the rougher noise. When the Saari family, sedate Finns from Wisconsin, commemorated their accession to their five-room bungalow of spruce logs, they first sprinkled salt on the doorstep and then conducted a service of prayer in the living room where the carpenters' shavings still littered the floor. And one colonist woman, I remembered, had set up a hand loom, intent on weaving the tapestry for the much-needed furniture which her cabinetmaking husband had patiently pieced together. Always, from that busy home, I'd carried away the feeling that our Matanuska Project couldn't be entirely a failure.

It was the incompetents, of course, who'd caused the most trouble, the incompetents like the prolific and indolent Betsy Sebeck and her unkempt brood of offspring. But even in their sloth they remained instruments of destiny. For it was the mountainous Betsy's two-year-old daughter Azalea who tried her best to swallow an open safety pin, while playing about a littered tent floor, the safety pin already alluded to. The pin stuck in the child's throat, and the mother, thinking it was choking to death, ran out screaming for help. It wasn't long before Katie and her Black Maria arrived on the scene. She failed to find the pin and suspected it had slipped down to the child's esophagus. But as she was without either X-ray machine or bronchoscopic instruments, she decided the case was serious and took matters in her own hands. In the absence of her Ruddy she radioed for a plane to carry her patient down to a properly equipped hospital.

Most of the colony was there, waiting for the answer to that call and garrulously sympathetic with the rotund Betsy, who, before being given a sufficiently cogent sedative, made the valley ring with her outcries.

The answer came, three hours later, when we heard the drone of a motor through the hilltops. I even felt a small thrill go through my body as I stood watching that gray-winged beetle so intent on its errand of mercy. It brought home to me that the wilderness was no longer the wilderness, that the cunning of man had ended the isolation of the North, that the loneliest corners of the world could no longer be entirely shut off from those helmeted couriers of the skies.

The courier of the sky, in this case, proved to be Slim Downey, the Cordova pilot, who had picked up the summons when he stopped to refuel at Fairbanks, on his way south from the upper Porcupine. He swung down between a furry colony of mountain clouds and was quickly surrounded by an army of rapt-eyed watchers.

But while the colony children pawed about the knees of that helmeted Viking and fingered and patted his plane struts, Katie did an odd and altogether unexpected thing. When she noticed her little patient in greater distress and giving every evidence of a choking fit, Katie took the child by the heels, and, holding her upside down in those muscular big hands of hers, abruptly cracked-the-whip with that limp and unprotesting little body. She swung and jerked it as a busy housewife shakes a floor rug to rid it of dust. It seemed like sudden madness. But an equally sudden shout went up from the watchers.

For there, in plain view, they saw a safety pin fall out between their feet. Even Katie gave a little cry of relief touched with gratitude. And Betsy Sebeck's wails of happiness as she hugged her child to a heaving and mountainous breast were almost as loud as her earlier wails of distress.

"I guess that puts a kink in my mercy flight," observed Slim Downey as Lander pushed through to his side.

I saw the two men standing there, talking together. And I saw a quick and affirmative nod of Slim's helmeted head. But it wasn't until Lander shouldered his way through to my side that I realized the import of their hurried conference.

"We've got our break," he said with an exultant light in his eye.

"In what?" I asked.

"In Trumbull's blockade," was the grim-noted reply. "Slim's to fly us in to the Chakitana."

It was while Lander was stowing away our duffel, half an hour later, and I was waiting to climb into the cabin, that the culminating touch came to that drama of speed.

It came in the person of Salaria, mounted bareback on one of her father's horses. She came galloping out of the distance, for all the world like something out of a western movie, with a rifle sling holding a long-barreled gun across her shoulders and a kit bag swinging from her belt. The figure she made was, in a way, almost humorous. Yet that rough and brown-skinned rider, behind all the frontier dowdiness, still carried an inalienable air of gallantry.

She swung off her horse and came straight to my side. Then she caught at my arm, as though to hold me back from climbing up into the cabin.

"Kin I come?" she said. She said it roughly yet almost imploringly.

"What for?" I asked, at a loss for words before such impetuosity.

"To swing in, if there's any fightin'," she announced. "I kin be a two-legged wildcat when there's call for it."

I had to tell her, of course, that there'd be no call for it. But I noticed that Salaria's dusky eyes continued to hold a look of desperation.

"You've got Sid Lander," she said with a shoulder-movement of comprehension touched with abnegation. Then she slowly nodded that tousled head of hers. "I'm as dumb as a fool hen in a snowdrift," she dolorously confessed. "I never savvied."

"Savvied what?" I questioned.

"I never savvied until that silk-skinned Trumbull cat put me wise," was Salaria's embittered reply. "But I sure gave her an earful when I had the chance. *I* may not git him. But *she won't*."

"What does that mean?" I parried, a little breathless before such primitiveness.

But Salaria refused to answer that question. She merely renewed her rough and manlike clasp on my coat sleeve and looked at me with dusky and doglike eyes.

"It's all okay with me, big girl," she said with a meekness that was new to her. "You deserve anything you kin git out o' this scramble."

I wanted to say more, but there was no chance. For Slim Downey pushed in between us and began loosening his mooring lines.

Salaria fell back a step or two, still looking up at me.

"I'm strong for you, chalk-wrangler," she called out, with an equally manlike wave of her arm, as the propeller blades began to spin in the clear northern air.

CHAPTER XXI

I HAD NEVER FLOWN before. That, I suppose, is why the thrill and throb of life in the thing carrying me sent answering thrills through my own crouching body as we took off and the earth fell away from us.

A creeping spirit of exaltation made me forget Lander's clouded brow and overtensioned watchfulness during those last hurried minutes that preceded our take-off. I could only remember that we were in flight. The valley, which had once seemed so big to me, became a narrow shadow between clustering peaks, peaks as white as wolf teeth, that lost their sharpness as we climbed. I sat thrilled at the thought of how an engined thing of metal and wood and linen could lift me like that into the heavens, how it could fight against wind and mist walls and roar through lonely mountain passes and soar on like a trumpeter swan above a rambling glacier of twisted white and green.

Then the world beneath us darkened and lost color. What had been a river became a thin and winding thread of silver. We drifted over a parliament of jagged peaks, with white striations of snow, over valleys and traverses and hummocks and bergs, over blue-green ice fields and gloomier mountain country where the south-facing slopes were furred with timber growth and the north-facing slopes stood almost bald.

Then the country became rougher again and the air pockets bumpier. We climbed higher to overstep a scattering of fog. It was the altitude, I suppose, that began to make me feel drowsier and lose a little of my earlier feeling of exaltation. Or it may have been the desolation of the world beneath me. For I could see no towns, no settlements, no signs of life. It left me with a feeling of being both placeless and timeless, unable to tell whether it was a minute or an hour that flowed past my foolishly staring eyes.

But the roughness of the wilderness into which we were rocketing rather frightened me. And some shadow of that fear must have shown on my face. For my fellow passenger, catching my eye, flashed me a reassuring smile.

I smiled back and caught comfort from his nearness, from the thought of his quiet self-reliance. And then, at a bluster of snow between the jagged white peaks under our floats, my heart sank again in the face of so much slowly unrolling desolation.

Then I heard Lander's voice behind me, uttering casual words that brought me out of my trance again.

"Why do you call this ship the *Snowball Baby*?" he inquired of the singularly silent man at the stick.

Slim Downey laughed.

"That's what they christened her back at Bear Lake," he answered. "Up at Eskimo Point they used to call her the *Igloo Queen*."

Still again I heard Lander's voice.

"Why aren't you carrying radio equipment?"

Slim laughed for the second time.

"I'm a bush pilot. What good is two-way radio to us when we're belly-dragging through a thousand miles of wilderness?"

"You know the Chakitana, of course?"

"Sure," answered Slim. "I was grounded and frozen in there two winters ago. Since then we've kept a gas cache at Carcajou Lake." He scanned the welter of peaks and valleys over which we were arrowing. "You'll be seeing it in half an hour, if the fog holds off."

But the fog didn't hold off. Cloud-ridges rolled up between the foreshortened white peaks and shut out the valley shadows and the snow fields and the shimmering greens of the glaciers. From those dark and drifting ridges we could see the trailing fringes of snow as it swirled and eddied down through the universal gray emptiness. A new uneasiness crept through me as we went higher, to climb into the clear. My eye, in fact, sought Lander's, who was still able to smile back at me.

Yet most of his attention, I noticed, was given to studying what glimpses he could get of the terrain below us when those cloud ridges thinned and twisted apart. Our pilot also seemed to be watching the valley bottom over which we were winging. He dropped lower as the cloud floor fell away under us. He gave me the impression that he was peering about for familiar landmarks.

Then I saw him stiffen and cry out, at the same time that Lander leaped to his feet.

"What's that?" was the latter's sharp demand.

Slim Downey didn't turn as he shouted back. But there was indignation in his voice.

"It's rifle shots. There's some fool shooting at us."

"Turn back," I heard Lander's voice call out.

"And go down like a duck?" was Slim's sharp-noted reply. "Not on your life!"

Instead of going lower, in fact, I could see that he was climbing, climbing steadily above the crevassed valley in its narrowing frame of mountain peaks, until the spruce-stippled lower slopes looked like dark patches of fur on an animal's back.

Then I saw the helmeted head stoop closer to the instrument board. This was followed by a series of hand movements that were meaningless to me. But even before I heard the stutter of the engine I could read alarm in that forward-bent figure.

"They got my fuel tank," Slim suddenly shouted over his shoulder.

"What'll we do?" asked Lander. The quietness of his voice was a surprise to me. "Sit tight," called Slim. "That's Blackwater Lake on our left there. I think I can make it. I've *got* to make it."

We veered a little as we slid down an invisible stairway that was nothing but crystal-clear air whistling through our struts. I could see the earth coming up to meet us. And I could feel Lander's hand groping for mine as we catapulted over ragged cliffs with little patches of snow between them. Then the valley widened again and between the lightly wooded slopes beneath us I could see a dark-surfaced pool of water that became much more than a pool as we drew down on it. I thought, for a moment, that we were about to dive into it headfirst, like a kingfisher diving for a minnow. But we flattened out, in some way, and heeled down on that dark water like a mallard heeling down in a slough.

But a ton of metal and humanity isn't easily stopped. I was stunned by an abrupt sense of concussion, of rocking and tearing and roaring, as our floats took the water and threw up a twin cloud of spray. I still felt shaken and strained when the wavelike weaving of everything about me slowly diminished and weakened into a glide. I heard Slim's throaty shout of gratitude and felt Lander's hand tighten on mine. But we merely sat there, in silence, as we taxied to a stop and saw the wind begin to beat us back over the ruffled dark water.

It carried us into a crescent-shaped cove framed by broken rock slopes, with a sprinkling of white birch along the shoreline. Beyond those slopes was an ice-worn rampart of hills, and beyond the hills were the snow-covered peaks of a mountain range that gave the impression of being illimitable.

It was very lonely looking country. I had to take a grip on myself, to keep from shuddering, as Slim poled ashore and with his mooring lines made us fast to the stunted birches.

"What do we do now?" asked Lander with what I recognized as purely achieved casualness.

Slim took out a cigarette and sat down on a rock. Then he mopped his face.

"We've got to get gas," he announced, "from our Carcajou cache. But it's no good to me, of course, until I've plugged that hole in my tank."

"Can you do it?" I rather tremulously inquired.

Slim laughed at my woebegone look.

"It'd surprise you what a bush-hawk can do when he has to. When I was iced down on Cranberry Lake last winter, with a dead battery and no starting crank, I was blacksmith enough to turn an oil-screen wrench into a hand crank. There's always a way, young lady."

I realized, from the lengthening shadows, that the day was coming to an end. My face, I suppose, was a stricken one. For Lander, after a glance into my eyes, placed his consoling big hand on my shoulder and said: "It's all right. We're not licked yet."

"I know it," I said with a foolish little surge of faith.

"We've grub for two weeks," he pointed out, "whatever happens. We've fuel, all the fuel we need. And a chance for snowshoe rabbit or caribou if we need it. You'll sleep in the plane cabin tonight and Slim and I'll camp on shore here."

"And then what?" I asked, trying to keep the desolation out of my voice.

"Then in the morning, when Slim's working on his ship and packing in his gas, you and I will start overland for Big Squaw Creek. We should do it in a day. And every day counts."

It was easy enough to say. But out on the trail, ten hours later, I realized there was little romance in mushing over the broken terrain of the Alaskan hinterland. There was no path through the spruce groves and no foothold on the hillside rubble. There were rock ridges and arroyos and canyons and gravel beds. There were sloughs to be avoided and steaming muskegs where mosquitoes swarmed. There were niggerheads and soggy tundra and oozy silt to be crossed and rock barriers to be mounted. Twice we worked our way up rough traverses that came to a dead end and compelled us to retrace our steps. Our shoulder packs, trimmed down as they were to essentials, seemed to grow in weight with the growing hours. I even came to resent the tugging burden of Sock-Eye's old six-gun swinging from my belt holster. But I could see that my own burden, compared to Lander's, was trivial. For my trail mate carried a belt ax and rifle and grub bag and blankets. Sometimes he had to use the ax to cut a way through the undergrowth. Sometimes he had to stop and help me over an especially forbidding rock wall. And sometimes I had to sit and rest while he checked up on his next line of advance.

When I felt I couldn't go further I found fresh strength in the thought that, many a year ago, my own father must have mushed through that unmapped country and battled alone against much the same obstacles. But I was not alone, I reminded myself as I struggled on in Lander's wake. I was with the one man I wanted to be with. And from that, being a woman, I should have wrung some rewarding taste of happiness.

But worry and weariness took the savor out of any such thought. We were merely two plodding animals, forgetful of self, swallowed up by the wilderness, fighting our way through from one peril to another. And when we slept out that night, with a campfire between us and the aurora borealis brushing the blue-white peaks of the mountains above us, I lay stunned with a slowly widening sense of solitude touched with unreality.

It was the far-off howl of a wolf that brought a final cry of protest from my lips.

"What's wrong?" asked the blanket-wrapped figure on the other side of the fire.

"Nothing," I said, startled by the thinness of my own voice.

But some forlorn note in that answer caused Lander to sit up. He sat there for some time, staring at me across our dwindling bed of coals.

"It's been tough going," he finally said. But he remained where he was. He merely reached out, meditatively, and threw a stick or two on the fire.

"I'm all right," I murmured as I moved about for a softer place in my rock bed. And then my heart thumped faster than it should have. For I could see that he had thrown aside his blanket and was crawling over to me, on his hands and knees. It made him look like a bear. But there was nothing ursine in his movements as he carefully wrapped my blanket closer about me, so that only my face showed. Then he squatted beside me, in the vague light of the campfire, and sat looking down at what he could see of my face.

"I'm not much good to you, am I?" he quietly announced.

I detected a new timbre in his voice. And it was both a joy and a peril to me.

"You're a good fighter," I told him.

"But that isn't everything," he suggested.

"No, it isn't everything," I agreed.

His gaze went, for a moment, down the dark valley, and then returned to my face.

"I know what you mean," he said in that overdisturbing low voice of his. "But our fight isn't won yet."

"But aren't we letting something better slip through our fingers?" I was foolish enough to cry out.

Lander sat considering this.

"You call me a good fighter," he finally said. "But any fighting I've done for you is easily explained."

"How?" I asked. And again, somewhere between the blue-white peaks, I could hear the far-off wolf howl.

"Because I've always loved you," he said with his face a little closer to mine.

Then he stooped still lower, and pressed his cheek against my cheek. His face was rough and unshaven. But in its very roughness I found something infinitely soothing.

It prompted me, in fact, to try to free my arms from the blanket. But he prevented that abandonment of reason by pressing the heavy folds closer about me.

"I've always loved you," he repeated as the hand pressure through the blanket grew perceptibly stronger and then relaxed again. "But this isn't the time for saying so."

CHAPTER XXII

WHEN WE BROKE CAMP the next morning Sidney Lander seemed surer of himself. Through his binoculars he examined the wide and twisting valley country and announced that we'd have to climb up into higher territory. The air was clear and windless and the crystal peaks that ramparted the sky looked less hostile in the slanting sunlight.

Along that higher terrain, too, we could now and then find a semblance of a trail, with firm rock taking the place of treacherous muskeg and obstructing swamp. The going was still hard, but much less precarious.

When we stopped to rest Lander mounted a glacial boulder and once more studied the lower valley through his binoculars.

"I begin to know these hills," he told me. "We're at last getting somewhere."

He pointed into the remote distance.

"That's the Chakitana," he called down to me. I detected a note of excitement in his voice. "And in an hour we ought to be spotting the Big Squaw."

So we pushed on again. But my trail mate's rise in spirits was not an enduring one.

"I don't like this loss of time," he said as he glanced at the sun. "It's three days now. And we may be too late."

"Too late for what?" I questioned.

"We'll know that when we get there," he said with a curtness which I wrote down to overtensioned nerves.

So still again we went forward. We went clambering over mammillated rock ridges and dipping down into blue-shadowed canyons. We forded tumbling streams opaque with silt and pushed through buck-brush as high as our heads. Far up in the hills I could see a mountain goat, motionless as a tuft of white cloud in the clear air. Far away, between two huddles of peaks, I could make out the twisted blue-green of a glacier, flashing back the sunlight. But it made a picture I'd seen often enough before.

"It's great country," Lander called back over his shoulder.

I couldn't agree with him. It seemed wild and torn and empty, the outpost of the world, a scarred battlefield where titanic forces had clashed and enmities older than man had left desolation in the wake of tumult and warfare. And tangled up in that matrix of burnt-out violence and in that debris of forgotten battles were little streaks and pebbles and grains of a yellow metal which men searched and dug and toiled and fought for. In that search no waste was too wild and no cold was too deep to turn them back. For the very word, "gold," I'd long since discovered, held a touch of magic in its allotted four letters. And Lander himself, I felt as I followed after him, step by step, with my eyes fixed on the pack-burdened high shoulders so resolutely swinging ahead of me, was being played on by that endless impulse.

The man in front of me, I felt, was in his element. He could even exult, in his own way, at the thought of peril and the approach of contest. He called himself my champion, but I was only a woman, a trivial factor in the enterprise. And as weariness once more crept through my body, an inner inertia of the spirit shadowed and darkened my mind. I felt cheated out of a companionship that had been proffered and then taken away from me.

Yet it was no time, I knew, for the softer emotions, for leaning on a sustaining shoulder and demanding what had to remain inarticulate. There were more serious things afoot. And to ask for tenderness, in the face of so many uncertainties, was as foolish as demanding consoling words when a house was afire and falling about one's ears. There was, I remembered, an end to be reached and an issue to be settled. And actions, I tried to tell myself, spoke louder than words.

Yet I was glad when Lander came to a stop, at the end of a traverse that led to a wide rock ledge overlooking the westerly running valley. The valley itself widened out, with a cleft or two in the hill ranges where a series of canyons and smaller valleys radiated out from the lower wide bowl, with gravel beds and groves of stunted spruce interspersed along its broken slopes. Those slopes looked empty and lonely.

"We've made it," I heard Lander say.

I stood watching him as he moved forward and mounted a glacial hardhead that had all the appearance of a pagan throne carved out of granite. He had a little trouble, because of his heavy pack, in getting to the top of it. Then with his glasses he scanned the wide stretch of valley that lay before him.

"That's the Big Squaw," he said with an unmistakable note of triumph in his voice. Yet all I could see, in the distance, was a meandering ribbon of water, an uncertain thread of water muddy with glacial silt as it twisted between broken rock and gravel beds fringed with dwarfed birch trees and in the blue-shadowed distance lost itself in what must have been a small lake.

"There's no plane at Cranberry Lake," I heard him say. "And the Trumbull mine's shut down. Everything's empty there."

He stooped and handed me the glasses, pointing into the valley. I finally made out the mine buildings, deserted and idle. And in all the broken terrain beyond them I could detect no sign of life.

"I don't understand this," Lander said as he reached for the glasses again. And even as he spoke a sound that was neither a whine nor a whistle smote on my ears. A moment later the sound was repeated, followed by the splash of a bullet against the rock on which Lander was standing.

"Get back," he called out to me. "Keep low."

His own drop from the rock top was so abrupt that the binoculars fell at my feet. He motioned me down as another bullet whined overhead.

"So that's how they welcome us!" he said as his eyes narrowed and yet remained alight with a grim sort of humor.

Still another bullet cut across the top of the rock behind which we crouched.

"They're getting their range," my trail mate sardonically observed.

"But who is it?" I gasped as tremors of fear mouse-footed up and down my spine.

"That's what I've got to find out," said Lander as he reached for his own rifle. But instead of bringing it into use he crowned the barrel end with his hat and slowly lifted it above the top of our sheltering rock.

There was a far-off report, and I saw the hat that had been on the barrel end whisked ten feet away. Lander, when he guardedly recovered it, found a bullet hole through one side of the felt brim. He looked at it ruminatively. Then he put the hat back on his head.

He sat in the rock shadow, studying the wide amphitheater of runneled and canyoned mountain slope that surrounded us.

"We'll crawl back," he quietly announced, "and come on him from another quarter."

"On whom?" I queried, trying in vain to match quietness with quietness.

"The man who's trying to murder us," was Lander's curt reply.

But he said nothing more. He merely motioned for me to flatten out on the rock slope and follow him in that wormlike retreat until we reached the shelter of an ice-worn traverse. There he adjusted his pack, looked over his rifle, and announced that we'd have to do a bit of backtrailing.

That backtrailing, however, turned into a quartering and cautious advance, once we had climbed to higher ground. There, between the parapeted ridges on our right and the freshet-torn slopes on our left, we crept forward in a westerly direction, crawling closer and closer to the heights overlooking the Big Squaw and the empty mine buildings. Our one object, Lander explained, was to keep out of sight. That meant more than one long and laborious detour and much creeping along sheltering ridges and a never-ending search for cover. Sometimes it was a clump of jack pine and spruce that concealed us; sometimes it was a scattering of hardheads. Once we dropped into a ravine as deep and narrow as a city subway, to emerge, after a quarter of a mile of guarded crawling forward, on a rubbled plateau screened with a scattering of white birch. Across this we crept like crabs, keeping always to the shadows. Then we wormed our way down a narrow arroyo fringed with alder and fire-weed. This brought us out on a rock shelf that overlooked the valley bottom, a rock shelf cut in two by a small stream that sparkled silvery-blue in the sunlight. In the moist ground between two converging shoulders of basalt grew a curtaining little congress of clump-willow.

I was glad to sit and rest while Lander crawled cautiously forward and, through that tangle of willow, carefully studied the valley beneath him. He studied it for a long time. Then he crept back to my side, his somber eyes quite without any look of satisfaction.

"Let's eat," he said as he reached for his discarded shoulder pack.

Instinctively I looked about for fuel; but he stopped me with a gesture.

"No fire," he warned. So we squatted Indianlike on the rocky floor of our sheltering bowl and ate as the shadows shifted and a wood-warbler twit-tered and hopped between the clump-willows. It struck me as odd that a little brown bird could sing through such an hour of tension. But Lander, I noticed, paid no attention to that incongruous musical accompaniment. His narrowed gaze, after he had drunk from the stream, was directed about the rock shoulders that held us in.

"You'll have to stay here," he said, "I've got a little scouting to do."

"Where?" I questioned.

He pointed into the valley below us. Then he reached for his rifle.

"Just sit tight here," he said with an effort at casualness, "until I get back. You're well hidden, and nothing can happen. If anything should happen, give me a couple of signal shots from that six-gun of yours."

"But I can go where you go," I maintained.

Lander studied my face. Then he smiled a little.

"I don't want you in this," he said with a quiet but steely firmness.

"But if it's dangerous for you I want to be in it," I persisted.

"I know what I'm doing," he said. "And you've still got to believe in me."

He didn't even say good-by. He merely slipped over the edge of the rock and lost himself in the fireweed and balsam fringing the stream that went singing down into the lower valley.

I crouched behind my clump-willow, watching for some sign of him. I saw him at last, flattened Indian fashion in a narrow crevasse as he inched his way down into that hollow of uncertainty. He went very slowly, so slowly that I was conscious of the shadows lengthening and the lavender tone on the higher mountain peaks deepening as I waited. He made me think of a Piute creeping up on a wagon train. For there was something snakelike in his movements as he advanced and waited and so craftily moved forward again. When he found better cover and disappeared for a time from sight I let my gaze travel on to the farther terrain, searching for some sign of life in its emptiness, wondering who and what lay waiting there, nettling with resentment at the thought that I was compelled to sit idle when action of any sort would have come as a relief.

Then my heart leaped into my mouth. A rifle shot echoed through the valley, tearing a hole in the silence. And before its echoes died away it was followed by another shot, and still another.

I saw Lander drop beside a boulder; and I thought, for one frantic moment, that he had gone down with a bullet through his body. But I could see him edge up over the crown of that boulder, with his rifle extended, pointing across a rock-stippled stadium to where a small whiff of smoke was drifting off between a sprinkling of hardheads. I could see him suddenly bend low and run toward the shelter of a larger boulder, where he again guardedly trained his rifle and fired at some undecipherable target.

If it was a battle, I told myself, I had a right to be in it. I forgot my trail mate's warning and went scrambling over the shelf edge, groping for my six-gun as I went.

I knew it was dangerous, but I didn't much care. All I remembered was that I was Alaska born and my blood was up. I couldn't see a man killed for a cause that was essentially mine. To stand aside, at such a time, was more than cowardly.

I disregarded Lander's shout of warning and ran on, scarcely thinking of cover.

Then an odd thing happened.

Instead of the bark of a rifle I heard the bark of a voice, half in protest and half in anger.

"*Sock-Eye*," was the shout that fell on my ears. It came from the tall figure which was no longer crouching behind its rock shelter. And that, I knew, was Lander, a startled and indignant Lander who wasn't even trying to wave me back.

"Sock-Eye, you old fool, stop it," was the repeated shout that echoed across the valley. And it was answered, a moment later, by a call that was halfway between the howl of a timber wolf and the ki-yi of a happy cowboy.

I could see the shaggy old figure that emerged from its hiding place and stood in startled wonder, staring at his equally startled enemy.

"I'll be hornswiggled if it ain't Sid Lander," cried the embattled old-timer as he lowered his firearm. "And me a-tryin' t' blow him out o' the valley!"

"What do you mean by it?" demanded Lander, striding toward him.

Sock-Eye stood scratching his head, a picture of bewilderment touched with contrition. His wandering gaze fell on me and he emitted a second triumphant ki-yi.

Then Sock-Eye turned back to the taller figure confronting him, the squint of incredulity going out of his bearlike eyes as he studied the newcomer. Then he spat and leaned on his rifle.

"I thought you was that yellow-bellied coyote Trumbull planted in these parts t' do his dirty work for him."

"What coyote?" questioned Lander.

"That fire-eatin' Ericson," Sock-Eye answered. "He's still snakin' round this valley tryin' to ease the hate out o' his system by puttin' lead in folks."

This fact brought a frown to Lander's face.

"Then it was Ericson fired on the plane two days ago?"

I could see a look of guile creep over the seamed old face. Then a smile widened the brown-stained and slowly relenting old mouth.

"I reckon them pot shots came from me all right," he slowly acknowledged. "I was under the deloosion it was Trumbull comin' back t' trump my ace when I had him already licked."

"You might have killed somebody," cried Lander.

The bearlike old eyes lost the last of their benevolence.

"There's jus' one snake I'm aimin' for t' git," Sock-Eye slowly affirmed. "And right now he's hidin' and huggin' a rifle somewheres between here and Cranberry Lake. And if you don't git him he'll sure git you."

Lander's narrowed eye studied the valley bottom.

"Why is he here?" I asked, chilled by the thought of unseen menace all about us.

"B'cause he's fuller o' venom than a cage o' copperheads," was Sock-Eye's deliberated reply. "He's so plumb sour with hate he can't see straight. And Trumbull cashed in on that when he posted him here as an armed guard t' protect his property. It was like leavin' a trap set with pizen bait behind him."

But Lander brushed that thought aside.

"What did you mean by saying you had Trumbull licked?" he demanded.

Still again I saw the look of guile on Sock-Eye's crafty old face. His eyes, when he spoke, were not on Lander, but on me.

"I ain't got nothin' aginst college-dood engineerin'," he said. "Least-a-ways, when a high-collar plootocrat tries t' change the face o' nature, there's always two can play at the same game."

"What do you mean by that?" Lander questioned.

"I mean, mister," was Sock-Eye's quiet-toned answer, "that I happened t' mush in here afore Trumbull and his survey officials dropped into this valley. They was bankin' on the Big Squaw t' show 'em ol' Klondike Coburn's claim couldn't lie along the crick bank where his patent sure said she ought t' lie."

I waited for Sock-Eye to go on. But as he stood silent for a moment or two, with a somber light in his crafty old eyes, he seemed to be turning a succulent thought over in his mind, very much as a squirrel turns a nut over in its paws.

"I reckon an earthquake must've run recent through these regions," he blandly suggested. "For there was the ol' Big Squaw, right back in the bed where she belonged. And when them engineerin' sharps got through with their maps and sightin' tools they sure had t' tell Boss Trumbull the mine was located proper and the claim stood as recorded. And the ol' skunk was so sprayed with his own scent that he——"

"Wait a minute," interrupted Lander, fixing the other with a steady eye. "How much dynamite did you pack into this valley?"

Sock-Eye scratched his head and spat. Then his leathery old throat shook with a chuckle.

"I reckon, tenderfoot," he observed, "I savvied how t' handle blastin' powder afore you was born."

"Then it was you changed the course of the Big Squaw?"

"I put 'er back where she belonged," Sock-Eye stubbornly maintained, "where she was on the original survey."

"But that doesn't mean the issue's settled," contended my champion.

"Sure she's settled," Sock-Eye proclaimed. "Them gover'ment sharps flew out three days ago, headin' for Juneau t' register their findin' and confirm the claim. And when the coast is clear I'll lead you over t' the Big Squaw and show you where your location posts is all set reg'lar and your limits defined."

"Why do you say when the coast is clear?" Lander exacted.

Sock-Eye's narrowing gaze went slowly over the shadowed valley bottom.

"B'cause there's a hate-soured son o' misery skulkin' around behind them rocks," he announced, "and he ain't consoomed with love for any one of us. Fact is, folks, we've got t' git under cover." He turned and pointed toward a rock ledge that wavered along the water-torn mountain slope. "I've got me a nifty little hide-out up that hillside there. She's tarp-roofed and bedded down with balsam and plumb out o' sight from pryin' eyes down here."

I knew a sudden sense of weariness touched with homelessness as I waited for Lander to retrieve our overlooked shoulder packs. I should have felt triumphant, I told myself. But any sense of triumph that came to me came without a tang of joy in it. All I knew was lassitude after tension.

"You've had hard goin,' girlie," Sock-Eye observed after a glance into my face. "But you've got your mine. And your ol' pappy'll rest easier knowin' you ain't been done out o' your rights."

"It doesn't seem so important," I said out of my backwash of weariness.

Sock-Eye wagged a shaggy head.

"I guess you're right, girlie. It ain't the gold that stacks so high in this game. It's the doggoned joy o' diggin' it out."

"But I'm not a miner," I reminded him. It was the toxins of fatigue, I concluded, that had turned their embattled valley into a place of gloom for me.

"But you're a claim owner," argued the old belligerent, "whether she's good or bad. And I may as well tell you, straight out, she ain't no El Dorado. There's a showin' of color all right. But accordin' t' the test pits I put down she's goin' to run thinner than your ol' pappy counted on."

Lander plainly resented that decision.

"You can't appraise a mine by a scratch or two on the surface," he said as we made our way up the broken mountain slope, slowly step by step.

Sock-Eye's gaze, as he stopped and blinked at the taller man, was one of asperity.

"I ain't no college dood," he affirmed. "But I panned these cricks afore you was a pulin' infant. And I reckon I kin still sniff out a payin' pocket when she's under my nose."

It seemed very futile and foolish. And I had trouble in finding my footing along the fan-shaped gravel bed that lay in our path. I even staggered a little.

"This girl needs rest and sleep," Lander said as he shifted his rifle and reached out an arm to hold me up.

I could feel that arm tighten about my tired body as we moved on again. And it meant more to me, in the slough of weariness that hung like liquid lead about my heart, than any mine.

CHAPTER XXIII

WHEN I WAKENED, THE next morning, I was puzzled by the scent of balsam close about me. I was equally puzzled by the scolding of two Canada jays that hopped about a dwindled campfire beside which stood a skillet and a coffeepot. Then I looked at the shoulder pack leaning companionably against the balsam bed on which I lay, and then out at the panorama of the snow-clad mountain peaks that sparkled in the morning sunlight.

It wasn't until I studied and recognized the second blanket that covered me against the morning chill that I was able to orient myself. And then I remembered. That tarpaulined lean-to belonged to Sock-Eye. And that second blanket belonged to Sidney Lander. And that stream which raced down between the gravel bars and silt beds of the valley bottom was Big Squaw Creek. It was running strong, at the height of the summer thaw, and as it tumbled over bar and boulder I could hear the noise of its hurrying in the clear mountain air.

Then a second sound intruded on the morning quietness. It was a faint and far-off drone that grew stronger as it rose and fell with the vagaries of the breeze. It became a throb of power, a purposeful and electrifying throb that promptly took me out from beneath my blankets. It took me scurrying down to the open cliff edge that overlooked the Big Squaw where the racing waters tore at the base of a cut bank. There, between the towering peaks, I could see the small and toylike plane that grew bigger as it came nearer, sometimes dark and sometimes bright in the crystalline sunlight through which it arrowed.

I shouted and waved, as it throbbed overhead, for I knew it was Slim Downey and his ship. The solitude, of a sudden, seemed less oppressive. I no longer worried as to the whereabouts of my two camp mates. For there above me, defying time and space, was an engined shuttle that could weave mountains and rivers together and carry us out of the wilderness.

But the plane went on, without sign or signal. And, for a moment, my heart sank. Then I gave a little cry of relief. For I saw how the tilted wings were dropping lower, banking and heading back into the breeze over the irregular silver expanse of Cranberry Lake. And even before its pontoons heeled down on that surface of ruffled silver I remembered that Slim could come to a landing only on water. And Cranberry Lake was the water that lay nearest the Chakitana claim and the Big Squaw.

My first impulse, at that happy discovery, was to find Sidney and shout the good news to him. He and Sock-Eye, I assumed, were somewhere down along the claim limits, probably checking up on measurements and monuments. So I moved out to the cliff edge, scanning the valley for some sign of life. I even gave a gulp of gratitude at the thought that noonday would see us joining Slim and his waiting plane and night would see us whisked back to a world of men and women and orderly life.

My searching gaze coasted the valley bottom, and then the opposing hill slopes, and then the nearer broken ground through which the Big Squaw twined. But I saw nothing.

I saw nothing until some obscure sixth sense prompted me to turn and study the rock ridge along which I had edged my way out to the cliff front. Slowly over the dark curve of that ridge I saw a hand appear, and groping fingers feel for a hold there. Then another hand showed itself, followed by a body that quietly wormed its way up over the ridge crown.

I thought, at first, it was Sock-Eye. But in that, I soon knew, I was mistaken. For there was something so malignant and reptilelike in that crawling advance I felt it must be the movement of an enemy, even before I caught sight of the short-barreled rifle trailing beside the flattened body.

At my instinctive cry of alarm that flattened figure abruptly lost its stealthiness. It dropped over the ridge wall, caught up the rifle, and stood foursquare in front of me, with a low laugh of derision.

I knew then it was Ericson. And my blood chilled as I fell back step by step as he advanced. He laughed again when he saw me come to the cliff edge, where I could go no farther.

He looked gaunt and harried and a little mad. But what troubled me most was a snakelike air of fortitude about him, the careless persistent knowledge of some venomous power in reserve.

"You can't get all the breaks, bright eyes," he said as he confronted me with his crooked smile. And the mockery in it, the familiar old tone of flippancy, still had the power of sending a wave of nausea through my body.

"What are you going to do?" I said, ashamed of the quaver in my voice. Still again Ericson laughed. Solitude, I felt, had played tricks with his mind.

"I'm going to get what's coming to me," he proclaimed, after a quick but pointed survey of the valley below us. "And you're *it*."

"I've done nothing to you," I cried, trying to keep my hands from shaking.

"Oh, yes, you have," was his hate-embittered answer. "And more than once. But I told you I wouldn't always be the underdog. And this deal I'm not."

His movement was quietly deliberate as he pumped his rifle.

"You're not going to kill me?" I gasped.

His teeth showed in a second crooked smile.

"That'd be too easy," he announced. "But it's wise, my dear, to be ready for the unexpected."

"But this isn't human," I cried. "It can't do you any good. It can't get you anywhere."

He cut those cries of protest short.

"Come here," he commanded, with a new and deadlier sort of intentness.

I could feel my brain telling my feet to obey, to take the steps demanded before that menacing small "O" at the end of a rifle barrel could spit death in my face. But my feet refused to move.

"Come here," repeated my enemy, with a note of wildness in his voice.

"Wait!" I called out, foolishly. I even more foolishly fell back a step or two, in an instinctive retreat of fear. And that, my brain told me, was a mistake. For I could see the barrel end steady and the hate-twisted face press closer to the balanced gunstock.

I knew what was coming; and I cried out, without willing that cry, as my body forlornly stiffened to receive its shock.

But through that call of helplessness came a sharper sound, a sharp bark that produced an incredibly abrupt change in the poised figure confronting me. I saw the rifle fall, I saw Ericson throw up his hands and suddenly twist about in a ludicrously frantic half-circle.

His hands were still above his head as his legs crumpled under him. And for one uncertain second he balanced on the cliff edge, like a tightrope-walker fighting for equilibrium on some fragile footway. Then I saw the collapsed body tumble over the cliff edge. It went sprawling and rolling along the steep cut bank until it struck the waters of the Big Squaw, where the current caught it up and churned and tossed it, with now an arm showing and now a leg, along the white-water course that twisted between its shouldering banks.

I was conscious of Sock-Eye standing at my side, leaning almost nonchalantly on his long-barreled rifle.

"He's dead," I gasped, staring at the churning watercourse that had swallowed up that receding tangle of limbs.

"I had t' git him," announced Sock-Eye, "or he'd a-got you."

"But you'd no right to shoot a man," I cried, still shaking from shock, scarcely knowing what I was saying.

Sock-Eye reached out and quietly pulled me back from the cliff edge.

"There's times, girlie, when a *hombre's* got t' make his own laws out here in the hills. And this was one o' them."

"But you killed him," I repeated, leaning on the shaggy old shoulder beside me.

Sock-Eye's laugh was low and mirthless but altogether untroubled.

"That ain't botherin' me none," he said. "Any jury north o' Fifty-Six'd say that snake killed hisself."

My earlier sense of homelessness and helplessness swept back on me. I knew a craving for security where no security was to be found.

"Where's Sidney?" I cried out in that tightening clutch of desolation. "I want Sidney."

I wondered why Sock-Eye so deliberately drew his shoulder away from my clinging hand.

"I'm here," called Sidney's voice, close behind me. He was out of breath from his hurried climb up the hillside. But there was steadiness in the arms which he clasped about my swaying body.

I could feel the throb of his heart and the subsiding panting of his lungs as he held me close to him. And those quieting hammer throbs of strength slowly beat the terror of homelessness out of my own hammering heart.

"It's all right," he soothed as he brushed the hair back from my brow and held my wet cheek close to his.

"Don't leave me," I said as my arms tightened about him.

He drew back a little, at that, and held my face between his two brown hands. Then his hungry eyes searched mine.

"We'll always be together, after this," he said. His arms closed about me again and I shut my eyes as I felt his lips on my lips.

"I've waited a long time for this," he said when he was free to speak again.

But instead of answering him I reached for his face and drew it once more down to mine.

It was Sock-Eye's voice that brought time and the world back to me again.

"I reckon it's a pot o' coffee you two cheechakos need t' steady you down a bit," he observed. "And while I'm wrastlin' that, jus' kind o' remember there's a bush-hawk's still waitin' for you over t' Cranberry Lake."

It took Sidney a little time to come back to earth. But he still clung to my hand.

"And what'll *you* do?" he questioned the old-timer. "Head back to Matanuska?"

"Back t' that mess o' misfits?" was Sock-Eye's answer. "Not on your life. I've got me two burros outspanned over in the next valley bottom and I'm a-goin' t' mosey out t' the open hills where I belong."

"But you can't do that, Sock-Eye," Sidney objected. "You're going to be needed before this is cleared up."

Sock-Eye reached for his chewing plug.

"She's plumb cleared up a'ready," he maintained. "And since you two dunderheads've finally made sure where your pay dirt lies and discovered how you was kind o' made for each other, from the first crack out'n the box, I don't see no call for me lingerin' around this neck o' the woods. No, sir. I'm goin' t' tote me and my stuff back into them hills where a man kin work a tommyrocker in peace."

I felt he was too old and spent for that sort of lone-fire adventuring through the valley bottoms of the North. But there was something still gallant and intrepid about the shaggy figure as he stepped over to the taller man and placed a hand on the shoulder that stood almost as high as his own head.

"You've got a straight-shooter in this gal of ol' Klondike Coburn's," he solemnly asserted. "She's a danged sight finer'n you deserve. And if you don't treat her right, down the years that's left t' you, I'll sure amble out'n these hills and fill your carcass so full o' lead they'll be usin' you for a plumb bob."

www.ingramcontent.com/pod-product-compliance
Lightning Source LLC
Chambersburg PA
CBHW011446170626
46816CB00008B/2538